J.C. FIELDS

THE
ASSASSIN'S
TRAIL

By J.C. Fields

The Sean Kruger Series

The Fugitive's Trail

The Assassin's Trail

The Imposter's Trail

The Cold Trail

The Money Trail

The Dark Trail

The Virtual Trail

The Ominous Trail

The Manchurian's Trail

The Michael Wolfe Series

A Lone Wolf

The Last Insurgent

A Matter of Payback

Dakota Storm

A Storm Does This Way Come

For my wife, Connie and our sons, Sean and Ryan

Vinci Books

vinci-books.com

Published by Vinci Books Ltd in 2025

1

A CIP catalogue record for this book is available from the British Library.
Paperback ISBN: 9781036706470

Chapter One

THE ASSASSIN WAITED on the parked motorcycle, a helmet obscuring his face. One parking space away was a black Mercedes convertible, its top down. His hand, hidden inside his leather jacket, held a suppressed SIG Sauer automatic. He watched the tall, well-dressed man exit the Starbucks and wave to someone inside. As the man approached the Mercedes, the motorcyclist's grip tightened as he prepared to withdraw the weapon.

Headlights flashed on the Mercedes as another car pulled into the empty parking space next to him and blocked his view of the tall man. A wave of panic engulfed him; his target was about to get away. As the man opened the driver's side door of the Mercedes, the motorcyclist realized he might have one more opportunity if he hurried. Leaving the gun inside his jacket, he started the motorcycle as the Mercedes backed out of its parking space.

Following the car toward the shopping center exit, he smiled as the Mercedes stopped at the intersection for a red light. The rim of the sun was barely visible above the horizon as dawn brightened. The motorcyclist calmly stopped the bike slightly behind the driver's side door, withdrew the pistol, and aimed at the man's head. In the act of checking traffic, the driver turned his head and suddenly noticed the muzzle of the gun two feet from his face. He cringed, instinctively raising his left hand in an attempt to defend himself, just as the pistol spat twice.

Calmly, the motorcyclist replaced the gun inside his leather jacket, revved the engine and accelerated into the intersection. The dead driver slumped against the seatbelt as the car rolled forward, his foot no longer applying pressure to the brake. It stopped when the right front tire made contact with a curb.

Several minutes later, one of the baristas inside Starbucks noticed the black Mercedes still sitting at the stoplight as the green light shifted again to yellow. She said, "Isn't that Mr. Rousch's car sitting over there?"

A tall skinny kid with acne and wild hair looked out. "Yeah, sure looks like it. I'll go see if he spilled his coffee."

He jogged over to the Mercedes. He glanced at the driver and the interior of the car. Staggering back, he gagged, turned, and ran as fast as he could back to the front door. As he entered the café, he yelled, "Call 911, Mr. Rousch's been shot."

Twenty minutes later, Detective Ryan Clark from the Alexandria, Virginia, police department, held his tie and sport coat against his body with his right hand and leaned over the driver's side door of the black Mercedes convertible. With his gloved left hand, he carefully reached for the ignition key and turned the engine off. That accomplished, he stood and stared at the man in the driver's seat. Two small holes were visible on the left side of his head. Red and gray matter were splattered against the passenger side seat and door. His partner, Detective Dan White, stood on the other side of the vehicle and grimaced.

"Looks like a drive-by to me. What do you think?"

Clark shook his head. "Don't know yet." He walked to the back of the car and wrote the license plate number down in a small note pad, then took a cell phone out of his sport coat pocket. He punched in a number and stared at the car as he listened to the phone ring.

"Alexandria Police Department, this is Sarah."

"Sarah, it's Clark, badge 398, I need registration on a plate."

He gave her the number, and thirty seconds later, she gave him details about the individual registered to the Mercedes. After hearing the name, he paused. "Sarah, I need one more favor. That name sounds familiar. Can you do a Google search on him?"

He heard clicking in the background as she typed. Ten seconds later, she said, "Wow, this guy must be important."

"What'd you mean, Sarah?"

"He's got a really long Wikipedia page. It says here he's the chairman of something called Citizens for Israel."

"Shit," Clark said softly. He continued listening and finally ended the call with, "Okay, Sarah, thanks."

White walked up to Clark as he stared at the dead man. "What's wrong? You look like you just saw the guy move."

Clark frowned. "This wasn't a random drive-by." He paused, looked at his partner and continued, "Remember the guy they found two weeks ago floating in his pool with a couple of bullets through the heart?"

White nodded.

"He was some big shot at the Israeli embassy," Clark nodded in the direction of the dead man. "This guy had something to do with Israel as well. I think this is much bigger than a random drive-by." Reaching into his back pocket, he pulled out his wallet, found a yellowed, folded business card next to two $20 bills and extracted it. He unfolded the card.

"Dan, we're going to need some help on this, and I know someone who can." He punched the number into his cell phone.

The call was answered on the third ring. "Federal Bureau of Investigations, Assistant Deputy Director Seltzer's office."

Chapter Two

Friday

HIS CELL PHONE vibrated as he passed the two-mile sign for the airport. Glancing at the caller ID, he briefly debated not accepting the call, but answered anyway, "Kruger."

"Sean, are you at the airport yet?" The caller was Alan Seltzer, head of the FBI profiling unit and Kruger's current boss.

"Well, I could lie and say yes, but it wouldn't matter, would it?"

"No, not really. I need you to meet a local detective before you leave." Seltzer's tone was blunt, and from past experience, Kruger knew not to invite debate. They knew each other from their academy years and were still close friends. But Seltzer had moved easily into administration and management, while Kruger made a name for himself solving some of the FBI's highest profile cases.

"How long will this take Alan?"

5

"Not long. You should be able to catch the afternoon flight to KC."

"I just missed the airport exit. Go ahead and tell me." Kruger's jaw clenched.

"Do you remember an Alexandria detective named Clark?"

"Yeah, works well with the Bureau and doesn't get his ego bruised like some of them. Why?"

"Well, he just called from a crime scene and asked specifically for you. Said he didn't want to discuss it over the phone. He also said you'd understand once you got there."

Kruger frowned. What could possibly be such a big problem that Clark wouldn't discuss it with the Seltzer? "Okay, where is he?"

Thirty minutes later Kruger parked his rental a block from the crime scene. Whatever Clark had called about was a big deal. A large crowd had gathered along the yellow tape perimeter. He counted ten patrol cars with emergency lights rotating, five unmarked cars and an ambulance. Plus all the major TV station news crews from D.C. and surrounding cities were broadcasting live segments for their morning news shows.

It took several minutes to make his way through the crowd and present his credentials to a uniformed policeman keeping everyone outside the tape. The officer said, "Glad you could make it, Agent. Detective Clark keeps checking to see if you had arrived." The young officer pointed toward a black Mercedes convertible. "He's over there."

Detective Ryan Clark was in his mid-30s. His dark brown hair was worn a tad longer than department regulations and helped hide the growing number of gray strands at his temples. The cheap dark pinstripe suit from JC Penney was wrinkled, but the white shirt was crisp and adorned by a red striped tie. Clark was stooped over, peering into the Mercedes, talking on a cell phone. He stood up and glanced in Kruger's direction over half glasses. His slender, handsome face smiled, and he started walking in Kruger's direction. "Hey, I've got to go, the FBI agent I called just showed up." He ended the call and offered his hand.

As they shook, Kruger said, "Ryan, what's the big mystery?"

"Thanks for coming, Sean. Sorry about the theatrics, but sometimes it's the only way to get results."

Kruger paused. "I get that. I'm here unofficially, right?"

"Maybe. At least for the moment."

"What does that mean?" Kruger said with a note of irritation.

"You need to see this. We'll discuss your involvement afterwards."

They walked to the Mercedes SL65 AMG. The roadster's top was down, sitting in the exit lane of a Starbucks. Its occupant slumped forward, head resting on the top of the steering wheel and the body restrained by the seatbelt. There was a small trickle of blood visible from two neat holes several inches above his ear. The victim was bald, except for a closely buzzed ring of gray hair. Kruger noticed a slight graying around each entrance hole. The right side of the roadster's interior was splattered with bone fragments and grayish red matter, indicating the severe damage on the other side of the victim's skull.

Kruger bent his six-foot frame to examine the bullet holes a little closer. "Hmm... Double tap at less than three feet with a 9mm."

Clark nodded, "That was my first impression."

"Looks professional. Who's the victim?"

"His name is Kyle Rousch. He is... or was the chairman of a PAC known as Citizens for Israel."

Kruger looked at Clark and back at the body. "Am I supposed to be impressed by that?"

Clark smiled and shook his head, "No, I suppose not. I doubt anybody would be impressed. Citizens for Israel is a lobbying group for the Jewish state. They spend millions of dollars on making sure support for Israel doesn't fade in Congress."

Kruger walked around to the right side of the Mercedes and quickly looked at the damage to the other side of the victim's head. He shook his head and walked back to Clark. "Looks like hollow points."

"I agree, but we're still looking for the brass. It appears the shooter may have taken the time to police the area before leaving. Pretty cool customer. Pops the guy with a double tap, collects his brass and walks calmly down the road. Early morning, no traffic to speak of, and no witnesses we can find."

Kruger smiled at his friend and calmly pointed at a security camera above the Starbucks drive-through window. "So, tell me, why the hell did you ask specifically for me? This looks like your jurisdiction, Ryan."

Clark looked at the camera, shook his head and called to another detective close by, "Hey, Mikey, go check the security tape on that camera."

Kruger bent over to look into the back seat, took a pen from his inside suit coat pocket and reached down into the back floor of the Mercedes. He slid the point of the pen into the open end of a cartridge shell and stood up. "The guy didn't pick up his brass, Ryan. The other one is lodged between the seat and the side panel. Definitely 9mm."

Clark shook his head. He looked around, found the

person he was searching for and yelled, "Hey, Roberto, bring your kit, the casings are in the back seat."

Just then, a man taller than Kruger walked up behind Clark and said, "Agent Kruger, I'm Ted Margolin with the Secret Service." The man offered his hand and Kruger shook it.

"Secret Service, what the hell are you guys doing here? You don't investigate this type of crime?" Kruger looked at Clark, then back to Margolin. "Okay, what the hell's going on?"

Margolin nodded at Clark, who said, "Ted's been investigating Rousch for over two years. Apparently he was laundering funds from the PAC and sending millions overseas to militant underground groups in Israel. The problem was he had a squeaky clean reputation and was always careful. He's never left a smoking gun, so to speak. He worked here in Washington during the week and flew home to the Hamptons on weekends."

Margolin continued, "We were probably two weeks away from a grand jury indictment. Since his routine was consistent, we didn't have him under observation all the time."

Kruger tried to resist the urge to say something, but couldn't. "Well, maybe you should have. See what happens." He motioned toward the Mercedes.

Margolin looked embarrassed. "No excuses, we screwed up this morning."

Kruger shook his head and said, "Alright, it happens, but you still haven't told me why you called for me."

Clark hesitated for a moment, glanced at Margolin and then turned to Kruger. "This is the second one. Two weeks ago Friday night, the Israeli cultural attaché was found in his pool with two .223 rounds through the heart. No witnesses. In fact, no one heard a sound. The girlfriend came back out from the house and found him. The wife was gone for the weekend." Clark paused for a few moments. "I'm not sure what we have, Sean, but I know it's bigger than my department. You're the only guy I trust at the FBI and I need your input."

Kruger looked back at the now deceased Kyle Rousch. "Shit, looks professional to me, Ryan. Are you sure the two are related and not a coincidence?"

Clark cocked his head to the side. "Right. You believe in coincidence just like I do."

"Okay, bad choice of words." Kruger stared at the Mercedes again. "I agree, you need to bring the Bureau in. It could be the same guy, but the different MOs bother me." He paused and looked back at Clark. "Look, I've been in D.C. too long, I need to go home for a while. I'll call Seltzer and see what he says. My guess is he'll transfer it to another department. If he sends it to profiling, it will land on my desk."

Clark nodded his agreement. "Okay, thanks, Sean. By the way, how are you and Stephanie doing?"

"We're good. I haven't seen her for a couple of weeks. She's been on the west coast and I've been stuck here in D.C. Lots of phone calls."

Clark smiled. "Why don't you two get married?"

Kruger hesitated before he answered. "Someday, maybe." The hesitation was more a realization of why he wanted to get home.

"Sean, take my advice, get married. I plan on getting married again, just haven't found someone like Stephanie."

Kruger smiled and shook Clark's hand. "We'll see. Expect a call from Seltzer." He turned and started walking back to his rental car. The last thing in the world he wanted was another prolonged case, one which would take him away from Kansas City. Was it time to retire? Twenty five years of dealing with the dark side of humanity might be enough. Over the past few months getting back to Kansas City and being with her dominated his thoughts. The realization Clark had verbalized his feelings made the decision easy. He would discuss it with Stephanie. She brought calm to his chaos, and right now, he needed calm.

———

RESCHEDULING his flight back to Kansas City was an exercise in frustration. Kruger's patience paid off and he was assigned the last seat on a US Airway flight at 7:30 p.m. Kansas City was his home, having lived there for over twenty years. His son was born and grew up there. His mother and father were buried there, and the woman he wanted to spend the rest of his life with lived there. There were other memories, many not as positive.

Considered by many to be one of the foremost FBI experts on profiling, Kruger was in high demand by police departments across the United States. Constant traveling came with the job. After earning a PhD in Psychology from the University of Oklahoma, he found teaching to be less challenging than expected. On the advice of an adviser at OU, Kruger applied at the FBI and was accepted. Now, twenty-five years later, the job was less challenging. He yearned for consistency, less traveling and a home life never realized.

The flight arrived early and he was at his car by 9:30 p.m. After putting his bags in the trunk, he retrieved a cell phone from his backpack and made a call. On the third ring, he heard, "Hope you're back in town."

"That's why I'm calling. I know it's late, just wanted to see if you were still up."

"Considering I just got to the condo twenty minutes ago and my body's still on Pacific Time, I'm not even remotely tired."

"How was LA?"

"Beautiful weather, great people, fantastic restaurants. There was only one thing missing."

"What was that?"

"You."

Kruger smiled, happy she was back. "It'll take about thirty minutes for me to get home. Are you hungry?"

"Not really, are you?"

"Nope. I thought if you were, I'd pick something up." He paused briefly. "What I really want is a beer. I think there's a few left in my fridge. Can you check? If not, call me and I'll pick up a six-pack."

"Sounds perfect. I'll see you when you get here."

Kruger ended the call and started the long drive from the Kansas City airport to his condo on the west side of The Plaza. Stephanie Harris was his neighbor in the condo next door. Both moved in soon after the building was remodeled and converted to condos. Strangers when they moved in, now four years later, they were close friends and in love. She was a senior VP with a greeting card company. Her traveling rivaled Kruger's; she was gone as much as he was. Their arrangement was simple: they were committed to each other. If both were in town, they would spend as much time together as possible. If not, long telephone calls were the norm. Since they lived in adjacent apartments, there was no need to move in with each other.

Kruger's first wife abandoned him and their 10-month-old son after three years of marriage. She simply packed a suitcase one day, left a note and disappeared. She would call their son on his birthday and occasionally on Christmas. After Brian started college, even those calls stopped. Now a senior at the University of Missouri, Brian had not heard from her in over four years.

Apparently, he was correct about the beer. Stephanie did not call him back. So he drove straight to the condo and parked his black Mustang GT in its designated parking spot. Their adjacent apartments were located on the second floor of the building with the back stairs entrance only ten feet from his car. Designed with an open floor plan, his living area blended into the kitchen and dining space. Dominating the space was a central see-through fireplace, one of his favorite features of the condo. Another favorite spot was a balcony off the living area. It faced east and overlooked The Plaza. Two bedrooms were located in an adjacent hall, each with its own bathroom. One was his bedroom. The other served as an office and spare bedroom when Brian came home from college. The wall separating the living space and bedroom area was highlighted by floor to ceiling book shelves and a built-in entertainment system. He preferred not to have a TV in his bedroom, but there were speakers on each bedroom wall fed by his main system. Normal music was smooth jazz, classical or the occasional classic rock.

Stephanie's condo was next door and a mirror image of his floor plan. He had laughed when he first saw her place, commenting about how the architect had pulled a fast one on the developer by charging for both designs. At one time, her balcony had a better view of The Plaza. But now new construction blocked her view. When they spent any time on the balcony it was always at his apartment.

As he opened his front door, he could see her on the

balcony sitting at a small bistro table, looking out over The Plaza and the well-lit bell tower in the distance. After depositing his suitcase and computer backpack in his bedroom, he found two beers in the refrigerator and joined her.

Stephanie was a beautiful petite woman in her early 40s, seven years younger than Kruger. Where he had straight dark brown hair, she had naturally curly light brown hair, which she wore past her shoulders. Her normal casual attire was one of Kruger's sweatshirts and faded blue jeans or shorts, depending on the weather. Tonight she wore only the sweatshirt. Her bare legs stretched out to a stool to her left. He kissed her, handed her a beer, and sat down on the stool across from her.

Smiling, she said, "How long's it been? Two weeks?"

Kruger nodded. "At least. I think I'm here for a while, how about you?"

"Nothing planned right now, but that could always change. All I have on my calendar next week are meetings at the office and lots of follow up." She paused, grinned and took a sip of beer. "Catch any bad guys lately?"

Kruger smiled as he took his second gulp of Boulevard Pale Ale. "From the way you're dressed, it looks like there's a bad girl I need to catch."

Her dark blue eyes twinkled in the lights from The Plaza. She laughed. "That might be possible later. You said you wanted a beer, so drink your beer." She paused, gazing out over 47th Street and all the hotels, restaurants and retail stores of The Plaza. She started to say something, but hesitated. After a few silent moments, "Have you heard from Brian this week?"

Something was on her mind. She was stalling, making small talk.

Kruger said, "His last email indicated the university finally offered the one class he needs for graduation. He has to take it this summer, which is a good thing since he starts grad school next fall. Other than that, he says things are great."

Stephanie was quiet again. Her gaze remained on the few cars on the street below as she took a sip of beer. "Sean, do you ever think about getting married again?"

"Yes." He watched her as her gaze returned to the brightly lit buildings. "Why do you ask?"

"Well, lately I've been feeling there has to be something more important in life than making sales budgets every year. It seems silly at times, constantly making sure the share-holders are happy, worrying about customer service, and keeping our sales team motivated. The challenge is gone." She paused and looked at him. "I'm not sure how much longer I want to keep doing it. Besides, I want to be a mother."

The statement caught him off guard. "Stephanie, aren't we a little old to be starting a family?"

"Other women have done it." She paused, keeping her eyes on him. "I'm not sure having a child at my age is a good idea. Too many risks for the baby." She looked back at the view. "I've been thinking about trying to adopt."

In silence, she turned back to Kruger.

"Would you be willing to do that with me?"

Kruger was silent for a while as he stared into her eyes. There it was. Something they had never discussed. It was implied but never discussed. It was funny how, just this morning, Ryan Clark had told Kruger he should marry Stephanie. Adopting a child was a new idea. An idea, which surprisingly, didn't bother him. In fact, he found the prospect of raising another child exciting.

Smiling, he nodded. "Yeah." After a brief pause, "I would like to start a family with you." He took a swig of his beer. "Want to know something funny?"

She nodded, her eyes still focused on him.

"I spent half the day thinking about doing something different myself. I was planning on discussing it with you tonight. Apparently we're more in sync with each other than we realized. The adoption idea is new." He grinned slightly. "What brought this on?"

She shrugged, "Don't know. It's something I've been thinking about for a long time. I've missed you so much these past two weeks, I was miserable."

"I know, it was a long two weeks."

"After you called tonight, I decided it was time. I've known since I first met you, if I ever decided to get married and have a family, it would be with you. Funny how life works, isn't it?" She grinned and raised the bottom of the sweatshirt just a bit to expose a bare hip. "I'm not wearing anything under this sweatshirt. Got any ideas?"

Kruger smiled, finished his beer in one gulp and stood. "Yes, I do. Let me grab a quick shower and I'll let you know what my idea is."

Chapter Three

MEMPHIS, TN

Saturday

NORMAN ORTEGA SAT at a two-person table in the far rear corner of The Music City Bean. Sitting with his back against the wall allowed him to keep an eye on the comings and goings of the coffee shop. He didn't care for the coffee, but the Wi-Fi was fast and free to access.

Searching the online version of the Washington Post with his laptop, he was not particularly pleased, no mention of the events of Friday morning. Finally, at the bottom of page eight in the local section, he found a small mention of the death of Kyle Rousch. No details, just that he had been murdered in an early morning mugging. The article asked for anyone with knowledge of the incident to contact police.

A mugging? Really? The man had been dispatched by a trained assassin. This was the second time the Post had treated his team's activities as inconsequential. Before closing the web site, he found the email address for the editor and started writing a letter explaining why Rousch

17

had been executed. As he was about to click the send icon, he paused. With his frustrations subsiding he re-read the email. The contents revealed more information than he wanted to disclose at this early stage of the operation. The next event would make a bigger splash, a more dramatic example of the capabilities of his team. If the national media ignored the next assassination then, he would send an email. He deleted this one.

The next target was scheduled to arrive in Kansas City this coming Friday to prepare for important meetings the following week. As he read the information provided by one of his team members in New York City, an idea started to form. The man assigned to this operation lived in southern Alabama and would be heading toward Kansas City on Wednesday. He opened a Gmail account known to the man, changed the password, and then typed out a message. When the message was finished, he saved it as a draft and closed the account. His next step was to turn on his cell phone and send a text message to the man's cell phone with the new six-digit password.

This was the way the team communicated. Each had an email account known only to Ortega and the member. Before each member composed a message, they would change the password, write the email, save it as a draft, and text the new password. Receiving a text signaled a message was in the email account to view. Important operational details could be discussed without code words, leaving nothing open to interpretation. Their only stipulation was to never use names. Target information was sent via the post office, good old-fashioned snail mail. Because the emails were never sent through the internet, the giant computers at the NSA could not pick up on key words or phrases their computers were tasked with catching. It was a handy process he had learned during his final tour in Afghanistan.

So far, the communications system worked. He closed the lid on his laptop, placed it in his backpack and headed toward the post office.

Chapter Four

KANSAS CITY, MO

Saturday

KRUGER AWOKE WITH A START. What time was it? Frantically trying to remember where he was, he saw a digital clock on a nightstand, his nightstand. It was 5:14 in the morning. Realizing he was in his bedroom in Kansas City, he relaxed. Moments like this were occurring more frequently. The result of too many nights, in too many hotels, in too many different cities. When he was a younger man, he could sleep through fifteen or twenty minutes of blaring music. Now he often woke before the alarm. Feeling reassuring warmth next to him served as a reminder he was indeed home. Stephanie lay curled up with her back touching his, her breathing slow and rhythmic. His thoughts went back to their lovemaking late last night. He hated being away from her, but the homecomings were almost worth the time apart. Almost. However, he wouldn't mind if the traveling stopped.

Experience told him trying to fall back asleep would be

futile. Carefully getting out of bed, he found running shorts, a long sleeve t-shirt, running shoes and socks. Dressing quickly in the bathroom, he quietly left the bedroom and headed down to street level. One of the great benefits of running in the morning was how quiet The Plaza was at this time of day. He loved to run early, without traffic or crowds. It allowed him to clear his mind and think.

Being an active FBI agent, Kruger was required to be armed at all times, so he carried a fanny pack with his ID, cell phone and a Glock 26. Even though he had only used his firearm once in the line of duty, he trained constantly and was an excellent shot. Stephanie hated guns, but understood the need. She had been assaulted one night shortly after moving into the condo. Kruger had just parked his car when he heard her scream. He was able to disrupt the attack before anything serious occurred, and they had been close ever since.

Forty minutes later, he slowed to a cool-down walk when his cell phone vibrated. He checked the caller ID, involuntarily sighed and accepted the call, "Kruger."

"Where are you?"

"Wandering around in the early morning dawn of Kansas City. Are you aware of what time it is?"

Alan Seltzer responded, "Well, I know its half past seven in the morning here, so I figured your body was still on Eastern Time and probably up. I was right."

"I'm on vacation, Alan, or did you conveniently forget that."

"No, I didn't forget. I just don't care. There's a firestorm brewing here in D.C., and I need to know when you can be back."

Kruger would normally have hurried up to his condo, taken a quick shower and grabbed his go bag. But after his conversation with Stephanie last night, he wasn't going anywhere. He silently counted to ten and said, "Probably not for a week or two, there's some personal business I need to take care of."

"Sean, I realize you just got back, but the President is breathing down the back of the director and he's breathing down Paul's neck. Paul's a good deputy director and I like working for him, but as you know, shit rolls downhill and we're in the valley. The director wants to know who killed the Israeli attaché and the PAC chairman. The President had a call from the Israeli Prime Minister expressing his disappointment in our lack of effort to catch the killer. Bottom line—I need you here to get this investigation started."

Kruger took a deep breath. "No, you don't. There are at least a dozen good agents based in D.C. that can handle this."

Seltzer cut him off, "Sean, this is not a request, it's an order. Get back to D.C. today. Is that understood?"

"Well, Alan, you leave me no choice. I just retired."

"Sean, this is no the time for theatrics."

"I'm serious, Alan. I'm done. Find someone else to ask how high when you say jump."

Silence.

Finally Seltzer said, "Okay, take a few days and call me Tuesday." The call ended and Kruger smiled as he walked up the stairs to his condo. This new found sense of independence was fun. Maybe it was time to retire, find a teaching position at a university and start a new family with Stephanie.

The aroma of coffee permeated the condo when he opened the front door. With a mug of coffee in hand, Stephanie was watching the sun peek through the buildings of The Plaza from the balcony's sliding glass door. She turned as he came in and smiled. She was wearing one of his t-shirts and the light shining through the thin material outlined her curves perfectly. She said, "I saw you come back five minutes ago. What took you so long?"

He held up the cell phone and pointed to it. "Alan called right after I started my cool down. He wants me back in D.C. today." He saw her stiffen. "I told him no. I'm taking some vacation time. We have things to do."

She relaxed immediately and walked to the kitchen, filled another mug of coffee, and brought it to him. "You know, I think I'll go into the office this morning and wrap a few things up. That way I can go in early Monday and turn in my vacation request. A week of vacation sounds good. Let's start with dinner at Houston's tonight."

"Great idea. I'll walk up there today and talk to Max about reservations. What do you think, eight?"

"Perfect, now I need to go next door and get ready for the office. If I get there early, I can get back by noon."

As she walked past Kruger toward the front door, he stopped her, pulled the t-shirt off over her head, picked her up, and returned to the bedroom.

———

ONE OF THE benefits of living right off The Plaza was the ability to walk to an amazing number of great restaurants. Houston's was Stephanie's favorite. Kruger preferred O'Dowd's Little Dublin Pub, but tonight, Houston's was a better fit for their mood. For a Saturday evening in mid-April, the place wasn't too busy. The high school prom crowd wouldn't start until the next weekend, so they didn't have to deal with long tables of overdressed teens. Max, as promised, had reserved their favorite table, one in the far back corner. It was an old habit, sitting with his back to the wall so the front door and the rest of the restaurant were visible.

After they were seated, Stephanie said, "I want to start with a bottle of red wine tonight. What kind do you want?"

Kruger smiled. "Are you planning on more than one bottle?"

Stephanie continued looking at the wine list. "Maybe." She paused for a moment. "Yes, more than one bottle."

Leaning toward her, Kruger said in a low voice, "Do you have an ulterior motive to ply me with wine and take advantage of me."

"No, I do not have an ulterior motive. I already took advantage of you this morning. I just want to get mellow and enjoy the evening."

After deciding on a California pinot noir, Kruger said, "I called a few old friends while you were at the office today. It appears I wouldn't have a problem finding a teaching position. In fact, the head of the Psychology Department at OU wants me to fly there Wednesday for an interview."

Stephanie looked at Kruger with concern, "Oklahoma City? Sean, are you sure?"

"I told him I wasn't at that point yet, I was just testing the waters. I also talked to a buddy with the Missouri Highway Patrol. He's a captain and wants to discuss an opening they have in the investigation department. So there appears to be lots of opportunities out there."

As she took another sip of wine a slight smile appeared. Kruger continued, "There's one more option. I could ask for a transfer to the KC office. I wouldn't have to travel as much and we could start making plans."

"I like that idea better. I don't think you'd be happy working somewhere besides the Bureau."

"I don't know. I originally wanted to teach. But I was younger then, I got bored with it, and applied to the FBI. I'm not sure about the Highway Patrol job. I'd still have to travel to various parts of the state. After our talk last night, I'm not sure I want to travel at all. I'm tired of being away from you."

Stephanie placed her hand on his arm, scooted her chair closer and leaned her head on his shoulder. "I know, the more I think about it, we should have had that conversation a long time ago." She was quiet for a minute, then said, "A friend at the office gave me the phone number for a local adoption agency this morning. I called, and they have an opening on Wednesday. We have an appointment at nine."

Kruger nodded his head, "Kind of figured you'd start the process. Don't we need to be married first?"

She shrugged her shoulders, "Not sure, guess we'll find out Wednesday." She paused and looked up at him. "Was that a proposal, mister? If it was, it wasn't very romantic."

.Kruger chuckled, "Now when did you start wanting a romantic proposal?"

"Just because you don't think it's necessary, doesn't mean I don't."

"Hmm... Well, how's this?"

Kruger reached into the inside pocket of his navy blue blazer and pulled out a small box. Scooting his chair back away from the table, he got down on one knee and took her left hand. "Stephanie Harris, will you marry me?" He opened the small box to reveal a one-carat engagement ring.

Stephanie looked at Kruger with surprise. A tear appeared in her right eye. She ignored it as it slowly trickled down her cheek. All she could manage to do was smile and rapidly nod her head. When she finally found her voice, she said, "Yes, Sean, yes I will."

Unbeknownst to Sean and Stephanie, other diners at the tables around them had been observing the activities of the proposal. When she nodded and said yes, everyone burst into applause of congratulations. Kruger was surprised at the outburst and slightly embarrassed. All he could do was nod and sit back down in his chair. Max noticed the commotion and hurried over. Realizing what Sean was doing, he too joined the applause.

After all the congratulations were said, the other diners went back to their private conversations and once again ignored the newly engaged couple. Stephanie stared at the ring now on her finger. "When did you get this, Sean? It fits perfectly and it's so beautiful. How did you know my size?"

"Stef, we at the FBI do not reveal sources."

She laughed, took her glass of wine and raised it. "To us, a new beginning for two old friends."

Kruger nodded, raised his glass and lightly touched hers. A light clink could barely be heard in the din of the restaurant.

Chapter Five

SOUTHERN ALABAMA

Monday

"HOW MUCH FOR THIS ONE?" Thomas Cooper said as he opened the driver's side door of a white 2008 Ford Econoline van?

"Now there's an excellent vehicle. This baby only has a hundred and forty thousand miles on it, barely broke in. The manager of our service department told me he'd never seen one this well maintained." The overweight salesman smiled as he followed Cooper around the vehicle.

"I didn't ask about its pedigree. How much?"

The salesmen paused, a little taken aback by his new customer's attitude. But he recovered quickly. "Ninety five."

Cooper shook his head. "It's almost ten years old. That's too much."

The salesman shrugged. "Age doesn't matter on these fleet vans. It's how they're maintained. This one…"

Cooper cut him off and said, "Seven and new tires."

"Can't do the new tires, but I can let you have it for nine."

"I'm paying cash, dude. Seven and new tires."

The salesman stared at Cooper for a moment, then at the van. "Make it seventy-five and you've got a deal."

One hour later, Thomas Cooper drove the newly purchased van off the used truck lot with a 30-day temporary tag, four new tires and no intention of registering or licensing the van. Its purpose was to provide a means of transferring his equipment from his small farm in southern rural Alabama to Kansas City. His personal car was currently parked in the long term parking area at Hartsfield-Jackson International in Atlanta. If everything worked according to plan, he would be retrieving his car in a week.

Cooper was a veteran of Iraq and Afghanistan. He had a Purple Heart and an Honorable Discharge. The Purple Heart was from being the only survivor of an IED explosion that destroyed the Humvee he was driving. He had watched his two closest buddies die in front of his eyes waiting to be medevaced out of the explosion site. It was later discovered that all of the armor plates protecting the Humvees in theater had been manufactured with inadequate strength. It was a problem the Army eventually corrected, but too late for his buddies. Cooper didn't blame the Army; he blamed the company that supplied the armor plates. More specifically, he blamed the men who put profit above protecting the guys fighting for their country.

His second and third tour found him deactivating IEDs. He had become an expert in explosives. It became his mission to prevent more buddies from being killed. Now he was a civilian. Not too many IEDs needed to be dismantled in his part of Alabama. With employment hard to find, he lived on his deceased grandparent's farm and worked part-time for an excavating contractor. To fill the rest of his time, he served as a volunteer fireman.

But the rage and anger remained.

He met Sargent Norman Ortega on his second tour. During their off duty times, the discussions always came back to their anger at the men who were profiting from the war. Ortega was a kindred spirit, his anger even greater than Cooper's. Six months ago, Sargent Ortega had called him with a proposal, one he readily agreed to. His trip to Kansas City would channel his anger toward a specific action.

It was early afternoon when Cooper backed the van up to the largest of three storage buildings on his farm near Atmore, Alabama. Two hours later, the equipment and supplies he needed in Kansas City were loaded and stored for the thirteen-hour drive. The last task he had to complete was to attach license plates stolen from a wrecked Ford van in a U-Haul lot two weeks ago in Montgomery. He wasn't concerned about someone reporting the plates stolen. The van was waiting for the insurance claim to be settled before being hauled off, which would not happen for several more weeks. By then, it wouldn't matter.

He glanced at his wrist watch. Memphis was seven hours away and the halfway mark of his drive. If he left now, he could be there by nine, grab some BBQ and be in a strip joint before 10 p.m.

Chapter Six

Monday

STEPHANIE LEFT EARLY to turn her vacation request into Human Resources and finish up a project. Her plan was to be back by noon. Kruger waited until 10 a.m. on the east coast to call Seltzer, plenty of time for his boss to finish his Monday morning briefing with Deputy Director Paul Stumpf and return to his office.

His call was answered on the fourth ring. "I didn't think you were going to call until tomorrow."

"Well, Alan, since we didn't go to war with Israel over the weekend, I figured the pressure was off."

Alan laughed. "Sorry about the theatrics Saturday. I was pissed and took it out on you."

"I could tell. Anyway, I called to discuss something with you."

Seltzer didn't answer for a few moments. "Okay, I hope this isn't about you quitting or something similarly stupid."

"No, I'm not quitting. But those personal matters I

spoke about were true. Stephanie and I are going to get married this coming Saturday. Afterward I want to start the process of a transfer to the KC office, that's all."

Kruger heard a chuckle. Alan said, "Kind of figured that might be what you were planning. Congratulations. Will it be a big wedding?"

"No, just my son Brian, Stephanie's sister and her husband. We're trying to keep it low key."

"Sounds like a good way to get married. We had way too many people at mine. My wife couldn't say no to anyone." He was quiet for several moments. "About the transfer. Do you know who's managing the KC office now?"

The comment concerned Kruger. The last time he had been there, the office was headed by a friend from his academy days. "Isn't Charlie Brewer the Special Agent in Charge?"

"No, he was promoted. Mint Dollar was named to that position about a month ago."

"Good for Charlie. What office did he get?"

"San Francisco. It's a great opportunity for him, more agents and more visibility."

"I'll have to call him and congratulate him." Kruger was stalling, trying to think through what his next move should be.

"You still want that transfer?"

"Well, let me think about it. Mint Dollar and I don't agree on, let's say, management styles."

Seltzer laughed. "Sean, you're being polite. The guy's a jerk and has no management skills. But the director likes him, or at least that's the talk around here."

Kruger was quiet again. He took a deep breath and finalized his decision. "Alan, I won't work for him, or with him, for that matter. He's an idiot."

"I agree. Is this about you cutting back on traveling?"

"That's all it's about. I've been doing too much of it lately. Maybe it's time for me to really consider retiring."

"Sean, don't make a rash decision just yet. Let me work on my end to see what I can do to slow down the traveling. I need to keep you on my team."

"Okay, Alan, I'd appreciate it. I'll talk to you soon."

Ending the call he went back to the kitchen to pour another cup of coffee. After returning to the balcony, he sat down, stared at the early morning activity on The Plaza, and started thinking.

Of all the people in the agency to be managing the Kansas City office, why did it have to be Franklin "Mint" Dollar? The man was incompetent, uninspiring, lazy, and an ass-kisser. The last time he and Kruger had worked together, Dollar almost caused Kruger to end his career with the agency.

Almost seven years ago, Kruger was working as a consultant to the Salt Lake City police department on the investigation of the torture and murders of seven young women. At the time, Dollar was working in the local FBI office and forced himself onto the case as it started drawing national media coverage. All the evidence Dollar had pointed to a drifter currently under arrest. Dollar was ready to close the case, but Kruger did not believe the homeless man was even capable of committing the crimes.

Despite strong disagreement from both Kruger and the local police chief, Dollar scheduled a press conference to announce they had captured the suspect, and the case was officially closed.

Two days later, another young woman disappeared and was found dead, tortured like the others.

The morning after the eighth girl was found, Kruger

was waiting for Dollar in the Utah FBI office. When Dollar entered, Kruger said, "Dollar, you're an idiot."

He stared at Kruger. "What are you talking about?"

"The guy you have in custody is totally innocent of these crimes. He can barely read and has the mental capacity of a 10-year-old."

"He's our guy."

"The person who committed these murders planned them with great care and forethought. The guy you have in jail can't even plan his next meal, let alone a complex crime."

Dollar's face grew crimson. He screamed at Kruger, "Your fucking psychological mumbo jumbo hasn't produced one damn suspect. At least I've been doing something."

Shaking his head, Kruger said. "All you've accomplished is to embarrass the agency with this ridiculous arrest. The man isn't capable of this type of violence."

"Oh, the great Sean Kruger. The Bureau's savior and seer of all men's souls, I suppose you know who it is. Tell me, who is it?"

Kruger was tired of the exchange. He stood, headed toward the door and opened it. Before he walked out, he turned back to face Dollar.

"It's a cop."

The next night, a police officer was caught with a drugged young woman just before he assaulted her.

Dollar held a press conference the next day and took full credit for the arrest and closing the case. Completely disgusted, Kruger left Utah, flew straight to Washington and filed a formal report critical of Agent Dollar. When he was told Dollar had the support of upper agency management, Kruger offered his resignation.

What followed was a typical agency cover up. Kruger

was offered a promotion and a promise he would never have to work with the man again. He demanded Dollar at least be reprimanded. Needless to say, that didn't happen either.

Now the incompetent Neanderthal was in charge of the Kansas City Office.

Well, that made his decision easy. He would retire. He really didn't want to work for an organization that would promote someone like Franklin Dollar. Smiling, he stood up, walked to his bedroom, put on his running clothes, and left the condo.

———

STEPHANIE WALKED through Kruger's door at exactly 12:30 p.m. She had changed into jeans and sweatshirt and looked like she was ready for a vacation. She smiled and said, "Hi, how'd the phone call go?"

Kruger was sitting on his sofa reading. He looked up, removed his reading glasses, and said, "Not worth a damn. They promoted someone to the Kansas City SAC position I refuse to work for."

Snuggling up next to him on the sofa, Kruger put his arm around her and kissed her. She said, "So, now what do we do?"

"I changed my mind, I'm going to retire. I'll let them know officially next week. I'll work through June, then I'm done."

She nodded. "Are you sure this is what you want?"

"Yes." He paused for a few seconds. "I'm tired of putting up with people like Dollar. Seltzer said he would work something out so I could stay in his department and not travel. But I think it was BS, just trying to pacify me. It's time for a change."

Placing her arm around his chest, she held him tighter. "As long as you're comfortable with the decision."

"I am." Kruger took a deep breath and let it out slowly. "I'll listen to what Seltzer comes up with, and if it's a good proposal, I'll think about it. But I'm ready to move on." He stood up and looked at her. Smiling, he reached for her hand as she stood up. "What's on our agenda this week?"

With an impish grin, Stephanie said, "Let's go get our marriage license this afternoon."

"Good plan."

Chapter Seven

KANSAS CITY, MO

Friday

"I'LL BET YOU A DOLLAR, Brian and his girlfriend show up around dinnertime," Kruger said while putting fresh sheets on the bed in the guest bedroom.

Stephanie was cleaning the small bathroom attached to the bedroom and replacing dusty towels with fresh ones. "Of course they'll show up at dinner time. Where do you want to take them?"

"Well, I thought about O'Dowd's, but we have such a busy day tomorrow we probably won't get much of a chance to sit down and talk. Besides, on Friday night, the place can be loud. Not real conducive to getting to know your son's girlfriend. One I didn't know existed."

Stephanie peeked around the door of the bathroom and looked at Kruger. "Are you still mad about not knowing?"

"Not really. He's too much like me to be mad. More jealous than anything."

"Why would you be jealous?"

"He told you, not me." Kruger smiled at her and finished fluffing the pillows. "What do you say we fix dinner here? We can have a quiet evening and get to know this young lady?"

"That would be perfect. I may have known about her, but I've never met her either. Now, the age old question of having dinner at home. What are we going to fix?"

————

THEY ARRIVED JUST after 6 p.m. Friday, having left Columbia after Brian's last class of the day. Brian was the spitting image of his father, just over six feet tall, slender and muscled like a swimmer. He wore his dark brown hair long and pulled back into a short pony tail. His face was slender, like his father's. Where Kruger had crystal blue eyes, Brian's were hazel and changed shades with the prevailing light. The father and son looked more like twins, except for the age difference. Kruger's hair was short, which allowed a small amount of gray to show at his temples. He also had the beginning of worry lines on his forehead and around his eyes.

Brian embraced his father and Stephanie, then introduced his companion. "This is Michele Brickman," he said with a proud smile. "We've known each other since our sophomore year." He was holding her hand as he introduced her, but released it when he continued, "Michele, this is my dad, Sean, and his fiancée, Stephanie Harris."

Michele smiled, shook both their hands, "Brian has told me so much about both of you, it's really nice to finally meet you." She was a slender woman, five inches shorter than Brian, with long brunette hair, emerald green eyes that sparkled in the lights coming in the room from The Plaza. She was pretty in a subtle way, an honest beauty, not enhanced with make-up. Her smile lit up the room, displaying a natural confidence in herself. Kruger admired this in people, and he liked her immediately.

The evening progressed nicely. Michele was not a vegetarian, but preferred food dominated by fresh fruits and vegetables, so the stir fry and rice prepared by Stephanie and Kruger was a hit.

After dinner, Stephanie started the inquisition.

"Michele, when do you graduate?"

Michele smiled and looked at Brian. "We both graduate in August. I start my postgraduate work at the same time Brian does. We got lucky. The university offers programs for both of us."

Brian looked at his father. "Michele will be working on her master's in child development."

Kruger nodded. "Good field." He looked at his son. "Have you made up your mind about concentrating on software or hardware?"

His son shook his head. "I'm not sure. I don't have to make that decision for another semester."

Michele held Brian's hand. "We have something in common," she said by way of changing the subject.

Stephanie smiled. "Oh, what's that?"

"We were both raised by single parents. My dad divorced my mom when I was young. I really don't remember ever living with him. Kind of like Brian and his mom."

Kruger remained quiet, but looked at Brian to see his reaction. There was none.

Michele continued. "He remarried and lives with his

other family in North Carolina. I see him once in a while, but not very often."

Stephanie said, "Where does your mother live?"

Michele was quiet and looked at the tabletop. Brian said, "Her mom lived in Hazelwood, but she passed away last year."

Stephanie reached for Michele's hand and squeezed it. "I'm sorry, Michele."

She nodded, but remained quiet. Brain continued. "I met her dad a few weeks ago. He seems like a nice guy. He's helping with her college tuition."

Kruger nodded and said, "Good. He should."

The conversation changed abruptly when Brian said, "Why'd you two suddenly decide to get married?"

Kruger looked at Stephanie and nodded for her to answer.

"Brian, your father and I have been friends for over four years. During that time we both discovered something missing in our lives. Someone to come home to. It's something you don't realize is missing until you find it. We knew we loved each other. Unfortunately we just hadn't taken the time to talk about it until last Friday night. Getting married is the just the first step. The second step will be adopting a baby brother or sister for you."

Congratulations exploded from both Brian and Michele, with the hugging lasting several minutes. Finally Brian said, "When? Do you know yet?"

Both Kruger and Stephanie shook their heads, and he said, "No, not really, could be next week or it could be next year. They never know. We have the paperwork done, which took all week. We decided we would have a small wedding with just you two and Stef's sister and husband in attendance. On Sunday, a reception has been planned at the

Marriot over on Brookside. Her office surprised us with the news early this morning. So the plans are as follows, a minister will drop by here around six tomorrow evening, perform the ceremony, and then we're all going to Houston's for dinner."

Michele turned to Stephanie and said, "I didn't bring any clothes for a reception. Is there somewhere around here I could find a nice dress?"

Stephanie eyed Michele for a second and said, "Yes, there is. Let me take you to my apartment and show you a few things. Then we'll know where to go tomorrow." They both stood and grinned at Brian and Sean.

As they watched the two ladies walk out the front door, Brian said, "Dad, I'm really happy for you and Stephanie. Why didn't you do this earlier?"

Sean sighed. "Well, there were a lot of reasons, but one very important one, and you're old enough now to understand. When your mother left, I made a pledge to myself to never say or do anything that would make you to resent her. I knew the reason she walked out. She hated being a mother. I just kept hoping she would change." He shook his head. "She never did."

Brian stared at his father. "Was it something I did?"

Kruger shook his head rapidly. "No, it was nothing you did, it started before you were born. I should have seen the signs, but I was too busy with my new career and traveling all the time. At that stage, I was gone more than I was home. She was always a little self-centered, but being pregnant caused her to become extremely selfish. She hated being pregnant and wanted me home to take care of her. My job didn't allow me to cater to her every whim. One day, you were about 10 months old, I returned from a two-day trip to St. Louis. I found you alone in your playpen crying. Your diaper was soiled, you were starving and screaming your lungs out. She was nowhere to be found."

Brian was quiet, fascinated with the story. After a few moments, he said, "What happened?"

"I was pissed beyond words. I cleaned you up, got a bottle, fed and rocked you until you settled down. I couldn't put you in the crib. Every time I did, you'd start crying, afraid you'd be left again. So I held you until you fell asleep. Your mother had packed most of her clothes and personal things, and then left you in your playpen. I don't know how long she'd been gone, probably twenty-four hours, maybe more. I never did find out. I called a lawyer friend of mine and had an injunction filed against her. She wasn't allowed to be with you unless I or my parents were in the same room. The injunction didn't really matter. She never made an attempt to see you until you were five. By that time, I had secured the divorce and was granted sole custody."

Brian stared at his father and said nothing.

Kruger continued, "Another pledge I made to myself was that I would never leave you with someone I didn't completely and unquestionably trust. That's when my parents jumped at the opportunity to help. They moved here so they could keep you when I traveled."

Brian nodded. "Grandma always told me they felt blessed about being able to help. She also told me they were sad you didn't have anyone in your life to love you."

"I wasn't aware they felt that way. They never said anything to me, but that's the way they were." Kruger shrugged. "I just didn't take the time to look for another relationship. Stephanie and I just happened. We moved in next to each other by chance, became friends, then our friendship grew into something else." He chuckled and was quiet for a moment. "Love sometimes just happens, without looking for it."

Brian sat quietly staring out the window toward the lights of The Plaza. Finally he said, "Wow. I didn't know that about my mother. I always thought it was something I did. Guess it wasn't."

"No, it wasn't. I realize now I should have told you earlier. Sorry, Brian."

Brian shrugged and looked back at his father. "It's okay, I've always known she was my mother, but Grandma was my mom." He paused, his eyes grew moist, and he blinked a few times. "I miss her."

Kruger nodded. "So do I."

Stephanie and Michele returned, giggling like teenagers. Stephanie said, "Oh, we are going to have so much fun tomorrow. We know exactly where to go."

She saw Brian's somber mood and glanced at Sean. "Did we come back at a bad time?"

Brian quickly recovered from his funk and said with a grin, "Nope, just having the birds and the bees talk with my father before his wedding night. Can't be too careful, you know."

Stephanie grinned, and Michele's face turned red with embarrassment. After a few moments, they all started laughing. As the laughter died down, Kruger said, "What time are you two going shopping?"

"Early, then I have a few things I need to get done before tomorrow night," Stephanie said.

"Great, that will give Michele and me time tomorrow to run a few errands," said Brian. "Right now I'd like to walk around The Plaza and show her some of the sights. Do you two want to go?"

Kruger shook his head. "No, you two go have fun. We need to clean up."

After they left, he and Stephanie started gathering the dishes. As they loaded the dishwasher, she said, "While you were at the grocery store this afternoon, I got a disturbing phone call from my assistant at the office."

His turned his attention to her and frowned. "What about?"

"It seems a private equity group is trying to take over the company. Have you ever heard of a firm called White-rock Equities?"

He shook his head, "Nope, but then, I don't deal in financial crimes. Why was the call so disturbing?"

"I'm not really sure. She didn't go into detail, but Sally was very upset. Rumors have been flying all over the office this week. Kind of glad I wasn't there. Apparently this group is famous for buying a company, firing all the top management, breaking it up and selling pieces off to get their money back. I've never heard of them."

"Is this just a rumor or something else?"

"Sally said the CEO of the Whiterock is in town next week for a board of directors meeting. The investment firm has already bought enough shares to demand a seat on the board. From what I was told, once that happens, they just continue to buy shares until Whiterock owns a majority of the company and they control the board."

"Give me an old-fashioned crazy guy any day. At least you know his intentions when you see him running at you with a knife."

She lightly hit his arm with her fist. "You aren't taking this seriously. This could be a problem down the road."

"For whom?" he smiled as he said it.

"Both of us. We might have to rethink our remodeling plans. What if I lose my job before the baby gets here, what then?"

"You aren't going to lose your job."

"Sean, as smart as you think you are, you're clueless when it comes to the ways of big corporations."

"Oh, I am? How many corporations have you raided lately?" He was beginning to enjoy the bantering and grabbed her around the waist as he said it.

She put her hands on his chest and feebly—but briefly —tried to free herself from his embrace. Placing her head on his chest, she sighed.

"I know, I'm being paranoid. I'm so glad I have you. For the first time in my adult life, I have something besides my career to think about. But I just don't need a crisis at work right now."

He kissed the top of her head and embraced her tightly. "Well, whatever happens we'll get through it together." Kruger paused. "Hey, I could get Mint Dollar to arrest him."

She pushed away, frowned and looked up at him. "It's not funny. I'm worried about this."

"Okay, if you're really concerned, I'll call a friend in D.C. Who should I ask about?"

Stephanie gave him the name, and he went to his office. Closing the door, he found the number he was looking for on his iPhone and pressed the call icon. His call was answered on the second ring, "Detective Clark, Homicide."

Kruger smiled. He knew Clark would still be working on a Friday night.

"Ryan, it's Sean Kruger. How are you tonight?"

"Sean, good to hear from you. Thanks for getting the Rousch case off my desk so quickly. I knew it was beyond our jurisdiction. What's up?"

"What was the name of the Secret Service agent with you last Friday? Ed or Ted something?"

"That was Ted Margolin, good guy. I've known him for a long time. He used to be with our department before they recruited him. Why?"

"I was asked a question today, one I couldn't answer. I need to run a name by him to see if he knows anything, that's all."

"Well, I know he'll talk to me, not sure about someone he doesn't know. I don't mind calling him. Besides I owe you for last week."

"That would really speed things up. Got a pencil?"

Kruger gave him the information about Whiterock, and Clark said, "I'll call you back after I talk to him, might be Monday. Will that work?"

"Fine with me. Thanks, Ryan."

"I heard a rumor this week you might be getting married and retiring, is that true?"

"Yes to the first and no to the second." He didn't feel like getting into long explanations tonight.

"Glad you took my advice, congratulations. And I'm pleased you're not retiring. Not enough of us good guys left. When's the wedding?"

"Tomorrow afternoon."

"Really? Shotgun wedding?"

Kruger chuckled. "No, we figured we weren't getting any younger, so why wait."

"Yeah, I hear you on not getting any younger. I hope I find someone like her someday. Next time you're in D.C., call me, I'll buy you a beer."

"Sounds good, Ryan. Call me as soon as you talk to Margolin." Kruger ended the call and sat staring at the wall. He knew how rumors started and wondered who Seltzer had told about his plans.

The phone rang less than five minutes later with Clark's

name on the caller ID.

Without delay he took the call, "Kruger."

"What kind of shit storm did you get me into, Sean? Margolin almost bit my head off. He wants to know what you know, and he wants to know it right now."

Chapter Eight

Friday

HE READ the saved email draft for the third time, then pressed the delete icon on his Samsung smartphone. The corners of his mouth edged slightly higher. Clean shaven with black hair cut short, his dark eyes stared out from behind black-rimmed glasses sitting on a narrow aquiline nose. He could have been a resident of any country bordering the Mediterranean Sea. Norman Ortega knew the man as Eduardo Acosta, a Spaniard. The man was not from Spain.

"I take the message was good news?" The older bearded man sat at a table sipping strong tea from a short glass.

"Yes."

The older man nodded. "You should be proud of your deception, Aazim. So far, the infidels do not know jihad has landed on their shores."

"They soon will."

"Come, sit with me and tell me what you have planned.

The brothers will be interested in what their money is paying for."

Aazim Abbas did not sit down. He turned and began pacing the small apartment, which overlooked Marina Bay, near Richmond. It was small by American standards, but spacious compared to where Abbas had lived in Paris. He stared out the window facing the bay, his revulsion of American excesses reinforced by what he saw. Private yachts and sail boats populated the docks west of his apartment. Women, who thought nothing of exposing their bodies in public, littered the boats in the bay.

"Tell the brothers their money is being spent wisely. By this time next week, everyone in the United States will know someone is preying on them. But they will have no idea who."

He turned and looked at the cleric. "When the time is right, we will broadcast to the world who is responsible. Until then, we must keep a low profile. Inshallah."

The bearded man nodded. "Yes, yes. I agree. But I must warn you some of our supporters believe we should accept responsibility for each event. They grow impatient."

"Let them be impatient. They are not here, dealing with the security." Aazim's eyes narrowed and his brow wrinkled. "I will not be rushed. They sent me here to bring jihad to the Americans. I am doing that. Tell them it must be done my way, or they can replace me. It has taken two years for our planning to bear fruit. Now they expect instant results."

"They are not unhappy, just anxious." The older man stood and walked to Aazim. He placed his hand on the younger man's shoulder and said in a soft voice. "We are dealing with old men with too much time on their hands. Old men who do not understand the complexity of your task. Let them voice their concerns, as it makes them happy. Keep to your schedule. Do not let their words sway you."

Abbas stared into the eyes of his mentor and nodded. "I will keep my tongue quiet."

"Good. Now, sit, join me for tea. We will discuss the next phase of your plan."

Aazim sat next to the older man and sipped on a glass of strong, bitter black tea. He was quiet for several minutes. Finally, the Imam said, "My brother, I have seen that look in your eye before. What have you decided?"

"Do you have any believers in your mosque? Zealots who are anxious to be with Allah?"

"Yes, we have several." The older man nodded slightly and sipped his tea. "I did not think you wanted that sort of activity yet."

"Maybe the old men are correct. Maybe I am being too cautious." He took another sip of tea, carefully lowered the small glass to the table and turned to the Imam. "What is the one thing Americans cherish most?"

"Their possessions?"

"Yes, but they cherish acquiring those possessions more. They do not really care for what they buy; they just love to buy. What if we struck at the heart of the beast? The very embodiment of this obsession of buying things."

"Yes. Yes, I see where your mind is taking you, Aazim. But what of your other plan?"

"It will move ahead without interruption. This will be extra. We will strike in the heart of the country, at the very belly of the beast itself."

The Imam smiled. "Tell me what is in your mind, Aazim."

Abbas nodded and proceeded to tell his mentor.

Chapter Nine

KANSAS CITY, MO

Friday Evening

"RYAN, slow down. What exactly did Ted say?"

"When I gave him the name you asked about, he was silent for a few seconds. Then in a quiet voice, he said, 'Why are you asking about this person?' So I replied, 'Sean Kruger with the FBI, you know you met him a week ago when Rousch was killed. He's following up on a lead and was just curious if you had heard of them.' That's when he went psycho on me. First he wanted to know why the FBI was investigating the man, then he wanted to know why he was going through me, then... Well, he just didn't make any sense. I calmed him down and said you'd call him. Call him right now, Sean, before the guy has a heart attack."

Kruger suppressed a laugh. "Okay, obviously I hit a nerve. I'll call him right now. As far as I'm concerned, you were never involved. We did not have this conversation. If someone checks the phone records, we were talking about the wedding to see if you could possibly get here, do you understand?"

"Yeah, I appreciate that, Sean. Let me know how it goes."

"I will. Good night."

Kruger ended the call and sat for a moment, trying to make sense of what had just happened. Apparently the man he had asked about was on a watch list within the Secret Service. If so, why?

Stephanie knocked and opened the office door to check on him. "Have you found out anything?"

"At the moment I'm not sure. Give me a few minutes; I need to make another call. Maybe then I can make sense of the last one."

Stephanie had been around him long enough to know it was time to shut the door and wait, which she did. Kruger gathered his thoughts and dialed the number Clark had given him for Margolin. The call was answered on the fourth ring. "If this is Kruger, you have a lot of explaining to do."

"Obviously the individual I inquired about is known to your organization."

"Just what the hell do you think you're doing? Why are you investigating Fernando Guevara?"

"Actually, I'm not. His name came up, I became curious and made a phone call, that's all."

Margolin was quiet for a moment. "Why are you curious?"

"My fiancée works for a company Whiterock is interested in. Guevara has bought a lot of stock and is trying to get a seat on the board, or something like that. Hell, I don't know this crap. She and everybody in her office are nervous.

I was trying to help and find out what I could. Nothing diabolical or sinister, simply trying to get some information for my future wife."

Kruger could hear a sigh on the other end of the phone. "Okay, I understand, Clark said I can trust you. What kind of information do you need?"

"Tell me about Guevara. What's his story?"

"Fernando Guevara is the son of Spanish immigrants, Philippe and Isabelle Guevara. They arrived in New York City in the summer of 1940. The dad was a tailor, opened a small shop in the South Bronx. Fernando was born in 1950, graduated from New York City College and took a job as a stock broker on Wall Street. Made his first million by the time he was twenty-four, then lost it during the oil embargo years of the seventies. The eighties were kind to him. He worked for several firms, then found a home as a fund manager at Goldman Sachs in 1989. Apparently, he made a ton of money during the dot com period, left Goldman Sachs and formed Whiterock Equities. That's when he became politically active. He is a major donor to the current president's party."

"I see. Thus the Secret Service's interest."

"Yeah. Thus our interest. He and the president are very close. He dines at the White House at least once, sometimes twice a month. We've vetted him several times, for security reasons. Plus, there was a rumor he was going to be tapped for a cabinet position. So far, that hasn't happened. The only thing questionable we found about the man was his business practices. He's ruthless when he sets his sights on acquiring a company."

"How so?"

"He's an egotistical bastard. He surrounds himself with very intelligent individuals, but if they disagree with him, he fires them. One such individual told us he got into a discussion with Guevara about how a target company was being evaluated. Guevara told him he was wrong; the guy calmly showed him the data, insisting he was right. Guevara started screaming at the guy, firing him in the middle of a meeting. The only reason he keeps good people is he pays twice what they would make anywhere else."

Kruger thought about this for a moment, started to say something but decided not to. "Okay, he's a jerk, that's not a crime. Why is the Secret Service so sensitive about this guy?"

"Because of his relationship with the president. Individuals higher up the ladder than I scratch their collective heads on why the president likes the guy. When he buys a company, the first thing he does is start letting people go. We were told this practice has two purposes. One, it immediately cuts overhead, and two, makes the survivors work harder. He then reorganizes the company and sells it outright, or breaks it up into various smaller companies. He then sells these entities separately. Whichever way he does it, people lose their jobs. We were told Whiterock regularly produces profits in the eight to nine figure range."

"How much has he contributed to the president?"

"A lot."

"Well, there you go. Money has a tendency to create strange friendships sometimes."

Margolin sighed, "Yeah, I suppose it does."

"Ted, thanks for the info. I owe you one."

"Well, let's chalk it up to interagency cooperation, what'd ya say?"

"Sounds good, talk to you later." Kruger ended the call and got his laptop out.

He emerged from his office twenty minutes later and

went straight to the coffee pot. After checking to see if it was still on from dinner, he poured two cups. He looked at Stephanie, who was sitting at the dining room table checking emails on her laptop. He motioned for her to follow him to the balcony. He sat down at the bistro table and stared out at the lights of The Plaza. Stephanie sat down and waited for him to start talking.

"Stef, the guy who owns Whiterock does exactly what you told me. He buys his way into a company, takes it over, and then sells off the pieces. Fernando Guevara believes he can do no wrong. He buys and sells companies like a used car dealer. No concern for the employees of the companies. They're just part of the assets."

Stephanie sipped her coffee and said, "Should I warn someone at my company?"

Kruger shrugged. "I don't know, his tactics aren't secret. I'm sure your senior management is aware of how he does business."

Stephanie grew quiet and stared out past the balcony. After several minutes, she said, "What can I do, Sean? I have to warn someone."

"I'm familiar with the psych profile, individuals who have an inflated perception of their own importance. They surround themselves with people who agree with everything they say. The rest of humanity is here to serve their needs and bow down to them. His personality type is dangerous when they have a gun, but this guy is probably more treacherous in other ways. The only thing I can suggest is talk to Neil. I'm not sure he can do anything if Guevara buys the stock he needs."

Stephanie reached for his hand and squeezed it. "Thank you, I appreciate you making the phone call. As I told you Friday night, I've lost my lust for making sales goals, and if something happens to the company…" She shrugged. "Let's concentrate on ourselves for a change, not the job."

"Whatever happens, we'll get through it together," Kruger said with a smile. "Hell, who knows, Oklahoma City might look pretty good in a few months."

Chapter Ten

KANSAS CITY, MO

Sunday

SMALL TALK WAS NOT his favorite pastime, but he did enjoy observing corporate culture in action. The reception held for them by Stephanie's company on Sunday afternoon was a great place to observe the pecking order and who was trying to get promoted. After all the congratulations and hand-shaking, Kruger found himself standing next to the bar and drinking the first of his self-imposed two beer limit. While watching Stephanie introduce Brian and Michele to her co-workers, he thought back to last night's dinner after their wedding.

Stephanie had arranged everybody at the table so she could sit next to Brian. After the cocktails and wine were served, she turned to him and in a serious tone, said, "Brian, now that your father and I are married, I would like to ask you a question. I know I'm not your real mother, but I love you like a son. With your permission, I'd like to introduce you tomorrow, and in the future, as my son. Would that be alright?"

Brian smiled. Like his father, he was seldom caught off guard by unexpected questions.

"Only if you allow me to call you Mom," he answered.

From that moment on, the evening went perfectly.

He smiled with the memory and sensed more than saw someone approaching where he stood. Wine glass in hand, Neil Ross, CEO and president of the company, was walking over to Kruger. The two shook hands, and Neil said, "Congratulations, Sean, I'm happy for both of you. Stephanie's an extraordinary individual and a valued member of my team. She deserves a fulfilling personal life."

"Thank you, Neil. I agree, she is extraordinary."

Neil Ross was in his early 60s, and not a heavy man, but one who had the body of someone who spent more time behind a desk than on a treadmill. He was dressed in a dark gray pinstripe Armani suit, complimented with an open collar blue silk shirt. His once coal-black hair was now lightened by an increasing number of silver streaks. Ross was the same height as Kruger, but today he appeared weary, his posture was slightly slumped, and the dark circles under his eyes detracted from his handsome face. Neil looked out at the crowd and said, "Can I talk to you for a moment on a professional level?"

Kruger looked at him and raised an eyebrow. "About what, Neil?"

"Stephanie tells me you know a little about Fernando Guevara."

Kruger shrugged. "I made a few calls, can't say I know a lot about him."

Neil nodded his head. "I understand your reluctance to

discuss this, but I and some of the local board members have been asked to meet with Guevara later this afternoon here at the Marriott. His staff called on Friday and inquired if we would be available to meet with him."

Neil paused for a few moments and looked at Kruger. "How did the man know several of us would be here?"

"Neil, I don't believe in coincidences. He knew about the reception, which means someone inside your organization is feeding him information. Stef and I didn't even decide to get married until last weekend. This whole thing was thrown together this week."

"Yes, I'm afraid I agree with you. I can't for the life of me figure out who would benefit. Can you tell me anything about him?"

Kruger thought for a moment. He had met Neil Ross several times over the past four years and liked the man. He was ethical, loyal to his staff and managed the company with compassion.

"I honestly don't know much, but as a profiler I would consider him narcissistic and manipulative. Definitely deceitful. I wouldn't believe a word he tells you, and anything discussed, I would get in writing. Preferably notarized by the Supreme Court."

Neil smiled at the last part. "I called a few friends around the country yesterday trying to get prepared for the meeting. They all agree with you. He has a ruthless reputation and everyone suggested not trusting anything he says in conversation. He told Frank he wants to have a private meeting with just the two of us in the morning. Not sure what it's about, maybe to discuss his offer before the board meeting tomorrow afternoon."

"Can't you tell him the company's not for sale?"

"Unfortunately, it is my fiduciary duty to determine

what is best for the shareholders of this company. If he makes a good offer, I am bound to present it to the board. Now, they can vote to decline the offer, but I have to take it to them. If he does buy us, I'll be gone, and senior management will be dismissed and replaced within six months to a year. That's his pattern."

"Do you think the board will vote that way?"

"The board has always agreed with Frank and me on our decisions because we do what's right for the company, and they trust us. But we've never had to deal with a situation like this before, a semi-hostile takeover bid." He shrugged. "I don't know what to expect."

"Sorry, but I'm not in a position to say too much." Kruger was getting uncomfortable. He couldn't tell Neil about the conversation with Ted Margolin.

Kruger was about to tell Neil he couldn't discuss anything further when a slender man in an incredibly expensive suit walked up to Neil. He was slightly over five-and-a-half feet tall, with coal-black hair combed straight back, bushy eyebrows over a hawk nose. The man extended his hand and said, "Neil, I'm Fernando Guevara. I was told you would be here. Mind if I join you?"

Neil looked shocked for half a second, but recovered rapidly, shook the extended hand and said, "Why, no, I don't mind, nice to meet you. Mr. Guevara, this is Sean Kruger. He and his wife are the reason for this little get-together. They were married yesterday."

Guevara smiled and shook Kruger's hand. "Nice to meet you, Sean. What is your position in the company?"

Kruger smiled, noticing that Guevara did not say congratulations or hello, but simply addressed him by his first name and got to business. He had also addressed Neil, a man he'd never met, the same way. How interesting. Kruger was going to enjoy this next part.

"Actually, I'm not with the company," he replied. "My wife is the Senior Executive Vice President of Domestic Sales. I'm an agent with the FBI."

Normally, in social settings such as this, when he dropped the FBI bomb, people either got flustered or were fascinated. Guevara did neither.

He politely said, "Well, nice to meet you anyway." Then he turned his attention back to Neil. "I would really like to meet your staff. Can you introduce me?"

Neil appeared tense and upset about the intrusion, so Kruger said, "Neil, I have to make a phone call. I'll talk to you later."

With that comment, Neil lead Guevara toward a group of senior managers gathered around a TV watching a Royals game.

Kruger observed as Guevara was introduced to each of the managers, half of whom were women. As the introductions progressed, Guevara seemed to ignore the women and concentrate on the male members of the group. Kruger smiled and slowly shook his head. Stephanie walked up to him and nudged him on the arm.

"Was that Fernando Guevara? I heard he might show up. Did you meet him?

"Yeah, I met him. That's him with Neil, all business, no time for social niceties. Since I don't work for the company, I'm persona non grata. Interesting guy, but I wouldn't want to have a beer with him. Watch how he interacts with the group over there. He's basically ignoring the women."

Stephanie watched for a few minutes and said, "Great, just great. At least Neil isn't kissing his ass. That would make it even more disgusting."

Kruger laughed and said, "Neil doesn't look too thrilled either. Probably wanting another glass of wine. Or something stronger. Why don't you go get Neil another drink, take it over there and get introduced?" There was a hint of mischievousness in his voice.

Stephanie stared at him and shook her head, "You're impossible. I'm sure I'll meet him soon enough. I need to rescue Brian and Michele. I left them with Bill and Lucy Henderstill. I hope they're still awake when I get back."

She walked away, making a wide circle around the area where Fernando Guevara was standing.

Kruger was following her with his eyes, thinking about how great she looked, when he noticed the man in the navy blazer. He was sitting at the bar and staring at Guevara. His expression was blank. Every few moments, he would fiddle with what appeared to be a Bluetooth receiver in his right ear. Kruger immediately suspected it wasn't a Bluetooth receiver, but a hearing enhancing device. He had used something similar several times when he was on surveillance. However, this one looked more like something from Walmart.

As Guevara moved around the room meeting different people, the man would follow discreetly, always staying about thirty feet away.

He didn't appear to be part of a security team. He was slender and did not have the upper body strength of most corporate security personnel. Plus those guys usually stood closer to their client and were constantly glancing around. This guy wasn't; he was concentrating on Guevara.

Besides the blue blazer, he wore khaki pants, a light blue polo shirt and loafers. He was holding a short glass containing a clear liquid and trying to be inconspicuous.

Intrigued, Kruger didn't care if the guy was spying on

Guevara, but he did care if the man was working for Guevara and recording private conversations. He made sure his iPhone's camera would not flash and discreetly took several pictures from about fifteen feet. After watching the man for a few more minutes, his years of experience told him the guy wasn't working for Guevara. He was following him.

Thirty minutes later, Guevara finished his rounds at the reception and left. His shadow set his drinking glass down and followed at a distance. In Kruger's mind, this left no doubt the guy was following Guevara. As discreetly as possible, Kruger wandered over to where the man had set his cocktail glass. Reaching down, he used three fingers spread inside the glass to pick it up without disturbing any finger prints on the outside. He took the glass to the bartender, showed his FBI credentials and asked for a plastic zip-top bag.

Nodding, the guy found one behind the bar and handed it to Kruger. "You gonna pay for that glass or just take it?"

Kruger stared at the man. "It's evidence. I'm taking it. You got a problem with that?"

The bartender backed up and hurriedly shook his head no.

With the bagged glass in hand, he walked to a quiet section of the reception area and took his iPhone out. He attached the pictures of the man to an email and sent them to a technician at the FBI Facial Recognition Department in D.C. Hopefully, he would get a response in a day or two. The fingerprints on the glass would be taken to the local FBI office first thing in the morning for processing. If he was lucky, using both methods there was a good chance to identify the man by tomorrow afternoon.

Suddenly he realized there might be one more possibility. He found Ted Margolin's number on his phone and called. Ted answered immediately, "Do you know it's Sunday, Kruger?"

"Actually I do, but I just met Fernando Guevara. I also found something interesting and thought you might want to know." He paused. "If you don't, I can call you tomorrow."

"Don't hang up. What is it?"

"Did you know he has a shadow?"

Margolin was quiet for several moments. "What do you mean, a shadow?" He paused, but before Kruger could answer, he continued. "Hey, what's going on, are you harassing the man?"

Laughing, Kruger said, "No, he showed up at a reception my wife's company is holding for us. Remember, the company he is trying to take over."

"Okay, now what do you mean about a shadow?"

"Someone is following him. Not a pro from what I could tell, but definitely someone trying to listen in on his conversations."

Margolin was silent for a moment, and then said, "We don't have anyone following him, if that's what you wanted to know. Could be an investor trying to get a scoop on his next target. They'd start buying shares anticipating the announcement of Whiterock making an offer. Once the news is out, the stock price of the target company goes up, and the investor makes a profit. Or it could be a reporter for one of the financial publications."

"So you think this is just some guy trying to make a buck?"

"Yeah, that's how I would view it."

"Okay, Ted, thanks. Sorry to bother you."

Kruger ended the call and stood thinking. Was the guy just some investor trying to get a lead on a stock or a reporter? If either were true, he was wasting his time getting the fingerprints analyzed. But his instincts told him different, and those instincts had solved more than a few cases over his career. Finally he decided he would get the prints checked and wait for the facial analysis. No use getting excited, and if it turned out to be a false alarm, so be it. At least he was being proactive.

Chapter Eleven

KANSAS CITY, MO

Monday

A PATCH above the left breast pocket on his shirt read 'Jerry' in stitched cursive letters. His name was not Jerry. The time was 10 a.m., and busy shoppers were already competing for parking spaces around Kansas City's Country Club Plaza. Frustration growing, it took several passes before one of three parking spaces he had chosen the previous day where available. The spot was just west of O'Dowd's Little Dublin at the corner of Pennsylvania and 48th Street. After parking the white Ford van, he gathered his clipboard, opened the door, and walked to the back of the van for his tool case. Calmly strolling to the front door of the tavern, he knocked and waited. O'Dowd's was still closed at that time of the morning, but a manager unlocked the door and motioned for him to enter.

"Well, Jerry," the manager said, glancing at the name on his shirt, "about damn time you got here. We open for business in less than thirty minutes, so you'd better hurry"

"Sorry, couldn't find a parking space. From what I was told last night it shouldn't take very long." Thomas Cooper smiled. "Just show me which restroom and I'll get started."

"This way." The manager started walking toward the other side of the pub. "The men's room overflowed last night about closing time. What a mess. We had to pay a couple of guys overtime to clean it up." The manger talked like he was speaking to no one in particular, just complaining. Cooper liked that. The less attention the manager paid to him, the less likely he would remember a description. After all, he was just a plumber, and no one remembered what a plumber looked like.

After showing him the offending toilet, the manager said, "Please hurry."

He quickly left the room to attend to more important problems. After the door to the restroom closed, Cooper took a long wire out of his tool kit. Snaking the wire into the bowl, it only took a few seconds before he felt resistance on the probe. He quickly pulled the object out and deposited it in the trash can. He had clogged the toilet the night before right before closing time with a specially designed sponge. Making sure he was still in the bar when it backed up and overflowed, he handed the night manager a business card for a company called Just In Time Plumbers. It was an actual company; he had taken the business card the previous week from the company after applying for a job.

He said, "I can be here first thing in the morning to fix it. I would right now, but don't have my tools."

The night manager said, "Okay, I'll leave a note for the day manager. What time will you be here?"

With the toilet unclogged, Cooper sat down on the toilet and waited for a phone call.

He didn't wait long. Less than fifteen minutes later, his cell phone vibrated. He answered it by saying, "Yes."

"On time, twenty minutes, your position."

The call ended.

Cooper stood, left his tools in the restroom and strolled to the front door. A young college student was preparing the front of the bar for the lunch time crowd. She smiled at him.

He smiled back. She was cute, blond, petite but well-endowed, and her name badge told him her name was Crystal. "Hi, Crystal, I have to get more tools out of the truck. Be right back."

He waited as two gentlemen in suits entered the now-open restaurant, then he walked out and turned right toward the van. He stopped in front of it, pulled a cigarette from a box in his shirt pocket, lit it, and continued to walk away from O'Dowd's.

Five minutes later, he had doubled back. The shirt with Jerry above the breast pocket and the flesh-colored surgical gloves were gone. His chosen position was about a hundred yards due south of O'Dowd's at the corner of Pennsylvania Avenue and Ward Parkway with a perfect view of the van. He leaned against the building and waited.

After another six minutes, he saw the limousine turn off of 47th Street onto Pennsylvania Avenue and head toward him. It slowed and turned right onto 48th Street, stopping even with the back of the van. He had calculated correctly. The limo stopped exactly where he needed it to be located. The driver got out and hurried back to the rear passenger side door. Once the door was open, a man about five-and-a-half feet tall with black slicked-back hair exited. He paused to say something to the driver.

Cooper quickly glanced at a photo on his cell phone,

smiled, and with his other hand, pressed the button on the converted garage door opener hidden in his pants pocket. He then moved behind the building to avoid the concussion.

The van exploded with a massive force, violently shredding the metal, glass, wiring, and plastic on the right side of the limousine. The driver and passenger died instantly from the concussion and shrapnel. Their bodies were then incinerated as the limousine's gas tank ignited. In the ensuing chaos, Cooper joined a group of panicked pedestrians rushing to get away from the noise and dust of the explosion. Amid the screams, he quickly walked to the east side of The Plaza. It took him almost seven minutes to reach the spot where he had parked a rental car earlier in the morning. As he opened the car door, the sirens of first responders could be heard off in the distance. Not wishing to get caught up in a police blockade, he calmly got in the car, started it and eased away from the shoulder. He headed north.

The route he followed took him to I-70 East, where he merged onto the interstate highway and started the three-and-a-half hour drive to St. Louis. There was little worry about being stopped by police for a traffic violation, but he kept his speed to the posted limit, just in case. Cooper figured they had more important things to do. He was right.

Six hours later he was sitting in the last row next to the window on a Southwest Airline flight bound for Love Field in Dallas. His hair was now its natural color and his tinted contacts were discarded. As the plane began to taxi toward the runway, he allowed himself a slight smile. Leaning his head back in the seat, he closed his eyes and relaxed for the first time that day.

An hour and half later, as the plane taxied to the terminal at Love Field, he turned on his phone and texted a one word message to a memorized number. After sending the word Dallas, he deleted the number from the phone and shut it off.

After exiting the plane with his carry-on in tow, he noticed the airport was moderately busy. This suited him fine. Waiting for the taxi took several minutes, but no one paid unusual attention to him. He instructed the driver to take him to the Adam's Mark Hotel in downtown Dallas. After paying the driver, he exited the cab, waited for it to get out of sight, then hiked three blocks to the Westin City Center. There, he entered the hotel and went to the restroom. Waiting ten minutes, he exited the hotel, found a cab waiting and proceeded to DFW airport.

He boarded the 9 p.m. flight to Atlanta and arrived just after midnight Eastern Time. After working his way to his car in long term parking, he left the airport, found I-85 south and started driving. Pleased with his progress, he finally stopped at a Holiday Inn Express in La Grange, Georgia. Once in his room, he turned his cell phone on and found he had a text message waiting.

The message was simple, "Acknowledged check in 2." This meant his previous message had been received and for him to check his email in two days. Satisfied with the events of the day, he took a quick shower, laid down and slept until noon.

Chapter Twelve

KANSAS CITY, MO

Monday Morning

AFTER THE FURIOUS activities of the weekend and the lateness of the prior evening, Kruger opened his eyes and stared at the digital clock by his bed, 9:59 a.m. "Haven't done that in a long time," he mumbled to himself.

Stephanie was curled up at his side with her back to him, her steady and rhythmic breathing a calming force to his sudden alertness. Had he heard something, or was it a dream? Probably a dream. His sleeping patterns had been so irregular of late, he was amazed he had actually slept till mid-morning.

He gently pushed the sheets aside, got out of bed and headed to the bathroom. He pulled on his boxers and went to the kitchen to start a pot of coffee. The sun was already past the balcony overhang as he opened the patio door and stood by the rail looking down on the Plaza traffic. The day was going to be warm. A good day to be with Stephanie and start figuring out their new life together as husband and wife, or wife and husband, whichever, he didn't care, just as long as they were together.

When the coffee was done, he went back to the bedroom to check on Stephanie. She was stirring, so he sat down on the bed to watch her. Last night, after the passion of making love, they lay together making plans. He had not realized until their conversation how relieved he was to be retiring at the end of June. The constant traveling, long periods away from her, a frustrating bureaucracy within the agency, and the realization his job was no longer challenging—all this merged into a sudden realization of his own weariness. In the past five years, he had solved several high profile cases. But recently, he had not felt challenged.

Why? Was it because he was bored, or was it due to loneliness? He went back into the kitchen and poured two cups of coffee, one with a little Sweet N Low and one with half 'n half for Stephanie. Taking the cups back to the bedroom, he set hers down on her nightstand. She stirred and opened one eye. With a slight grin on her face, she said, "I don't suppose you know what time it is, do you?"

"I do."

"You said that Saturday." She grinned.

"Yes I did."

"Well? Are you going to enlighten me about the time, or do I have to guess?"

"Guess."

"Seven-thirty?"

"Nope."

"Eight."

"Nope."

"Sean, don't tease me, it can't be past eight."

"It's exactly ten-forty. You slept in."

Stephanie groaned, rose up to look at the digital clock,

then fell back to her pillow. "I was supposed to get my hair cut at eight-thirty. Guess that didn't happen."

"Nope, guess it didn't."

"Can you say anything besides 'nope' this morning?"

"Yes. I love..."

He didn't finish. The explosion rattled the windows of the condo. It intensified as the concussion and dust cloud reached the balcony and swirled into the condo through an open sliding door.

"What the hell..." was all Kruger could say as he reached first for a pair of jeans, then tennis shoes, a polo shirt, badge, cell phone, and gun.

He was out the door before Stephanie could say anything. When he got to the street, he stopped, clipped his badge to his belt and tried to determine the direction he needed to go. Sounds were echoing off buildings and masking their true direction; he saw a reflection of flickering light and took off running.

He ran down 47th Street to Pennsylvania, turned right and saw the chaos two blocks to the south. Heading that way, he reached the corner at 48th and witnessed pure bedlam. As he turned, he saw the tangled metal of what was once a limousine in front of O'Dowd's Little Dublin. Body parts were strewn on the sidewalk and street, while individuals with blood streaming from their face sat on the sidewalk dazed. A woman screamed as she cradled a young infant in her arms. An elderly man held a similarly aged woman in his arms, stroking her face and trying to keep her calm. Trees in front of O'Dowd's were smoldering as first responders started to arrive. The scene reminded him of a terrorist bombing in Bagdad he had helped investigate a few years after the downfall of Saddam Hussein.

Kruger's trained eye went to the burning limousine. The

right side was a twisted tangle of metal and melted plastic. The roof line was sheared and angled perpendicular to the body. He positioned himself to see if there were any survivors; what met his sight told him the answer. The interior of the limousine contained two bodies in the rear portion, both charred beyond recognition. He had seen this type of destructive power before, but it was always military in nature. He made a mental note to make sure explosive residue was tested. His guess would be C4.

A fire truck screeched to a halt next to the shattered limousine. Several firemen leapt to the ground with fire extinguisher and started spraying the burning car. Kruger backed off and let them do their job. He walked back to O'Dowd's and went in through the shattered glass of the front lobby. The scene was grim. A young lady, with whom he had flirted on several occasions, lay unmoving on the floor. He bent down, felt her neck and did not find what he was searching for. Her unfocused eyes stared at the ceiling, confirming her condition. The tables and chairs next to the front window had been thrown back into the interior and shattered. Apparently the only person in the front of the building had been the hostess. Lucky her.

He headed to the rear of the restaurant to see if he could assist any of the injured. There had been few customers at this hour, but he found two he knew.

Neil Ross and Frank Bonner were in the back of the restaurant on the floor, covered with debris from the ceiling and broken tables and chairs. Neil had a bad gash on his forehead, and Frank Bonner stared blankly, a large shard of glass protruding from his half-severed neck. Kruger bent down to check on Neil. There was a pulse, although weak.

"Neil... Neil... Can you hear me?"

With a raspy voice, barely above a whisper, Neil Ross said, "What happened?"

"Don't move, you've been in an accident. Help will be here shortly."

Neil opened his eyes and stared at Kruger. At first not recognizing him, the older man finally nodded. "Sean, is that you?"

"Yes, sir, don't move until the EMTs get here."

"Where's Frank?"

Kruger noticed several first responders moving toward them and said, "I've got a severe laceration on the upper forehead here, probably a concussion."

The EMTs nodded and pointed to Frank Bonner. "What about that one?"

Kruger shook his head. The fireman understood and knelt down next to Kruger.

Neil said, "Sean, where's Frank?" with a note of desperation in his voice.

Kruger had to tell him something. "Neil, Frank's hurt, they're working on him right now."

"How bad, Sean?"

Kruger gave him a slight smile, but said nothing.

"We were supposed to meet Fernando Guevara here at ten-thirty. He…" Neil closed his eyes and seemed to lose consciousness.

The EMT gently shook him. "Sir, don't go to sleep, I need you alert. Stay with me, sir." He shook him again and Neil opened his eyes. Tears formed and slid down his dust covered face.

Kruger thought about what he had just heard. Fernando Guevara was meeting them here. More than likely one of the bodies in the limo outside was him. He shook his head. Rich guy number three.

74

Later, after he watched Neil being loaded into an ambulance, he surveyed the area. He was surprised to see Franklin Dollar, the Special Agent in Charge of the Kansas City FBI Office, talking to several men in FBI windbreakers. He wanted to go back to his apartment, but thought he needed to get Dollar the information about Guevara. As he approached the group of FBI agents, Dollar noticed him and waved him over.

"Kruger, what the hell are you doing here?"

Kruger glared at Dollar and said "I live about five blocks from here. Heard the explosion and thought I could help."

Dollar nodded, "Did you see anything?"

"No, it was pure chaos when I arrived. The limo appears to have taken the greatest force of the explosion." Kruger pointed to the now smoldering car and then pointed at the damaged front of Dublin's. "Two dead in the restaurant, with at least half a dozen injured, some critically."

Dollar turned back to his men and said, "Start looking for anyone who saw the explosion. Everyone knows the drill." Both men nodded and took off in different directions. Dollar turned back to Kruger. "I know you and I don't see eye to eye on a lot of things, but we need to work together on this as a team. Are you on board?"

Kruger stared at Dollar, trying to determine his motive, but finally stuck his hand out and said, "Yeah, I'm on board. This was too close to my home not to be."

Both men shook, understanding they had a truce for the moment.

Kruger pointed to the limousine and said, "I can give you a pretty good guess on one of the victims in the limo."

Dollar looked at the destroyed vehicle. "Who?"

"Fernando Guevara, CEO of Whiterock Equities. He

was meeting two gentlemen here at the restaurant. Looks like someone knew he was going to be here."

"How do you know?" Franklin looked at Kruger with skepticism.

"Because my wife's boss was the one he was meeting and they just put him in an ambulance. That's how I know."

"You said two."

"Yeah, the other one didn't make it. Look, I was at a crime scene in Washington a week ago that may be related."

"How?"

"Two other high profile businessmen were killed in Washington, D.C. Guevara fits the profile, but this is an extreme way of killing him. The others were executed, one with a close range double tap, and the other with a rifle from long range."

Franklin looked at Kruger, sighed and said, "Go home, clean up, and be in my office this afternoon at 4 p.m. I'll arrange a conference call with Washington."

Kruger glanced at his watch, but it wasn't there. He had left the condo so fast, he'd forgotten it. Walking west on 48th Street, heading back to their condo, he saw Stephanie helping several women sitting next to a building. She had apparently followed Kruger after he rushed out of the condo. As he got closer, she saw him and rushed into his arms.

"Sean, thank God you're okay. I was so worried."

"I'm fine, Stef, what are you doing here?"

"When you bolted out of the apartment, I started hearing the sirens and thought I needed to go and help in some way. I found several people wondering around in a daze, so I got them to sit down until the EMTs arrived. Where've you been?"

"The explosion was in front of O'Dowd's. It's bad, Stef, really bad. Neil and Frank were there waiting for Guevara. Neil is on his way to the hospital." He paused for a second, "Frank... I'm sorry. Frank didn't make it."

Stephanie looked at him with terror in her eyes and then buried her face in his chest. He could feel her sobbing. Taking her hand, he started walking back to the condo. Halfway back he thought of something. He pulled out his cell phone and dialed a number in Washington, D.C. The call was answered immediately, "Lab, Luke Riley speaking."

"Luke, it's Kruger."

"Hey, Sean, I haven't run that picture yet. Hope that's okay, your email said it wasn't urgent."

"Yeah, I know, Luke. About thirty minutes ago, it jumped to Urgent High Priority. There's been an explosion here in KC, and the guy in the photo may be someone of interest."

There was silence on the phone, and then Luke said, "It's on CNN right now. Looks bad."

"It is, Luke. I know of at least four dead, and the total may climb before the day is over."

"Okay, Sean, I'll run it right now. Is this official or what?"

"Luke, I hate to ask you this, but I would prefer you keep it between you and me for now. If this person is not involved, I'm the only one who will catch the heat."

"That's why everybody likes you, Sean. You watch out for us backroom guys. Not too many agents do that anymore."

"I appreciate the kind words, Luke, but I just need to know as much about this guy as I can. He may have just killed a friend of mine."

"Understood. I'll email the results as soon as I have something, okay?"

"Works for me, Luke, thanks." Kruger ended the call just as he and Stephanie reached their condo.

When they were inside, Stephanie turned to him and said, "What photo?"

Kruger crossed the room, pulled the sliding glass doors shut, closed the blinds, turned to Stephanie, and said, "There was somebody following Guevara yesterday. He had a listening device in his ear. Probably eavesdropping on Guevara's conversations. He may be involved with this, or maybe not. I took several pictures of him with my phone and sent them to the lab in Washington. That was the lab tech, a good man, and if the software can find him, Luke will do it."

Stephanie nodded. "How bad was Neil?"

"Not sure, but it might be a good idea for you to head over to the hospital to check on him. I have to be on a conference call at the KC office at four. I'm not sure how long it will take either. Plus, if I get a response from our guy in Washington, I might have to take a quick trip to Springfield."

"JR?"

Kruger nodded. "The agency will require too much paperwork and court orders for the kind of internet search I need. JR can do it with his eyes closed and not ruffle any feathers."

She nodded, "Okay, I'll clean up and go to the hospital and let you know about Neil as soon as possible. Sean…"

"Yes?"

"Be careful."

"I will."

Stephanie went to the bathroom, and Kruger heard the

shower start. He went to his desk and retrieved the glass in the plastic bag with the fingerprints. He stared at it and said to himself, "Guess I need to get you to Fed Ex for a quick overnight. Maybe this will help give us the name of our eavesdropper."

Kruger looked at his wrist. His watch still wasn't there. Glancing at the digital clock, he determined he had a few hours before the conference call. Plenty of time to clean up and get to the KC office. He had a bad feeling the events of the day would suck him into the investigation of the other two murders. All three were rich. The first two had connections to Israel. He realized he needed to know what connection Guevara might have to the Jewish state and he needed to know it before the conference call at the KC office. It was time to call Seltzer and bring him up to speed.

He didn't know his phone call would set in motion a cascade of events affecting Stephanie and him for the foreseeable future.

Chapter Thirteen

KANSAS CITY, MO

Monday

BY 3 P.M., Kruger was checking emails in an empty cubicle on the second floor of the Kansas City FBI Office. Nothing from Luke yet, but after this amount of time, he was not optimistic about getting results from the photos. The drinking glass was another matter; Fed Ex Priority Overnight was scheduled to deliver it directly to Luke Riley's attention first thing in the morning. Hopefully by Tuesday afternoon, he would have a name and face.

Kruger understood when Dollar told him to go home and clean up, he meant for Kruger to put on a suit and tie before the conference call. He had no intentions of wearing a suit to the office, so he showed up in khakis, FBI polo shirt, light tan socks and his Docksider loafers. At least he was comfortable, and hopefully sending Dollar a message he wasn't Kruger's boss.

Promptly at five minutes to four, a young agent stopped at his cubicle and said, "Are you Agent Kruger?"

Kruger looked over his reading glasses at the agent and nodded.

"They're ready to start in the conference room. Agent Dollar sent me to find you. Ah... sir, Agent Dollar has a strict dress code for the office. Coat and tie at all times."

Kruger stood, closed his laptop, placed it in his backpack, walked around the desk, patted the young agent on the shoulder, and smiled before answering.

"I don't work for Mint Dollar. Besides, I'm on vacation."

He exited the cubicle farm and headed for the conference room.

When Kruger entered, Dollar glared at him, shook his head, and said, "You're late, Agent Kruger."

Kruger glanced at his watch, it was exactly four o'clock and the conference call had not started. He said, "No, I'm not, it's just now four." Pointing at the large screen monitor on the wall, he added, "No call yet."

"In this office, we anticipate, we are professional, and we are punctual."

Kruger rolled his eyes, shook his head, and found an empty chair on the far end of the conference table. He glanced around. There were eight other agents, all young and all in dark gray suits with red striped ties. Except for the faces, they were identical. He removed his computer from his backpack and placed it on the conference table. He stifled his urge to laugh at the absurdity of Dollar and his rules. Finally, he was saved by the big screen coming to life with the image of FBI Director Phillip Wagner. Sitting next to him was Deputy Director Paul Stumpf and Assistant Deputy Director Alan Seltzer.

Director Wagner started, "Thank you all for joining this call. I wish it was under better circumstances. Deputy Director Stumpf will brief you on what we currently know, and then we will hear any updates you might have. Last we will discuss how to move forward with the investigation. Director Stumpf..."

Paul Stumpf was in his late 40s. At one time a dedicated marathon runner, he still had the body to show for it. But after having both knees replaced, he was starting to add pounds to his five-feet-eleven frame. His hair was dark brown, perfectly styled, with no noticeable gray. Wireless glasses sat on an unremarkable nose in front of arctic blue eyes. Kruger knew Stumpf from his early career; he considered him a friend and still one of the good guys. On the other hand, Director Wagner was an unknown even though he had met him several times.

Stumpf started his review. "We have two cases here in the Washington, D.C., area that could be related to this morning's incident in Kansas City. The profiles of all three victims are too similar to be coincidental. All three have financial ties to the current president's political party. In addition, all three were active in lobbying for congressional support of Israel. While we do not want to draw conclusions from these facts, it does point us in a particular direction for our investigation. We want to thank Agent Dollar and his team for supplying the name of the KC target. His identification enabled us to reach out to the Secret Service. They are also investigating."

Kruger noticed that when Guevara's name was mentioned, Dollar smiled ever so slightly. The man was amazing. He would take credit for anything that made him look better. So much for being a team player.

Kruger's decision to pursue the identity of Guevara's shadow on his own had been correct. If Dollar knew about it, there would be an instant news conference and the guy would go into hiding.

Stumpf continued, "A sample of the explosive residue is being flown to our lab here in Washington for analysis. But after reviewing videos from the scene, our explosives experts suspect military grade C4."

Wagner said, "Thank you, Director Stumpf. We'll let the KC team give their report."

"Thank you, Director," said Dollar. "Agent Wright will review our findings."

Kruger listened but didn't hear anything new. In the few hours he had been at the apartment and here in the office, the local team had failed to find anything of significance. Their only new information was identifying the license plate from the van. It had been stolen from a wrecked van in a Montgomery, Alabama, U-Haul parking lot. Unfortunately, two more victims had succumbed to their injuries, making the death toll six. He wondered if one of those was Neil. But he doubted it. Stef would have texted or called him.

Alan Seltzer took control of the video conference after the KC review. He started by saying, "We will divide responsibilities in the following manner. On-site investigation will continue to be handled by the KC team with Agent Dollar in charge. Profiling will be handled by my office with Agent Kruger as lead, and he will report to me. Agent Dollar will report directly to Paul Stumpf. This will give us a broader view of the whole investigation."

While Seltzer continued, Kruger sent a brief text message to Seltzer's cell phone: "Thanks, I owe you."

After Seltzer finished speaking, Kruger watched him as he inconspicuously checked his phone, smiled and nodded.

The director took control of the meeting again. "Gentlemen, we will consider these incidents to be acts of domestic terror. We will not speculate to the press. Furthermore, we will keep our findings within these walls. Is that understood?"

Everyone around the table nodded vigorously, except Dollar. He was too busy looking around the room, making sure everyone was agreeing. Kruger nodded, but not to the degree the other agents were nodding. He hated talking to the press and avoided it when he could. People far more important than he were paid to do that.

As the conference call ended, the wall monitor went blank. Dollar cleared his throat loudly and said, "Thank you, everyone, good work today. Let's get back to it. Everyone is dismissed."

The sound of chairs scooting on carpet, shuffled papers and the clamor of multiple conversations was interrupted by Dollar saying, "Agent Kruger, don't leave yet. I need to discuss something with you."

Kruger sat back down, waited until the room was clear and the door closed. He stared at Dollar and said, "What?"

"First, your appearance and attire is inappropriate for this office."

Kruger shook his head, but said nothing.

"Also, how did you manage to avoid reporting to me? Did you call and whine about having to work under my supervision?"

Kruger smiled, but maintained his silence.

"Don't think I'm not aware of the report you filed against me after Utah. You delayed my career advancement by several years. I didn't appreciate the accusations, which were unfounded and misleading."

Kruger knew that if he stayed any longer, the situation would become volatile. So he stood, placed his computer back into his backpack and lifted it onto his shoulders. He walked to the conference room door, opened it, and before leaving, turned, and said, "I really don't care if you believe it or not. I had nothing to do with the decision. I came here in the spirit of cooperation, hoping you'd changed. But after this little conversation, and the fact you reported Guevara's name to the director without verification, confirms my original perception of you."

Dollar's face turned red and he stood. "And what the hell does that mean?"

"That you're still an idiot."

Chapter Fourteen

GERMANTOWN, TN

Tuesday

MEDIA COVERAGE of the Kansas City explosion continued nonstop on both cable and broadcast news networks. The talking heads continued to speculate on motive and which group was behind this latest terrorist attack. One network went so far as to blame the current president of relaxing the nation's vigilance and willingness to defend itself. Several senators were even calling for his impeachment. Norman Ortega laughed when he heard this. Politicians would use any excuse to further their media presence.

He was impressed when one financial correspondent mentioned the two murders in Washington, D.C., and a possible link. Finally, his team was getting the attention it needed to further its cause.

But, the stupidity of seemingly intelligent men and women sitting around tables and putting forth theories on something they knew nothing about, disgusted him. Shaking his head he continued to be amazed that people actually watched this banality on TV.

Ortega was ex-Army. Everyone on his team was ex-Army. He had personally recruited them from soldiers he had served with during his four tours in Iraq. These were men disaffected by a civilian world dominated by rich and apathetic business owners. The very individuals whose freedom to build their businesses was guaranteed by the sacrifices of men like Ortega and his fellow soldiers. Yet, they remained hesitant to interview returning veterans.

He snapped out of his funk and got back to business. Once again he was connected to the internet in a public place, this time a McDonald's in Germantown. It was time to start planning the team's next target, a job that would finally make it clear to the politicians and public what his team was doing.

Ortega contemplated the skill sets needed for the next target. Spreading the assignments around was essential. It would keep his team from getting careless and making mistakes. Mistakes led to getting caught. For now his team had not made any obvious ones. At least, he didn't think they had.

He was not delusional. He knew one or more of his team would be caught eventually. But with its current structure, the trail would end there. He'd been careful. Their communication methods would be hard to trace, and no one knew who the other team members were. His recruiting had been done after the men returned home, so no one knew the others' identities. He was the central hub of the group; each man knew Ortega, but no one knew where he was located. This was done on purpose. No one on the team would be able to tell the authorities his location. If compromised, he would disappear for a while and change his identity, but his team would survive to operate later. He was a realist and prepared for this eventuality. It was just the cost of doing business.

Since no one had been compromised so far, it was time to press on with their plan. The new target was a rich first-term congressman from California. The man had made millions in the telecom industry, finally selling out and running for congress. This would really throw off any theory the FBI might have about rich businessmen being targeted.

He typed out the email, signed off the internet and then sent the text message with the new email password. It was time to check out of his hotel and drive to the next city, probably St. Louis, or maybe Little Rock. The decision would be made as he drove out of the hotel's parking lot.

His protocol was simple, travel light and always be mobile. A habit learned from his beloved 1st Calvary Division.

Chapter Fifteen

KANSAS CITY, MO

Tuesday

INTERNAL FBI EMAIL traffic concerning the explosion had increased tenfold since Monday afternoon. Most of Franklin Dollar's emails contained little helpful information. There were, however, several from one KC agent worth reading. The agent had found plumbing tools in the men's toilet at O'Dowd's, but no plumber. After questioning the injured manager of the restaurant, the agent determined the plumber had been the driver of the van and had waited to park in a specific location. The manager had asked the plumber about being late, and remembered the plumber say he had a hard time finding a parking space.

Kruger made notes as he reviewed the emails. He printed this particular one, wrote a few questions on it and placed it in his file. Clearly the driver knew where to position the van for maximum destructive power on a vehicle dropping someone off at O'Dowd's. But how would he have known Guevara would be in a limousine and at O'Dowd's at a specific time?

Suddenly Kruger knew how. Because he had overheard Neil Ross and Guevara making specific plans on Sunday at the reception. He would need to confirm with Neil if their meeting plans for Monday were discussed during the reception. While not definite, odds were increasing that the man following Guevara was a person of interest.

His cell phone broke his concentration. He glanced at the caller ID, a Washington, D.C., area code. He answered, "Kruger."

"Sean, it's Luke."

Kruger glanced at his watch, noted it was 11:30 a.m. in Kansas City, afternoon Washington time. He said, "Good afternoon, Luke, what's up?"

"Nothing on the pictures, but the fingerprints hit pay dirt."

"Yeah? Who is he?"

"Military, U.S. Army. His name is Thomas Cooper. I compared his military ID photo with the pictures you sent, and it's the same guy."

"Does it give a current address?"

"No, but he's originally from southern Alabama, around Mobile. Mustered out about three years ago with an Honorable Discharge. He did a couple of tours in Iraq and one in Afghanistan, plus received all the usual commendations for being in a combat zone. Nothing heroic, just the standard ones."

Kruger was quiet for a few moments. "They found a license plate from the van. It was stolen in Montgomery. The van wasn't, just the plate."

"It fits, doesn't it?"

"Yes, it does. Can you send me everything via email?"

"Yes, I'm sending it now."

"Thanks, Luke. Remember, you don't know anything about this, right?"

"Got it. Thanks, Sean." Luke was about to end the call, but quickly said, "Almost forgot to tell you one thing."

"What?"

"Guess what he did in Iraq?"

Kruger thought for a second, smiled and said, "Explosives."

"Yeah, he disarmed IEDs."

"So if he can disarm an IED, he can probably build one, wouldn't you agree?"

"I would agree. I think you have a good lead, Sean. Good luck."

Kruger ended the call and noticed a large file from Luke downloading into his email account. As soon as it was finished, he opened the file and stared at the face of Thomas Cooper, ex-military explosives expert, and the man following Fernando Guevara forty-eight hours ago.

He said, "Hello, Thomas Cooper. I need to find you, and fast.

———

BARBARA WHITLOCK HAD BEEN an analyst for the FBI for as long as Kruger could remember. Having worked with her on numerous cases, he found her work exceptional. She was also discreet. He found her direct number on his cell phone, a number only a select number of agents possessed, and pressed the send icon.

The call was answered on the third ring. "I haven't heard from you in a very long time Agent Kruger. Why is that? Did you find another, younger, better looking analyst to call and harass?"

Smiling, Kruger replied, "No, Barbara, you will always be my favorite. I enjoy harassing you."

There was laughter on the other end of the call. "Good, I wouldn't want to have to go to HR and accuse you of harassing another analyst. Heard you got married. Who's the lucky girl?"

"News travels fast. Yes, we were married last Saturday. Stephanie and I finally figured out we weren't getting any younger."

"Good for you two. You know, when we heard the news, it broke a few hearts around here. Some of us thought we might have a chance."

Kruger chuckled. "That's very nice of you to say, but I don't believe it."

"Probably for the best. So, what can I do for you, Sean?"

"I'm working on the profile of the guy who did the Kansas City bombing."

"Saw the videos; it looked nasty."

"It was. I need a deep dive on three individuals: Charlton Wheeler, Kyle Rousch and Fernando Guevara."

"Were all three in the bombing?"

"No, just Guevara. The others were separate incidents, but I believe they're related."

"Got it. What are you looking for?"

"Common threads, business associates, personal habits, social connections, political beliefs, anything you can find that might tie them together. No matter how slim."

"Send me the case file numbers and I'll get right on it."

"Thanks, Barbara. One more thing."

"Yes?"

"Be careful who you mention this to. Mint Dollar is involved."

"Shit." There was silence on the phone for over five seconds. "That moron, I wouldn't give him the time of day. Don't worry, I'll only discuss it with you."

Kruger ended the call and leaned back in his desk chair. It was time to visit his friend in Springfield. He sent a short text message to a number he had memorized a long time ago. The message was simple. "Call me K." His cell phone vibrated fifteen minutes later with a caller ID of UNKNOWN. He smiled, answered it, and said, "Kruger."

"I haven't heard from you in six months."

"Yes, you're right, sorry. I've been busy, but you could have called too."

"Yeah, you're right, but I really don't like calling FBI agents, even if they are fishing buddies."

"Speaking of fishing, I was planning a fishing trip. How're they biting?"

"Don't know, haven't been lately. Guess we can find out together. When are you coming?"

"Early tomorrow morning, same place?"

"See you then."

The call ended. The total call time recorded on his phone was exactly one minute and twenty-two seconds. The maximum JR Diminski would stay on a phone call was two minutes, and he never identified where he lived. It wasn't that he was paranoid. He was a man who didn't exist within the system and didn't want the NSA listening to his conversations. The fishing nonsense was JR's idea; when Kruger needed his help, he would just ask to go fishing. He shook his head and smiled as he thought about the first time he'd met JR Diminski.

Kruger had been assigned to help track down a fugitive

accused of killing one man and wounding another in New York City. Politics, and the fact the fugitive fled to another state, brought the FBI into the case. Through various sources, whom Kruger refused to identify, he tracked the fugitive to southwest Missouri in the city of Springfield. During his investigation, evidence was found that contradicted the known facts of the case—namely, the dead and wounded men were actually hired thugs who were going to kill JR and dump his body in the Hudson River.

JR had been a computer software analysis for a large privately held software company. The owner of the company decided to bring in new investors to help expand his business. The new investors, through stock manipulation, suddenly owned a majority of the outstanding shares. They proceeded to dismiss the entire analysis team and outsourced their jobs to India. Within a year, the company was broken up and sold, reaping millions for the new investors.

After being dismissed, JR had hacked into the laptop of the new owner and found multiple files outlining illegal activities by the individual. He copied the information and tried blackmailing the man, thus the reason he found himself in the company of so-called security guards. JR managed to escape, but in the process, killed one and wounded the other.

Their first conversation was the night Kruger sat down next to him at a local pub in Springfield. An old friend of Kruger's had been helping JR establish his new identity. When Kruger sat down, the friend said, "JR, this is someone you need to talk to. He's fair and will listen."

Joseph stood up, looked at the man he had called JR, and left.

Kruger said, "Before you wet your pants, I'm not here to

take you back to New York. I know the truth and I'm here to help you."

The man looked at Kruger calmly and said, "Don't know what the hell you're talking about, man. I'm just sitting here drinking a beer and watching a baseball game."

Kruger nodded, "Okay, here's what I know."

He proceeded to tell JR everything he knew while JR stared at a TV showing a St. Louis Cardinal baseball game. When Kruger was done, JR said, "And what do you plan to do with this knowledge?"

Kruger sipped his beer, stared at the TV, and said, "Nothing. I need someone like you to help me once in a while. If you want to help me, fine. If you don't, I'll walk out of here and you'll never hear from me again."

JR turned to him and said, "How do you know Joseph?"

Kruger shrugged and said, "Old family friend."

"If I help you, what's in it for me?"

"I'll start the process of clearing your real name."

JR looked at the Kruger, smiled and said, "My name's JR Diminski, glad to meet you."

They had been friends ever since.

Chapter Sixteen

MEXICO CITY

Wednesday

THE GULFSTREAM G280 taxied toward the private aviation area of the Benito Juarez International Airport in Mexico City, far from the scrutinizing eyes of the airport's two main terminals. As the plane came to a stop in front of an open hanger, two white Toyota Land Cruisers with dark tinted windows pulled up next to it and parked. The front cabin door of the aircraft slowly lowered. Aazim Abbas stepped cautiously onto the first step and surveyed the surrounding area. Large passenger jets taking off and landing contributed to the constant din in this section of the airport.

Satisfied he was not under surveillance, Aazim hurried down the steps and immediately entered the back seat of the second Land Cruiser. As soon as he shut the door, the two vehicle caravan started moving.

The man in the seat next to him smiled and said, "I trust your flight was uneventful?"

"Yes." Aazim looked at the man with an icy stare. "Why did you call me down here? It was unnecessary."

"Oh, quite the contrary. We needed to talk, away from the prying eyes and ears of the American NSA."

The man sitting next to Abbas was dressed in a dark blue suit with a faint lighter blue pinstripe. His black hair was trimmed and professionally styled. A neatly trimmed beard accentuated his oval face. Black eyes stared out through square black spectacles perched on a prominent nose. As he smiled, his brilliant white teeth betrayed his real age.

Abbas blew out a breath with disgust. "We are careful, your highness. Very careful."

"Yes. Yes, you've told me how careful you are. Maybe too careful. The Americans think these attacks are the work of one man. A deranged man, not an attack on their way of life."

Abbas said nothing.

"Aazim, we chose you because you are aggressive. But so far your actions are that of a woman."

Closing his eyes and taking several deep breaths, Abbas said, "On purpose. The next attack will prove we have brought jihad to their homeland. They will no longer be able to deny its existence."

The prince nodded. "My brother and I were hoping you would dispel our concerns. When will this glorious moment occur?"

"Is my shipment still on time?"

The prince nodded his head ever so slightly.

"Good. Here is what we have planned." Aazim Abbas proceeded to outline his proposal.

When he was done, Prince Bandar Farad Saud sat back and laughed. "I like it. This will be a glorious moment.

Now, you will be my guest until tomorrow. Then you can fly back."

"Prince, I must be back in Dallas by tomorrow afternoon.

"You shall be, but tonight you are my guest."

———

THE SPARSELY FURNISHED one-bedroom apartment occupied by Billy Reid reflected his total lack of concern for frivolous possessions. His sofa and coffee table were purchased at a yard sale for twenty dollars. Gaming magazines were stacked in various locations throughout the room. His dining room consisted of a single barstool scooted under a three-foot long, waist-high breakfast bar separating the living area and kitchen. An unmade twin mattress lay on the floor of his bedroom. An old lamp atop an upside down milk crate provided the only light in the room.

However, he had a different standard when it came to his electronics. A high-end ASUS gaming laptop was his most recent acquisition. But his pride and joy was a new 60-inch 3D HD TV and Play Station purchased with cash at a local Best Buy two weeks earlier. A TV stand bought at a local Walmart provided plenty of storage for his numerous games. The TV and Play Station were procured the day after he had received the biggest paycheck of his life. Actually, it was an electronic transfer from a bank in Europe. He didn't know which one, nor did he care. The money was there.

Billy was 32 years old, ex-Army with two tours of Iraq and one in Afghanistan. His final tour in Iraq derailed what he thought would be a twenty-year army career. A roadside

IED destroyed the Humvee he was driving and left him burned and deaf on his left side. The burns on his arm, chest and leg had healed, but the scars were a permanent reminder of the accident. After months in a VA hospital and an Honorable Discharge, he came home broke, divorced and bitter.

The large payday was the result of a sergeant he had met in Afghanistan contacting him with a proposal. After several months of careful thought, he accepted the challenge.

Billy had a talent, one the Army recognized with EIC Silver Badges, one for pistols and one for rifles. He was an excellent marksman and a trained sniper. Not a very marketable skill in the civilian world, especially when accompanied by deafness and scarring, but he had found a part-time job at a pistol range. The money wasn't much but it allowed him time to work at the challenges Ortega offered.

He slipped into the role of assassin easily. After following and observing the two men for several weeks, he devised the plans and methods for their demise.

The first one gave him an opening when the man's wife left for the weekend and his girlfriend came over for a little swimming and sex in the mansion's pool. The shot was easy, 200 yards from an elevated wooded area overlooking the back of the house. After only an hour in his hide, the man sent the girlfriend into the house for more drinks. Billy shot him as he walked around the pool. Center mass shot, one .223 slug from Billy's Remington 700, perfectly placed in the man's heart and the other hitting the upper torso as the dead man's body fell into the pool.

Billy didn't wait for the girlfriend to return poolside. He simply crawled back over the rise, calmly walked back to his pickup and drove away. The Remington 700 had been disassembled and disposed of at various spots along the Potomac. He could always buy another 700; they were accurate right out of the shipping carton, one of the reasons he liked them.

At first he thought it would bother him, but when he saw the man, it didn't. The target had black hair with a dark complexion, reminding him of the type of men who planted the IED in Iraq. He slept fine that night and every night after.

The second target posed more of a problem. The guy worked all the time, and other than when he left for the airport, the only places he went were his office and apartment. Billy had specific instructions: the job had to be completed in Washington, D.C. Finally he decided the best opportunity would be after the man got his morning coffee. The guy followed the same routine every morning, went to the same Starbucks, got the same coffee, and then drove to his office with the top down on his expensive convertible.

The night before Billy did the job, he borrowed a motorcycle from a guy who lived in the same apartment building. The best part was the guy didn't know Billy had borrowed the bike. He returned it before the neighbor left for work. Both the SIG Sauer and the suppressor were tossed into the Potomac River later in the day.

Now Ortega had given him a new challenge, one he was concerned about. The first two men were obviously rich, but nobody knew who the hell they were. At least Billy didn't, and since there was very little mentioned in the newspapers or on TV, apparently nobody else did either.

But this job was different. The target was a congressman, a relatively new and little known one, but still a congressman. His planning would have to be more precise and careful.

While not under a strict timeline, the job had to be completed anytime during a three-week window starting this coming Friday. Details of the congressman's itinerary for the next three weeks were provided in a package, post-marked New York City. As he read it, three opportunities were pointed out, but he would observe the congressman for a few days and see for himself. If he could find other open-ings, they would be preferable. Better to be unpredictable, just in case he was being set up.

He trusted Ortega, but only so far. Ortega had been a Master Sargent and Billy a Corporal, and while not close buddies, they knew and respected each other. Ortega had witnessed some of the inter-squad marksmanship competi-tions the Division put together. Billy was proud of the fact he won every time he entered one. After being wounded, he lost track of Ortega and never saw him again. Then one day out of the blue, Ortega made contact. But complete trust wasn't part of the deal.

Glancing at his watch, he was due at the pistol range in an hour. After his shift, there would be time to drive by the congressman's house and start his recon.

Chapter Seventeen

SPRINGFIELD, MO

Wednesday

KRUGER PARKED his Mustang in the back of a nondescript three-story building in the center section of Springfield at half past nine in the morning. Not knowing how long it would take, he had told Stephanie not to expect him until later that evening.

JR was waiting for him in the lobby with a cup of coffee in his hand and said, "Restroom's next to the stairs. When you're done, come on up to the second floor. I'll be in the computer room."

Kruger smiled, took the coffee and said, "Hi, JR, nice to see you again. Yes, I had a nice drive. I'm doing well, and you?"

JR stared at Kruger, then chuckled and shrugged. Without a word, he turned and headed for the stairs.

When Kruger got to the second floor, he saw JR sitting at a work station on the far wall of the room. The room itself was the entire second floor. Support columns were used for the load bearing areas, but otherwise there were no walls. Waist-high cubicles, each one a computer terminal or Wi-Fi access station, formed a maze on the floor. After navigating the labyrinth, he joined JR at the work station.

Without turning from the two side-by-side monitors, JR said, "Joseph told me to tell you hello, and if you have time, stop by."

"I was planning on it, as long as you don't screw around and take all day."

JR turned around and stared at Kruger. Once he saw the smile on Kruger's face, he nodded and said, "I deserved that, didn't I?"

Nodding, Kruger grinned, "Let's get busy."

"Okay, what've you got?"

Taking the laptop out of his backpack, Kruger opened it. After the computer booted, he opened the file on Thomas Cooper, showing his photo to JR.

"I need to find this guy. I have a hunch he's responsible for the KC explosion on Monday."

JR studied the picture. "How do you know?"

"Because I saw this man stalking one of the victims at a reception on Sunday. I acquired his fingerprints from a drinking glass he touched. He's ex-military and specialized in disarming IEDs. If he knows how to disarm explosives, I bet he can build them. The blast in KC used C4, Washington confirmed it this morning. I need to talk to him."

"Good enough for me." He handed Kruger a thumb drive and continued, "Copy the file to this and I'll see what we can find."

As JR worked, Kruger wandered around the room. Four years earlier, using his computer skills, JR had changed his identity. Now, still living under his new identity, JR had built a successful business providing computer security to financial and commercial enterprises.

Ten minutes later, as Kruger wandered back to JR's work station, he heard, "Okay. Here's what we're going to do. First I'll input his picture into a new facial recognition program I've been working on for the last few years. It's more advanced than the one you guys use in Washington. If he was photographed by a security camera somewhere, we'll find him."

Kruger pulled a legal pad from his computer bag. "Let's assume he left the KC area, probably flew out of a local or an airport within driving range. I would start with KC, Omaha, Wichita, Springfield and St. Louis. All are within a few hours' drive of The Plaza."

JR nodded as he typed on the keyboard. "Makes sense. I'll tap into the TSA system and run a routine comparing departing passengers at all five airports starting Monday at ten-thirty."

Kruger looked concerned.

JR smiled, "Don't worry, it sounds complicated, but it's not."

"How long will it take? I don't have all week."

"Not long. There's a group of us like-minded individuals who have tethered our computers into a secure bot-net system. It allows us to tap unused processing power among the group."

Exactly two minutes later, a series of files popped up on the left monitor. JR pointed to it and said, "Let's take a look at this one." He opened the file and saw the smiling face of Thomas Cooper handing his ID to a TSA agent. "Well, well, look at what we have here," JR mumbled to himself. He checked the file. "You nailed it, Sean. This is St. Louis, time stamp three-thirty-two p.m. Monday."

Kruger smiled, glad his hunch was right. "Can we determine his destination?"

Shaking his head, JR started typing again. "No way of telling his departing flight from this picture, but let's look at a few more files."

Many of the returned files were false hits, until finally JR said, "There we are, look at this one." He pointed to a picture of Thomas Cooper handing his boarding pass to an agent as he entered the boarding gate.

Kruger read the time stamp, "Southwest to Dallas Love Field, Monday, four-thirty-two p.m."

JR's fingers flew over the keyboard like a maestro pianist. As he typed, JR said, "Okay, now we shift our search to Dallas. I'll check parking lot surveillance, auto rental agencies, hotel check-in, etc. This may take a little longer because I have to access different servers instead of just one in the previous search."

Kruger rubbed his chin with thumb and forefinger. "Can we check the flight manifest with Southwest in St. Louis to determine if he's flying under his real name?"

"Already did, and he isn't. However, if he boards another flight in Dallas, my software will compare flight manifests and determine if any names match."

The computer started returning files rapidly as JR continued to type more instructions. Kruger could not even imagine the programming and computer power needed to process what he was witnessing. Finally, JR lifted his fingers from the keyboard.

"Now, let's see what we've got."

Searching through the files, they determined that Cooper had traveled to the Westin City Center in downtown Dallas. He'd been caught on the hotel's security camera getting into a taxi. The next positive ID was another

TSA security camera shot of the man going through the security check at DFW. Comparing the passenger manifest of the Southwest flight from St. Louis to Dallas, the system found a similarly named passenger on an American Airline flight to Atlanta.

Kruger said, "I'll bet Atlanta is his last stop; he's from southern Alabama. Can you do the same search in Atlanta?"

JR nodded and started typing again. The search results were plentiful in Atlanta, but the most important security camera shot was of Cooper getting into a car in a long term parking lot. This picture revealed a critical piece of information. A perfect view of the car's license plate.

Kruger sat down and glanced at his watch. It was just after one p.m. He now knew that Cooper was somewhere in the south. He heard JR mumble something as a laser printer whined and spit out several pieces of paper. After examining them, he smiled and handed both to Kruger. One was an image of a driver's license with Thomas Cooper's picture and an address in Atmore, AL. He looked at JR and said, "I'll be damned, you found him."

"Yup, sometimes I even amaze myself. Now what?"

Kruger thought for a moment.

"The best thing for me to do is take a trip to Atmore. Unlike my fellow agents in Kansas City, I don't believe this is the only individual involved. I think there are numerous individuals involved." Kruger stared at the papers in his hand. "Since we know his address, is there any way to see if he has an email address you could access?"

JR turned back to his keyboard and typed. After studying the response, he turned back around, "He doesn't have internet access at the address, which is a meaningless statement because of cell phones. He just doesn't have any hard-wired internet access. Without some clue as to his email address, I wouldn't be able to hack into it. I'd need his laptop or cell phone."

"Okay, I'll try to get one of those for you."

After leaving JR's building, Kruger sat in his car and thought through his next moves. First, he determined he wouldn't report his findings to Mint Dollar. No way, not this time. But it was time to call Alan.

"Good afternoon, Sean. Any progress on the KC incident?"

Kruger decided to keep the information he shared with Alan to a minimum. "I think so. I have a line on a person of interest in the Alabama area. Nothing concrete, but I know he was in KC this weekend and has explosives experience."

"Should I ask how you came about this information?"

"No."

"Okay. Do we need to involve Dollar and his team?"

"Not yet. The information is circumstantial at best. But I think it's worth my time to check it out before wasting any additional resources."

"Fair enough. Fly down there and report back when you have more."

"Thanks, Alan, I'll keep you posted."

After ending the call, Kruger checked his watch. Plenty of time for a visit with Joseph before he headed back to KC. He'd fly down to Pensacola first thing in the morning.

There was no way he was going to involve Dollar at this point. No way in hell.

Chapter Eighteen

ALEXANDRIA, VA

Wednesday

THE UPSCALE NEIGHBORHOOD was dominated by BMWs, Audis and Mercedes Benzes. On his first drive-through the day before, Billy realized his beat-up 1990 Ford F-150 would draw attention. Attention he didn't want. After driving past the congressman's house, he noticed several landscape companies tending to the perfectly manicured lawns within the quiet neighborhood.

After the drive-through he found a sign shop and explained to a bored clerk what he needed. He was shown to an Apple Macintosh computer with a complete array of design programs. After several false starts, Billy saved the design and told the clerk the file name. One hour later, he left the shop with two magnetic signs for his pickup. Placing one sign on the driver's side door and the other on passenger's door, he stood back to admire his handiwork. The truck now represented AAA Mowing and Landscaping Services LLC, just another yard service vehicle tending to the lawns of the neighborhood. He could hide in plain sight.

After the sign shop, he drove to a flea market and bought two lawn mowers, a trimmer and gas cans to give the pickup more authenticity.

Billy's final stop was a bike shop, where he purchased a high-end mountain bike, helmet, riding clothes and other various accessories the well-heeled bike rider might utilize. Up-close recon was now possible. He could ride the bike through the neighborhood and blend in with all the other local cyclists.

By parking the truck in the shopping mall, not far from the neighborhood entrance gate, he could ride the bike and blend in. With these two methods, he felt comfortable he could watch the congressman's house without drawing too much attention.

It was early Wednesday morning, as he rode the bike down the congressman's street, he witnessed the congressman stretching, preparing for a run. It was 6:30 a.m. He stopped the bike and started inspecting his tire while keeping an eye on the congressman.

His briefing information had not mentioned anything about a morning run. It might take a few mornings to confirm the pattern, but here was a possible opportunity outside the ones suggested.

———

FRESHMAN CONGRESSMAN ROY GRIFFIN stretched before his morning run. This was his favorite part of the day, alone without any of his so-called colleagues pressuring him to vote their way or constituents wanting him to vote for a special bill that would benefit their business or cause.

Unfortunately, the only thing he enjoyed about being in Congress was helping individuals within his district deal with the massive government bureaucracy.

At 42, Roy was slightly over six feet tall. He wore his blond hair longer than current fashion and was male model handsome. He was also rich. Keenly aware his looks and money were part of the reason he was elected by his image-conscious Northern California district, he was determined to make a difference in Congress. He had unseated a Republican who, at the time, was under investigation for sexual assault. While the allegations were proven false, he still lost the election. Roy was halfway through his first term and frustrated with the congressional system. He served on the Foreign Affairs Committee. Even though he was just a first-term congressman, he served as the Chairman of the Subcommittee on the Middle East and Africa. Campaigning as a staunch proponent of Israel in an area with the third largest Jewish community in the country, Roy was a natural for the chairmanship. But with the chairmanship came demands for support of other bills he did not care for. Thus, his frustration.

His morning run was a must. The exertion helped him think clearer and work through problems. Regardless of the weather or temperature, he had to run. His normal path was a five to six mile route that meandered through his neighborhood. Sometimes he would run clockwise, sometime counter-clockwise, it didn't matter. Today he would run clockwise.

During this morning ritual, he normally saw fellow residents doing their morning workouts. He didn't know any of them, but he waved anyway. This morning, he saw the usual individuals, plus one he had not seen before. A bike rider. Possibly a new neighbor or someone just starting a new morning routine. Griffin noticed the rider, then promptly forgot about him as his thoughts moved on to other concerns.

———

BILLY PASSED the congressman once so he could be seen. Afterwards he carefully followed him, staying out of sight as best he could, making mental notes on the congressman's route. It would take several mornings to determine where the best place to complete his assignment would be, but he had time.

As he followed the congressman, three possible locations for the ambush were spotted. He would need a few more mornings of recon to confirm the running route, then he would determine the best location and devise his plan. In the meantime, he would explore the area with his truck.

Later that morning, while driving around the area, Billy found a road leading to the rear portion of the congressman's property. Although heavily wooded, he discovered several access points during his afternoon hike around the property.

He didn't trust the suggestions from the man in New York. This was his operation, and he didn't believe anyone not on site could tell him the best option. When Billy left the neighborhood late Wednesday, he had two contingency plans. Both presented excellent opportunities for success.

Chapter Nineteen

SOUTHERN ALABAMA

Thursday

THE FLIGHT from Kansas City landed in Pensacola, FL, a few minutes before 11 a.m. Eastern Time. The weather was perfect, mid-seventies with a few clouds blowing in from the Gulf of Mexico. Kruger had specified a four-wheel drive vehicle when he made the reservation, believing it might come in handy traveling the back roads of rural Alabama. He smiled when the Hertz agent handed him the keys to a Jeep Wrangler. A fun ride was always welcome.

Before leaving Kansas City, a Google Maps search showed Thomas Cooper's place located a mile north of County Road 3 about seven miles east of Atmore. With the aid of his GPS, he found the farm without difficulty. Driving around the farm several times, he became comfortable with the terrain and access roads. Knowledge of the ways in and out gave him an advantage if the suspect decided to bolt.

The small farmhouse sat in the middle of an oasis of trees, 300 yards down a gravel driveway, which was due west of a rural farm road. Cultivated farm land surrounded the island of trees and house. Behind the house and just outside the tree line sat a midsize barn and several smaller outbuildings. Each appeared to be equipment or storage sheds to Kruger. He made a note to keep those buildings under surveillance; hopefully they didn't contain any explosives.

As a courtesy, Kruger always contacted the local law enforcement agencies, so once he was satisfied he knew the area around Cooper's farmhouse, he headed for the Escambia County Sheriff's Department eighteen miles to the east in Brewton, AL. It would kill a lot of time Kruger didn't feel he had, but it was necessary. In his experience, a preliminary visit with the local authorities forged a team approach. Kruger liked to get them on board first, rather than after the fact.

Thirty minutes later, he pulled into the parking lot of the sheriff's department. It was a square building with a flat roof and a handicap ramp in between the building's two entrances. Kruger took the left-hand stairs and entered the door identified as the sheriff's department. He showed his credentials to the deputy at the front desk, asked for the sheriff and was told to wait.

While Kruger waited, he read all the wanted posters, garage sale notifications, public notices and miscellaneous town event fliers on the lobby bulletin board. After more than ten minutes, a thin man in his late 50s and several inches taller than Kruger entered the lobby. He was dressed in a light blue polo shirt with the words "Sheriff G. Lamb" and a gold star embroidered above the left breast. A holstered Smith and Wesson .38 Special was clipped to his belt. A sad and weary look reminded Kruger of a droopy bloodhound. The man offered his hand and said, "Sheriff Lamb. What can I do for you, agent?"

Kruger shook the offered hand and said, "Sheriff, can we talk in a less public location?"

The sheriff nodded and motioned for Kruger to follow him. He led him to a small room with a table and four chairs. Kruger recognized it as an interrogation room, but said nothing. Lamb motioned him to a chair, shut the door and sat down on the opposite side of the table. "Now, is this private enough for you, agent?"

Kruger recognized the wariness in the sheriff's demeanor. He had seen it a lot over the years. An FBI agent coming to a small county sheriff's department meant only one of two things: something bad had happened, or something bad was going to happen.

Kruger said, "Sheriff, I'm here on a tip concerning a person of interest in the Kansas City bombing this week. He may be living near Atmore. I would like to ask your assistance in my investigation." He sat back and waited for the sheriff to respond.

The sheriff blinked several times and nodded. "What's the name?"

Kruger reached into the inside pocket of his jacket, took out a picture and handed it to the sheriff. "Thomas Cooper, an ex-military explosives expert. We tracked him from Kansas City on the day of the explosion back to the Atlanta airport. I have an eye witness who saw this individual following one of the victims killed in the explosion."

The sheriff stared at the picture for several seconds, then got up and left the room. He returned a few minutes later and said, "The deputy that normally patrols Atmore is on his way in. I don't know this man, but he might."

"We retrieved the suspect's fingerprints from a drinking glass he touched during the time he was observed following the victim. He may not have anything to do with the explosion, but my gut tells me he does."

Lamb nodded, "Yup. Been doing this for thirty years. Always trust your gut."

A young deputy stuck his head into the room and said, "Sheriff, no wants or warrants on him. No criminal record either. Got in trouble once for toilet papering, but that's it."

The sheriff said, "Thanks, Nick." He then turned to Kruger. "Let's go to my office. We can wait for the deputy there and discuss how my department can assist you. Can I offer you some coffee while we wait, agent?"

Kruger shook his head. "No, thanks, I'm fine."

On the way to the sheriff's office, Lamb made a detour into a small kitchen area and poured himself a mug of coffee. "Well, I think I will."

After they were in Lamb's office, Kruger said, "My plan is simple. I will arrange for a federal search warrant. Timing is up to you and when you can be ready. If we find anything connecting him to the explosion, your department will arrest him and get credit for cracking the case. I'll question him and get out of your way. Good publicity for your next election. Unfortunately, after the announcement of his arrest, your small community will be overrun with FBI and media."

The sheriff nodded. Kruger continued, "I'm with a separate part of the FBI that profiles individuals like Cooper and I don't think he's the only one involved. However, my opinion is in the minority within the agency. There will be an agent arriving who's in charge of the overall investigation. He's a man you will want to shoot five minutes after you meet him."

Lamb's indifferent expression did not change as he said, "He hasn't met me yet."

Kruger was quiet for a few moments, then smiled and said, "Glad you have a sense of humor. You'll need it with Agent Dollar."

"I'm not joking."

Kruger looked Lamb in the eye and saw no hint of humor. No, I don't suppose you are, he thought.

Kruger spent the next half hour briefing the sheriff on the layout of Cooper's farm house and land. He was interrupted only a few times with questions, so it went quickly. A knock on the sheriff's door produced a quick "Yeah," from the sheriff.

A short deputy, no more than five-feet-seven, entered the office. His strong upper body, slim waist and skinny legs created the illusion of a Y. The deputy's head was shaved, with a dark brown and gray mustache and goatee. His eyes were green with dark black circles on the outside of the iris. He appeared to be in his 20s, but Kruger couldn't be sure. Sheriff Lamb said, "Agent Kruger, this is Deputy Dale Hickman."

Kruger stood and extended his hand, which the deputy shook briefly and then returned to a parade rest posture. He said, "You called me in, Sheriff, what's up?"

Lamb took the picture of Thomas Cooper and handed it to Hickman and said, "Can you identify this man?"

"Yes, sir. Name's Tommy Cooper. He's a volunteer fireman for Atmore. Why?"

"Do you know him?"

"Not real well." The deputy paused as he stared at the picture. "Worked a couple of fires and auto accidents with him, but I don't know him personally."

The sheriff said, "What do you know?"

"Not much. Talked about being in Iraq, said it sucked. Lives on the farm his grandparents gave him when they passed on. Don't know anything about his folks, don't think they're alive. What's going on, Sheriff, he done somethin' wrong?"

Lamb nodded to Kruger and said, "Agent, do you want to tell him?"

Kruger summarized what he had told the sheriff, excluding the explanation of what would happen when the media found out.

The deputy looked back at the sheriff and said, "He seemed like a good guy. Kind of hard to believe it."

Kruger said, "Deputy, it's hard to judge people sometimes. Like I said, my evidence is circumstantial, but I believe he's involved."

Sheriff Lamb stood up and said, "Dale, get the guys together, put your vests and helmets on, we're going to take a ride." He turned to Kruger, "I need that search warrant. Let's get this over with."

Kruger was impressed with the readiness of the small county department. While they didn't have an overabundance of sophisticated equipment, they had a dedicated and well-trained SWAT team. It was late afternoon when the caravan came to a stop in front of Cooper's driveway. Kruger had accompanied the sheriff in his squad car with five cruisers and the county's armored van following. After calling Seltzer, Kruger had a federal warrant issued for the search of Thomas Cooper's farm. The sheriff had it signed by a local judge, and they left for Cooper's property.

As Kruger watched the armored van and two patrol cars slowly drive down the gravel driveway, the silence of the afternoon was shattered by automatic gun fire from the farm house. Not small arms, but heavy, large caliber automatic rifle fire. The armored van stopped 50 yards from the farm house, steam spewing from under the hood. Kruger heard Sheriff Lamb curse, pick up the radio and yell, "Goddammit, return fire."

In the chaos that followed, the relatively small caliber AR-15s carried by the deputies had little effect on the farm house. The deputies had taken refuge behind their squad cars and were returning fire as best they could. Kruger heard Hickman call out over the van's loud speaker system, "Tommy, put your weapon down and come out with your hands above your head."

Even using Sheriff Lamb's binoculars, Kruger was unable to see inside the small farmhouse, so he directed his attention to the barn and outbuildings. He saw something inside the larger barn that brought back a long forgotten memory of a long forgotten investigation in Iraq. Realizing he had to get to the barn to confirm his suspicion, he tightened the tactical vest he had borrowed from the sheriff, zipped up his FBI windbreaker, and pulled his FBI cap down over his eyes. He laid the binoculars on the front seat of the sheriff's car and checked his Glock 19 to make sure it was primed. Taking it in his right hand, he looked for the best path to the barn. Then he bent over and started running. Lamb yelled for him to stop, but Kruger ignored the request as he used the squad cars and trees to avoid the attention of the occupant of the farm house. Several times, Kruger dove to the ground when bullets pinged close to his position. Finally, after zig-zagging his way to the barn, he arrived without getting shot.

Once inside, he holstered the Glock and went straight to a stack of boxes partially covered by a blue tarp. He yanked the tarp off and stared at fifteen shipping cartons. He looked around the barn and found a claw hammer to pry off the top of one of the crates. The contents of the carton made him shiver. Wrapped in their original factory protection were cushioned bricks of C4 explosives. He backed away from the cartons, retrieved his cell phone from his pocket and hit a speed dial.

Seltzer answered on the second ring, "What've you got?"

"Alan, get the military or somebody down here. I've got C4 coming out my ass. This is our guy. Hope he doesn't off himself before we can talk to him."

The explosion obscured Seltzer's response. The barn shook, dust fell from old rafters and the building creaked from the concussion. Realizing what had happened, Kruger brought the phone back to his ear and heard Seltzer yelling in the phone, "Sean! Sean, answer me, are you okay?"

Kruger said, "Yeah, I'm okay, we're too late. The house just exploded. I'll call you back when I know more."

All of the gunfire ceased with the destruction of the farm house and the silence was deafening. Sheriff Lamb's patrol car screeched to a halt several feet from the barn, and he ran into the barn. He stopped, stared at Kruger and yelled, "What the hell did you do that for?"

Kruger pointed to the crates and said, "Get several deputies and DO NOT let anyone enter this barn until the military gets here."

Lamb walked over to the open crate, stared at the contents and said, "Ah, shit." He immediately went back to his squad car and started barking orders.

Kruger walked out of the barn, stared at the smoldering remains of the farm house and mumbled, "Damn it, I needed to talk to him." As he watched, deputies started getting organized putting crime scene tape around the remains of the farm house. A few small fires were burning within the debris, but nothing seemed to be getting out of control.

Realizing more explosives could be stored in the other buildings, Kruger hurried over to check their contents. He carefully searched the first one and found only lawn mowers and garden tools. The second building was being used as a garage. Parked inside was a Chevy Malibu, the same car he had seen in the picture taken at the Atlanta airport long term parking. He checked the license plate and confirmed it was the car from the picture. And on the front passenger seat was a cell phone.

Using his windbreaker to cover his hand, Kruger opened the car door, grabbed the cell phone, slipped it into his pocket and closed the door.

Chapter Twenty

Thursday

ROY GRIFFIN WOKE, disoriented, to the sound of a phone ringing. By the time he was coherent enough to understand it was his cell phone, the call was sent to voicemail. He retrieved the caller ID and immediately knew it was not good news. His wife was in California visiting her mother and normally did not call after 9 p.m. Eastern Time. The cell phone showed the time as 1:05 a.m.

Skipping the voicemail message, he immediately called her back. She answered on the first ring.

"Roy, Mom's cancer is back."

Roy could tell she was crying. "How bad is it, Cheryl?"

"They're not expecting her to live through the weekend. Please come home, I need you. She needs you."

"Okay, I'll get the first flight I can find this morning. Are you at the hospital now?"

"Yes, she's asleep. I'm planning to stay the night."

"Okay, tell her I'll be there as soon as possible. Try to get some rest."

"I will. Be careful. I love you."

"I love you too. I'll call you back as soon as I know about my flight."

Roy ended the call and started going through a check list of what he needed to do. His first step was to call his administrative assistant, then call United to make a reservation. He didn't have to pack; he was going home. But he would need a small suitcase with briefing papers. Finally, he would need to call the limo service for transportation to the airport.

By 2 a.m. he was done. His flight would leave Reagan International at 7 a.m. and arrive in San Francisco just after 11 a.m. Pacific Time. A limo service would pick him up in three-and-a-half hours.

Lying back in bed, his thoughts turned to his mother-in-law. She had been his biggest supporter during his run for Congress. In fact she was his campaign's primary fundraiser. Her contacts and influence paved the way for winning the election. Many a late night were spent sitting in her living room, enjoying a good Napa cabernet sauvignon and discussing what his priorities would be once he was in Congress. She never doubted for a moment he would win the election. In her mind, it was inevitable. The realization she would be gone soon brought a tear to his eye. He would miss her encouragement, her guidance and her sense of right and wrong.

Memorial Day was only two weeks away and Congress was already getting ready for recess. Knowing he would not get back to sleep, he got up, opened his laptop and sent his assistant an email outlining his plans. He would not return until the second week in June. Staying away from Washington for an extended period would make Cheryl happy. She detested the place. Now they would both need to stay in California for a while to settle his mother-in-law's extensive estate.

———

BILLY REID ARRIVED EARLY in the congressman's neighborhood. One more reconnaissance to confirm when Griffin started his morning run. This morning, something was wrong. He watched the limo driver place a black suitcase in the trunk as the congressman entered the car's back seat. Once the driver was behind the wheel, he backed the limo out of the driveway and sped away. With his pickup two miles away in the mall parking lot, following the limo was not going to happen. An unfortunate development. As he rode back to the pickup, he wondered where the congressman was going and how long he would be gone.

When he returned to his apartment, he checked the congressman's website, there was an update in his Schedule a Meeting link, The Congressman will be in his home district until after the Memorial Day recess. He will return to Washington the second week in June. Billy stared at the message. Griffin would be away from Washington for the next four weeks. A full week outside the timeline he was supposed to follow. He wasn't sure how Ortega would react, but there was not much he could do about it.

The communications to and from Ortega took most of the afternoon, but confirmed he would wait until the congressman returned. The job had to be done in Washington, D.C.

Billy had no problem waiting. He had plenty of money,

plenty of video games, and now plenty of time to immerse himself in the experience.

———

ORTEGA READ the first message from Billy, frowned, and deleted the message. He tapped his finger on the table next to his laptop. There would have to be another target before the congressman. There could not be a four-week gap in the assassinations. Pressure had to be kept up or the news media would lose interest. If the news media lost interest, so would Congress. If Congress lost interest, their demands—when made—would be ignored.

It was time to utilize Cooper's expertise again. After finishing the email draft to Cooper, he sent the text message with the new password.

The media coverage of the Kansas City operation had been splendid. Glancing at the clock on his laptop, it was time for a news update. He turned on CNN and stared horrified at the images on the TV. CNN had a helicopter hovering over the sight of a massive explosion on a farm outside of Atmore, AL. What shocked Ortega was the image of Thomas Cooper's driver's license picture superimposed on the screen.

Had Thomas accidently detonated one of his bombs, or was it something else? He turned the volume up: "…first reports from the scene tell us a routine arrest attempt by the Escambia, Alabama, County Sheriff's Department may have led to an explosion leveling the residence of Thomas Cooper. There are no details on whether Mr. Cooper was present. It is also unknown if actions by the sheriff's department triggered the explosion."

The image shifted from an aerial view of the chaos to an announcer sitting behind a desk.

"Preliminary reports indicate the detonation originated from within the house. In addition, we are told by a confidential source Cooper was a person of interest in the Kansas City bombing that occurred last Monday. No other details are known at this time."

Ortega tried to remain calm as he listened and stared at the TV. The anchor continued, "We now have a correspondent on the scene. We take you to Scott Burnett."

The view switched to a reporter standing in a road. Behind him, in the distance, the smoldering remains of the house served as a backdrop.

"We are standing at the entrance to a small farm seven miles east of Atmore, Alabama. This is as close as local law enforcement will allow us at this time. Neighbors have identified the owner as Thomas Cooper. He's described as an outstanding young man, volunteer fireman and Iraq war veteran. We are told he volunteers at a local animal shelter and helps his neighbors during hard times. The sheriff's department has not made any comments at this time. Scott Burnett, CNN."

Ortega started pacing. He rubbed his forehead with his hands and his breathing quickened. Mumbling to himself he said, "Has the FBI found one of us faster than expected? I knew someone would be caught, but Cooper had only completed one job."

He stopped pacing and stared at the TV again. "Did you set off the explosion yourself, Cooper? If you did, I hope you made sure your laptop didn't survive."

As he watched the images on TV, the question about the laptop, and wondering if the FBI could discover anything incriminating, made him breathe even harder. He placed his palms on his forehead and his eyes widened.

"Oh shit. Cooper's cell phone has my number on it."

He walked to the night stand of the hotel room, where his cell phone was located, and turned it off. Taking the back off the phone, he removed the battery and SIMM card. He flushed the SIMM card down the hotel toilet. Tomorrow he would get another phone and inform the remaining members of his team about the new number.

The CNN reporter was introduced again and said, "We've been told additional FBI agents are in route to this location to assist the lone FBI agent currently on site. Both the on-site FBI agent and the Escambia County Sheriff's Department have not issued a statement or answered any of our questions. One development we've observed over the past hour is an increasing number of deputies guarding a barn behind the house."

"Wait a minute." There was a pause as the reporter turned to his right. "I'm seeing a convoy of military Humvees rapidly approaching. They just made a detour across a corn field heading directly toward the barn we just mentioned."

Ortega continued to stare at the TV.

"Damn, they found the C4."

He closed his eyes and shook his head.

"Cooper, you idiot."

The camera followed as five Humvees sped across the field toward the barn, the lead vehicle stopping in front while the others parked strategically around the building. As each stopped moving, soldiers emerged in full battle dress armed with automatic weapons. An older uniformed man without a helmet stepped out of the lead Humvee. He was met by a tall man in a blue polo shirt and a man with a FBI windbreaker. They all hurried into the barn as two other soldiers quickly closed the doors to the barn. Two additional soldiers took up station outside the door and stood guard. As the camera continued to focus on the barn, the correspondent said, "I believe we just saw the sheriff of Escambia County and the FBI agent meet the commander of the military convoy."

Ortega stopped paying attention. He knew exactly what had happened. Cooper had stored all of their C4 in the barn. All the work they had done to secure it was now wasted.

He slammed his fist on the desk and screamed, "Damn you, Cooper."

After several more minutes of watching the events in Alabama, he started packing.

Chapter Twenty-One

ESCAMBIA COUNTY, AL

Thursday

KRUGER WATCHED as deputies set up a command post and roped off the smoldering remains of the house as they waited for the local fire department. Sheriff Lamb walked up to him and said, "Sorry I doubted you back at the office."

Kruger smiled, "No problem. You realize this is going to get real ugly, real quick. Reporters, FBI, military, you name it, they'll arrive shortly and the circus will begin."

"Son, this would have gotten ugly with or without you. Glad we found the C4 before someone used it."

"Let's hope this was all of it." Kruger turned and stared at the barn. "I don't think he was acting alone. How could he have gotten this much C4 by himself? He's been out of the military for several years."

Lamb stopped walking, looked at Kruger, and said, "Good question. That stuff's not exactly available at the local farm supply store."

Kruger shook his head. "No, it isn't."

In the distance, they heard sirens approaching.

"That will be the local fire department," Lamb said. "Guess I'd better make sure they don't spray down any evidence."

He walked toward the smoldering remains of the farm house with three deputies following.

Kruger's cell phone vibrated. He checked the caller ID and answered, "Kruger."

"Give me a rundown," Seltzer said. "The corner office is asking lots of questions and I can't answer any of them."

After briefly summarizing the fire fight, Kruger told him about the discovery of the C4 and the destruction of the house.

Seltzer said, "Okay, you've got Air Force Special Operations coming out of Elgin Air Force Base. They should be there within the hour and will take charge of the C4. Dollar commandeered one of the Bureau's jets and is bringing his team. They should be there before dark. The deputy director told me to tell you good job, but that's unofficial right now. Dollar is whining about being kept out of the loop. He's claiming you're grandstanding, again."

Kruger sighed. "Figures. He'll probably come down here, look around, and declare he solved the case. Wait till he meets the local sheriff."

"Who's the sheriff?"

"His name's Gordon Lamb."

Seltzer was silent for a few seconds and then started laughing. "About six foot four, looks like an old hound dog, doesn't say a lot?"

"Yeah, that's him. We got off to a rocky start, but after I told him what was going on, he jumped on board. Good man."

"You don't remember him, do you?"

"What do you mean?"

"He's ex-Bureau. One of the rising stars about twelve years ago. He was in line to be deputy director one day. The man's got more commendations than any other agent in the bureau's history. One day, he just walked into the director's office, told him to shove the job and resigned. I lost track of him after that. Guess he's been in Alabama ever since."

Listening to Seltzer, Kruger watched the sheriff. No wonder he liked the man so well. "It will be interesting to see how he and Dollar get along. My money's on the sheriff."

"Mine too. Keep me up to date, Sean, the director's personally involved."

Kruger ended the call and watched a helicopter circling the area, probably media. There was already a lot of activity along the farm road near the driveway leading to the property. The sheriff had the foresight to instruct several of his deputies to block the entrance with squad cars and maintain crowd control. CNN and Fox News already had news vans setting up, and he suspected others would follow. The circus was just starting.

He was about to head back to the barn when Lamb walked up and said, "Just got a report, a convoy of military Humvees are about a mile out. Deputy told them how to bypass the commotion at the end of the driveway and come directly to the barn. I suggest we meet them and present our little gift."

Kruger nodded. "Just heard you're ex-FBI. Why didn't you say something earlier?"

Lamb shrugged. "Didn't seem important at the time."

"Why'd you leave?"

"Same reason you'll leave one day. Got tired of the BS."

Kruger smiled and said, "Yeah, you're probably right. It does get deep at times."

Thirty minutes after the military took charge of the C4, an FBI forensics team from Montgomery arrived and took charge of the destroyed house. They set up a perimeter and started searching. Kruger knew the lead investigator, Charlie Craft. A few years back on a serial killer investigation, Charlie had been a rookie. Kruger worked with him and explained what an investigator needed. The young man had taken the advice and built on it. Now he was in charge of a medium size forensics department.

Kruger watched Charlie get his team started. After several minutes, Charlie noticed Kruger watching. He smiled, waved, and hurried over to where Kruger stood on the outside of the crime scene perimeter.

They shook hands and Kruger said, "How've you been, Charlie?"

"Couldn't be better, Agent Kruger."

"Charlie—you know my rules."

Charlie looked embarrassed. "Sorry, Sean, I forgot. I've been dealing with too many self-important agents lately."

Kruger laughed. "I can only imagine. Speaking of self-important agents, Mint Dollar will be here shortly. He's now the SAC in Kansas City and will be taking over when he gets here."

Charlie's happy-to-see-you demeanor changed immediately. "Ahhh, shit, are you kidding me?"

"Wish I was. He was promoted just before this case broke. Unfortunately he still can't find his ass with both hands behind his back."

Charlie chuckled. "Thanks, I needed to hear that."

Charlie was one of the techs involved with the case in

Utah and witnessed Dollar's lack of ability. Kruger said, "I hate to ask you this, but I need a favor."

"Sure, Sean. What is it?"

"I think this guy was the tip of the spear, just a soldier in a much bigger operation. No one guy has the ability to steal as much C4 as we found in his barn. If there was a computer or a laptop in the house, I need the hard drive. It might lead us to others involved."

Charlie looked at Kruger, then back at what remained of the house. "You want JR to look at it, don't you?"

Kruger nodded. "We both know if there's something on a hard drive, he can find it and a lot faster than anybody at the Bureau."

Charlie looked again at the search area and thought for a moment. "Okay, if we find it, I'll log it in, then slip it to you someway. But I have to have it back."

Smiling, Kruger put his hand on Charlie's shoulder. "You may have just saved a lot of lives."

As Charlie walked back to the search area, Kruger glanced at his watch. It was getting late. Mildly surprised Dollar hadn't arrived yet, he felt it was probably a good time to call Stephanie and let her know he was alright.

She answered after the first ring, "Sean, are you okay?" Her voice was noticeably stressed.

"Yes, Stef, I'm fine. It's a little chaotic right now, but at least we have a starting point for the investigation. Guess you've been watching the news?"

"Yes, I have, and so has Brian." Her voice an octave higher than normal. "He's called several times asking if I had heard from you."

This was the first time anybody had expressed a concern about his safety while he conducted an investigation.

However, it was also the first time he had ever been involved with an exploding house.

"Call him back and tell him I'm fine. I can't right now. I'll be heading back tonight. I have to make one quick stop, then I'll be home."

There was a long silence on the call. Finally he heard, "Okay, just make sure you're careful. I didn't get married just to become a widow."

Kruger suddenly realized he was acting different himself. In the past, he never thought about how quickly he could get home. He worked his investigation and it took however long it took. Today he was plotting the fastest way to get home. His decision to retire was the right one. He said, "I'll be careful, I promise." No more running through a firefight and dodging bullets, he thought. Damn, what was he thinking?

He noticed Charlie walking back toward him, and when he arrived, Kruger said, "Did you find anything?"

Charlie offered his hand. Kruger shook it as Charlie passed him a small flat object. Very quietly, he said, "I found it a few minutes ago. It's a solid state drive. They're extremely sturdy. I haven't logged it in yet, so get it back to me as quickly as possible. Okay?"

Kruger nodded. "Thanks, Charlie, I will."

As Charlie walked away, Sheriff Lamb came up next to Kruger and pointed toward the growing crowd of media vans at the end of the driveway. "I just received a radio call, three black Suburbans have arrived. Would that be your Agent Dollar?"

Kruger chuckled and nodded, "More than likely." He paused for a few moments and said, almost to himself, "Where the hell can you rent black Suburbans in Pensacola?"

Lamb shrugged, "Not sure, but it does seem pretentious."

Kruger nodded, "That's Dollar. By the way, since he's here, I need to follow up on a new lead. Can one of your deputies take me to my Jeep?"

"Yeah, how soon do you want to leave? I need to get a couple of these guys off overtime."

"As soon as someone can take me."

The Suburbans slowly worked their way through the swarm of media. Kruger could hear the commotion of questions being yelled all the way from where he stood next to the storage buildings. Once through the crowd, the three vehicles quickly drove down the long drive and parked just outside the tree line. The doors opened in unison, making Kruger suspect Dollar was on his radio saying, ready, set, exit. After he was out of the passenger side of the lead Suburban, Dollar surveyed the scene, buttoned his suit coat, straightened his tie and headed straight toward a deputy guarding the perimeter of the search area. The deputy pointed at Lamb, who was already walking toward Dollar.

Kruger smiled and followed. He wanted to hear this exchange.

Dollar offered his hand, which Lamb shook. Dollar said, "Are you Sheriff Gordon Lamb?"

Lamb nodded and said nothing.

"I'm Special Agent Franklin Dollar. I am now in charge of this crime scene. Thank you for your assistance, Sheriff. Now if you will have your men vacate the area, I will conduct the investigation from here."

Lamb stared at Dollar and in a thick Alabama drawl said, "Well, Agent Dollar, the good Governor of this fine state has told me different. You go ahead and conduct your little investigation, but my men will stay right where they are until I'm told different by him."

Dollar, unprepared for this type of response, said nothing. He simply turned, walked back to the Suburbans and started giving orders to the other agents. Kruger walked up next to Lamb and said, "First time I've ever seen him speechless. Well done, Sheriff."

Lamb looked at Kruger and with a slight grin said, "Guess I'd better call the Governor and tell him what I just said."

Kruger struggled not to laugh. "I'll have to remember that line."

Lamb delivered on his promise of a ride. Fifteen minutes later a deputy asked Kruger if he was ready to go back to the sheriff's office. Thanking the deputy, he told him he'd be right back. He found Lamb. "Thanks for the ride." He offered his hand to the sheriff and continued, "It's been a pleasure working with you, Sheriff."

Lamb gave Kruger a wide grin and shook his hand. "Pleasure was all mine. I do believe I'm going to enjoy messing with that Dollar fella's head."

Kruger walked back to the deputy's squad car, opened the door and was about to get in when Dollar yelled at him to wait a minute. Tempted to ignore him, Kruger decided to wait. When Dollar got to the car he said, "Where are you going? I need a full report from you about this crime scene."

Kruger smiled, looked at Dollar with disdain, and said, "If I remember correctly, I report to Alan Seltzer, not you. After I file my report and he reads it, you can request a copy."

Dollar's eyes grew wide and his face reddened as Kruger got into the squad car and closed the door.

On the way back to his Jeep, Kruger called the agency's

Travel Department, and was told the only flights back to Kansas City were in the morning. He wouldn't be back until almost noon and then have a three-hour drive to Springfield. Too much wasted time. He had to get the cell phone and disk drive to JR as quickly as possible.

The deputy driving said, "There's a charter service at the Brewton airport. Would that help?"

Kruger said, "It might. Is anyone there now?"

The deputy glanced at his dashboard clock, shook his head and said, "No, it will be morning before the airport opens again. Sorry."

They drove in silence for a long time. Finally, a slight smile appeared on Kruger's face. When they arrived at the sheriff's office, Kruger thanked the deputy, got into the Jeep, and activated his GPS unit. It estimated his arrival time at JR's would be just in time for scrambled eggs and coffee. He started the Jeep and began the long drive to Springfield.

Chapter Twenty-Two

Thursday Evening

"IT'S GOING to be another long evening, honey. I have no idea when I can get home... No, don't wait up for me... I'll grab a sandwich or something here... I love you too."

Alan Seltzer pressed the end call icon at the same time he heard a quick rap on his office door. Paul Stumpf, Deputy Director of the FBI, stood in the partially open door and said, "The director wants an update. Do you have a minute?"

"Yes, Kruger gave me an update a few minutes ago, have a seat." He pointed to one of the two chairs in front of his desk. Seltzer proceeded to summarize the events in Alabama, leaving out some of the details, like who the sheriff of Escambia County was.

His 45th birthday had been two days ago. Marking the event as special, he had purchased a high-end Cannondale carbon-frame racing bike. Due to current events, Alan had yet to ride it. Riding a bicycle ten miles a day and more on weekends helped him stay fit. Plus the solitude allowed him to think through problems. The birthday also brought another milestone, a prescription for no-line bifocals. Even though he had worn reading glasses for some time, the new glasses left his eyes fatigued and bloodshot.

Obtaining his current position within the FBI had taken hard work and perseverance. As one of the few African American assistant deputy directors, he was responsible for several divisions. Kruger and he had been classmates at the FBI Academy and made agent status on the same day. Even though their career paths were different, they had remained close friends throughout the years, with Alan rising into the ranks of management and Kruger establishing his reputation as a top investigator. Unbeknown to him, his current position was the result of a recommendation by Kruger after turning down a promotion. Seltzer had a lot of respect for Kruger, which meant he did not micromanage him, nor did he question his decisions. The results spoke for themselves: Kruger solved more cases than anybody else in his divisions.

Stumpf said, "Is Kruger still convinced there are more individuals involved?"

"More so now than before. He believes it's almost impossible for one person to obtain that much C4 without assistance."

Stumpf nodded. "The key word there is almost impossible, not impossible. But, I agree with him. Unfortunately, the director doesn't, and he's listening to Mint Dollar, who's convinced there's only one person involved."

"How does he know that when he's not even on site yet?"

Stumpf smiled. "Do I really have to answer your question?"

The absurdity of Franklin Dollar finally causing both to start chuckling. Seltzer said, "Yes, I imagine he will work the case very diligently until tomorrow afternoon, declare it solved and take full credit."

"Yes, and when he does, we'll expose him as the fraud he is. But until that happens, the director is listening to him."

Stumpf paused and leaned forward in his chair.

"Unfortunately he's demanding Kruger be taken off the case immediately."

Seltzer shook his head and folded his arms on his desk. "Kruger is thinking about retiring. Pulling him off will push him over the edge. He'll pull the plug. I know him. He told me after the KC explosion he thought Dollar might have changed his ways and wanted to work as a team. After the video conference, Dollar reverted to his normal ego-centric self. To Kruger, the man is dangerous and incompetent."

"Dollar is dangerous and incompetent, but there are only a few of us who recognize it. Let him hang himself, and then we can move forward with our plan. Pull Kruger off the case officially, let him take some of the vacation time he's been saving."

"What do you mean officially?"

"I'm not going to tell you what to do, Alan. But we both know Kruger works best without a net. Take his net away, turn him loose."

Stumpf stood and headed for the door. He turned just before leaving and said, "We didn't have this conversation."

Seltzer just nodded.

FINALLY AT 10:45 P.M., Seltzer turned the lights out in his office and headed toward his car. The call to Kruger needed to be made away from the office. No one ever knew who was listening at any given time inside FBI Headquarters. As soon as he had driven out of the parking lot, he made the call. It was answered on the third ring.

"Kruger."

Seltzer heard wind noise in the background.

"Sean, where the hell are you?"

"Just outside of Birmingham, why?"

"Are you driving?"

"Yeah."

"Why?"

"I couldn't get a flight until mid-morning, which puts me back in Kansas City late afternoon. I have too much to follow up on, and this way I can be there by early morning."

Seltzer hesitated for a moment and said, "Sean, you've been officially taken off the case."

"By who?"

"The director."

"Why?"

"He believes you are getting in the way of Dollar's investigation."

"Did he say that, or did Dollar put words in his mouth?"

Kruger's anger was growing, Seltzer could sense it, even though his voice didn't betray his emotions. He said, "Dollar complained he was left out of the loop about Cooper and it delayed his arrival at the scene."

Kruger started laughing. "Give me a break, Alan. Dollar was nowhere on this case. He had absolutely no idea how to move it forward."

"I know, you told me before you left for Alabama. But the fact remains, you are officially off the case."

"Alan, are you using code here? You've used the word officially twice now. Am I unofficially on it?"

"I can't say that, but you are officially off the case."

Kruger chuckled. "And everybody wonders why I want to retire. This is BS. What am I supposed to do, Alan, take a vacation?"

"I think that's an excellent idea. Why don't you take a trip to Springfield and go fishing with your buddy."

Kruger was silent.

Seltzer continued, "I'd like to join you, but I can't. Too much going on here."

Kruger's voice grew quiet. "Who else knows about my fishing trips?"

"No one, just me. We have a mutual friend who's invited me several times, but I've never been able to make it."

Kruger let out a sigh of relief. "How do you and Joseph know each other?"

"Who do you think talked me into applying for the FBI? He didn't always live in Springfield, you know."

Seltzer waited, hoping that revealing he knew about Kruger's information source would send the right message.

"Okay, I get it. You can tell the director that I will officially turn in my retirement papers in June."

"Sorry it has to be this way, Sean. Paul and I know you won't let us down. We also understand your frustration. Don't make a hasty decision."

"I have no intentions of letting you down. Dollar's the one everyone needs to worry about. He's going to embarrass the agency one more time, Alan, probably tomorrow."

"Paul and I know that. I can't say any more. I'll explain it the next time I see you."

"I'll let you know how the fish are biting."

Seltzer ended the call and continued his drive home. If

Dollar declared the case closed with the death of Cooper and Kruger proved more individuals were involved, it would effectively end Franklin Dollar's career. But if Cooper did act alone, Dollar's career would be sealed. He'd be in Washington in some high-profile position making everybody's life miserable. If events proceeded in that direction, Seltzer would join Kruger and retire.

As he pulled into his driveway, he thought of Joseph. It had been too long since they had last spoken. He missed Joseph's clarity of thought and his wisdom. Yes, he would have to call his uncle as soon as possible.

Chapter Twenty-Three

DALLAS, TX

Thursday

THE HERTZ RENTAL car agent looked at the driver's license and then at the customer. He smiled, typed on his computer key board, handed the license back, and said, "What type of credit card will you be using, Mr. Acosta?"

Aazim Abbas smiled back and handed the clerk a platinum American Express card in the name of Edward Acosta. "I reserved the car for two weeks. Can I extend the reservation an additional week?"

The agent nodded and continued typing on his computer. Several minutes later, he handed Abbas the completed rental agreement and told him where the car was parked. As he walked toward the exit, he stopped, his attention drawn to a flat-screen TV in a waiting area. CNN was showing an aerial view of Cooper's destroyed house and the crowd of sheriff's deputies, firemen and FBI agents. Walking closer to the TV, he started reading the crawl at the bottom of the screen.

After a few moments, a man in his late 50s approached the TV. "Goddamn terrorist, got what he deserved." The man shook his head and walked off.

Abbas took a deep breath. His nostrils flared, and his lips tightened. He closed his eyes briefly, then continued on to the parking area where the rental car was located. Once behind the steering wheel of the car, he pounded his palm against it and stared out the front windshield. His breathing was short and rapid.

After several minutes, his breathing returned to normal. Finally he started the car and pulled out of the rental area parking lot.

Thirty minutes later, he was in his motel room and typing his first message to Ortega.

"Is all C4 gone?" He texted the new password and waited for a return text.

Ten minutes later, he received it and opened the email account again.

"Yes."

Following the same tedious procedure, he wrote, "When can you get more?"

It was twenty minutes before he received a response.

"Four to six weeks, maybe never. Source is being watched by CID."

Abbas took a deep breath and replied.

"Not good enough, need more by end of month."

This time the response took almost an hour.

"Cooper's supply took over two years to assemble. It will take time."

Abbas stood and paced the room for five minutes. Ortega would have to be dealt with later for this unforgiveable offense. He walked over to the window, opened the curtains and stared out over the hotel's parking lot. As an idea started to form, he finally smiled and nodded his head.

———

THE DALLAS-FORT WORTH area was heavily populated with Walmart stores. Abbas spent several hours visiting various stores in the area and buying pre-paid cell phones from each. By the time he was back in his hotel room at midnight, he had over twenty phones. He only bought one phone per store, never more, and he paid cash. The next step was to contact the Imam in Richmond, California. Leaving the hotel room again, Abbas drove three miles to a 7-Eleven that still had a payphone outside the store. After putting the necessary number of quarters into the machine, he dialed the number for the Imam. The call was answered on the third ring. Abbas said, "As-salamu alaykum."

"Wa-alaykum salaam. How are you, my brother?"

"I am good, Imam. I apologize for the lateness of the hour. I need counsel."

"Ah. How can I help?"

"The matter of which we spoke earlier. It is time. Can you send three to help?"

There was silence on the other end of the call. "Maybe. When do you need them?"

"A week."

"Yes, a week will be good. I will arrange for their trip."

"Thank you, Imam."

The call ended abruptly without a response from the Imam. Abbas frowned, hurriedly returned to his rental car and drove back to the hotel.

Sleep did not come easily. The abruptness of the call

ending continued to dominate his thoughts. Finally at 5 a.m., he rose, packed his suitcase, and checked out of the hotel.

Chapter Twenty-Four

SPRINGFIELD, MO

Friday

DRIVING at night eliminated more than an hour from the GPS's estimated drive time to Springfield. The lack of traffic in Memphis at 2 a.m. saved thirty minutes with the remaining time made up along the route. He pulled into JR's parking lot at exactly 7:58 a.m., and by 8:30 a.m., the disk drive and cell phone were in JR's hands. Since Kruger knew very little about what JR was doing, he quickly dozed off.

JR's mumbling and sudden animation woke Kruger from his impromptu nap. Because the desk chair he occupied was not designed for a person six feet tall to sleep, he had a sharp pain in his back and his neck was stiff. JR was leaned forward on the edge of his chair, his fingers flying over the keyboard typing instructions. His head turned rapidly as he checked data on the three large monitors sitting on his desk. Finally he sat back in his chair.

"Kruger, you just hit the Powerball."

Still half asleep, Kruger yawned, "What've you got?"

"These guys are clever. If I just had the cell phone, I wouldn't have found it. If I just had the hard drive, same results. Zip, nothing. But with both, the puzzle comes together."

Kruger was tired, barely awake and out of patience. "WHAT FUCKING PUZZLE?"

JR looked at him with a smug grin and pointed to the computer screen. "How they communicate."

Suddenly awake, Kruger walked to where JR was seated. "Okay, start over. What've you found and who are they?"

"THEY are, at minimum, six distinct individuals, probably more. But I can only identify six unique email addresses they are utilizing on a regular basis. They're probably—no, not probably—definitely either ex-military or still in the military. The codes and abbreviations they use are military. They use a twenty-four hour clock and their messages are brief. Plus, their communication system was developed by individuals in Iraq and Afghanistan who knew their emails were being monitored by the NSA. Our guys discovered the system and reported it back to the Pentagon. I saw some of the classified memorandums several years ago."

Kruger stared at JR. "I won't ask how you saw them, just explain how they communicate."

"It's simple. Email addresses are set up using one of the free email services, like Gmail or Hotmail. Anyone can set up an email account and use it on any computer they want. Are you with me so far?"

Kruger nodded. "Yes, yes, I'm aware of how email works. So?

"So, let's say you set up six email accounts, one for each member of the group. The leader knows all of them, but the members only know their email address and the leader's. If the leader wants to send a message to member A, he opens that member's email account and types a message. He then saves it as a draft. He changes the password for the email account and sends a text message with the new password to member A. When member A gets a text message, it's the signal he has a new email. He opens his email account with the new password and reads the draft. He has now received an email without sending it through a bunch of servers via satellites. Those types of messages can't be intercepted by the NSA."

"Why?"

"Because they've never been sent."

Kruger thought about it for a second and said, "What about the text message? It's sent via cell phone towers."

"There's the beauty of their system. It's just a bunch of random numbers and letters. It has no meaning unless you know what it's for. It's not even a code, it's random. It wouldn't be tagged by the NSA's computers because it doesn't contain any key words their computers search for. It's brilliant."

"Brilliant in its simplicity." Kruger started pacing. "Can you find out who the email accounts belong to?"

"Probably not a specific name, unless they access the internet on their home network. But as smart as these guys appear to be, I doubt they're doing that." He paused and grinned. "However, I can identify where the computer accessing the email is located."

"Okay, could the agency figure this out with just the hard drive?"

JR shook his head. "No, it's too badly damaged. I was

only able to figure this out by finding several server addresses I'm familiar with."

"Could they figure it out with both the hard drive and cell phone?"

"Maybe, depends on the tech."

"Could they if you provide a roadmap?"

JR looked at Kruger and said, "I try not to communicate with those types of law enforcement individuals."

"You'd talk to Charlie, wouldn't you?"

JR thought about it for a few seconds and said, "Yeah, I'd talk to him. He's cool with my situation."

"Okay, I'm not sure I have to do it yet. It depends on a particular individual. If he decides to embarrass the agency, we'll send these items to Charlie. At that point you can walk him through it."

JR's face grew animated and suddenly he burst out, "Whoa, Sean, I just thought of something. I could put a fire alarm on each of the computer addresses. That way I would be alerted when any of the computers were online. If, and this is a big if, they use a certain ISP on a regular basis, it would suggest their home address. From there, I could tell you the person's name and physical address."

"How?"

"Just hack their ISP and get their billing information."

"Isn't that illegal?"

"Yes, but it's the fastest way to find these guys. Do you have a problem with it?"

Kruger shrugged. "I don't, do you?"

JR smiled and said, "I knew I liked you for a reason. You've got a larceny streak as long as mine."

KRUGER WAS PREPARING to drive to Kansas City when he thought to check CNN for the latest news on Dollar's investigation. JR had several flat screens on the wall for this purpose. It was right at 2 p.m. and the top of the hour news recap was in progress. Finally, the anchor said, "We have breaking news from yesterday's explosion near Atmore, Alabama. Scott Burnett has the latest. Scott?"

The remains of the house served as the backdrop, with yellow crime scene tape, little yellow flags in the yard, and a reporter standing off to the side. Scott Burnett said, "Late this morning, FBI Special Agent in Charge Franklin Dollar announced he will make a statement to the press at 2:30 p.m. No word on what he will say, but we hear there has been a new development in the investigation. We'll be here for his news conference. Back to you, Jim."

Kruger looked at JR and said, "At least the man is predictable. I'll bet you a dollar he says the case is closed, wanna bet?"

JR shook his head. "I'd lose."

At 2:30 p.m., CNN cut to Scott Burnett again. "Jim, I was just told Agent Dollar will make a statement to the press in five minutes."

Just like Dollar. Loves to keep people waiting, Kruger thought. He muttered, "Figures."

JR said, "What'd you say?"

"Nothing. My original assessment of Dollar's personality has been correct for the past seven years. He hasn't changed a bit."

Burnett continued to recap the events of the past twenty-four hours for the twenty-fourth time. Finally, the camera panned to a make-shift podium with the FBI seal on it. Franklin Dollar stood behind it and began reading from a prepared statement.

"Good afternoon, I am Franklin Dollar, Special Agent in Charge of the FBI Kansas City Field Office. Last Monday at the Kansas City Country Club Plaza, a deplorable act of terrorism was committed against the citizens of Kansas City. This act killed eight innocent civilians and wounded fifteen others. Since that time, the Kansas City FBI office has been diligently working non-stop to identify the perpetrator of this cowardly act.

"On Wednesday, an agent based in Kansas City identified a person of interest and tracked him to this rural community in southern Alabama. At approximately 3:30 p.m. yesterday, a federal warrant was issued in the name of one Thomas Cooper of Escambia County, Alabama. With the aid of local authorities, a legal arrest was attempted. During this attempt, the suspect commenced firing high caliber weaponry on local authorities, deputies returned fire, resulting in a lengthy exchange of gun fire.

"During the exchange, the suspect detonated ordinance inside the house. Forensic evidence suggests these ordinances were set as booby traps in the event of a police raid. After the detonation, several hundred pounds of C4 explosives were discovered in the suspect's barn. The explosives used in the Kansas City attack were of the same type.

"In addition to the explosive ordinance, multiple firearms matching the type used in two additional killings in Washington, D.C., were discovered in the remains of the house. Travel records place the suspect in Washington, D.C., during the time of those murders.

"In light of these facts and additional evidence discovered during our search of the property, we are prepared to announce that Thomas Cooper was responsible for these heinous crimes. I will now answer a few questions."

The reporters all shouted at once, until finally one question was heard.

"Agent Dollar, what was the name of the agent who tracked Cooper to this area?"

Kruger smiled, interested in how Dollar would respond to the question.

Dollar said, "The agent has requested his identity remain anonymous. Next question?"

JR had walked over to where Kruger was standing and said, "What an asshole."

"Well, technically he didn't lie. He just didn't give anybody else credit. Guess it's time to send the cell phone and hard disk drive to Charlie. Dollar just stepped on himself."

Additional questions were being yelled at Dollar, and he chose to answer very few. Finally someone said, "Agent Dollar, internet chatter says this is the work of a new domestic terrorist group. Can we have your response to those accusations?"

Dollar straightened his tie and said, "Conspiracy theories have been with us since the assassination of Lincoln, there is no factual basis this was the act of terrorists, foreign or domestic. This was the work of one man, and one man only. Thank you."

With this statement, he turned and walked back to the investigation area. The camera returned to Scott Burnett, who started to recap the press conference.

Kruger turned the sound down with the remote. "Send the cell phone and hard disk drive to Charlie's home address, I'll call and tell him they're coming. You'll need to provide a roadmap for him on how to retrieve the data. In the meantime, set those alarms on the emails. I want these guys."

THREE HOURS LATER, Kruger walked into his living room. It was late and he was starting to feel the effects of less than three hours of sleep in the past two days. Stephanie greeted him with a kiss and said, "Hi, I missed you."

He smiled and hugged her. "I missed you too."

"Saw the press conference today. You weren't mentioned. Why?"

"For one thing, I didn't want to be mentioned. Plus, the less I am associated with Franklin Dollar, the easier it will be to catch these guys."

"What do you mean?"

"The man has no basis for stating Cooper was responsible for all three attacks. He got anxious and wanted the credit for solving a high-profile case. He doesn't realize we have evidence suggesting there are at least five additional individuals involved."

"Didn't you give that information to Dollar?"

Kruger shook his head. "No, we discovered it just a few minutes before his press conference. Dollar wants to get this over with as quickly as possible. He's over his head with his new position and the only way to keep the director from seeing his shortcomings is to declare the case closed. I feel sorry for the guys in the Kansas City office. Most of them are good, solid agents."

"So what are you going to do now?"

"Don't know." He closed his eyes briefly while he yawned. "I'm officially off the investigation. But Seltzer implied he and Paul want me to continue to work it. Seltzer knows about JR, seems he and I have a common friend who knows all about my fishing trips."

"Joseph?"

Kruger nodded.

"Apparently Joseph has known Alan a long time. Like me, he was the person who encouraged Alan to join the FBI. Right now, I'm tired and need to go to bed. I'll be able to think clearer in the morning."

She hugged him. "I'll go with you, I didn't sleep very well last night."

Chapter Twenty-Five

SPRINGFIELD, MO

Saturday Night

A DESIGNATED laptop in the computer room was tasked to monitor the tracking cookies JR Diminski had attached to each of the identified computers. Using a program written for a client several years ago, he modified the software to send an email when any of those computers accessed the internet.

At exactly 10:14 p.m. Saturday, one of the target computers went active. JR's cell phone vibrated with the receipt of an email alert. Rushing to the second floor, he checked to see which computer had gone active. He quickly downloaded a computer worm to the active machine. His virus would attach itself to any email account the target computer accessed. Once another computer accessed the email account, the worm would attach itself to the new computer and record all keystrokes. Once the process was complete, when the now-infected computers accessed the internet, the worm would send files with the keystroke recordings to JR's laptop.

When he would receive any of those files was unknown, but at least the process to monitor the group's communications was starting. All he had to do now was sit back and wait. With a grin on his face, he walked back upstairs.

———

JR RETURNED to the computer room at 2:28 a.m. Sunday morning. As usual, when he worked on a problem, he couldn't sleep. So he checked the tracking computer and found numerous downloads, more than he had anticipated. The time stamps on the files indicated they had arrived somewhere between 11 p.m. and midnight. Had something important occurred within the group today? He accessed some of the files and by 3 a.m., he was confident something was going on. Files continued to be received, and JR became increasingly confident he would soon be able understand and monitor the group's communications. Finally at 4:30 a.m. his initial problem of monitoring the group was solved. Walking back upstairs, he crawled into bed and fell asleep immediately.

By 9 a.m. Sunday morning, JR was back on the second floor confirming what he had. He was now in possession of recordings of all messages typed on the group's computers. In fact he found two previously unknown computers not found on Cooper's cell phone and hard drive. The narrative contained within the keystroke files was disconcerting. He decided to call Kruger, a direct violation of his communication protocols. But something had changed within the group. The messages, though vague in content, contained a note of urgency. This was way beyond anything he had helped Kruger with in the past.

————

ALAN SELTZER WAS UP EARLY SITTING at the breakfast bar of their house with his first cup of coffee and reading the Sunday Washington Post. His wife was still asleep, allowing him a few minutes of quiet before they got ready to leave for church. After ten straight days without a break, the thought of an actual day off to relax was appealing. As he turned to the Op-Ed section, his cell phone vibrated.

He glanced at the caller ID, sighed and answered. "This is Alan."

Paul Stumpf said, "I just got a disturbing call from our counter-terrorist division."

Seltzer closed his eyes, the twinge of a headache suddenly making itself known. "About?"

"They have several radical Islamist groups under surveillance in northern California."

"I've heard about it. Is something going on?"

"They're not sure. But, one of the Imam's received a phone call from a payphone very late on Thursday night. The call itself seemed innocent enough, except for the lateness of the hour."

Seltzer was quiet for a few seconds. "Go on."

"It seems the normally reclusive Imam is suddenly making house calls on members of his flock. The surveillance team has followed him to over fifteen apartments and houses. He stays about an hour and then leaves."

"Do they know who he's visiting?"

"Yes, every single one of them is a young adult male between 19 and 24."

Taking his time to respond, Seltzer took a deep breath. He exhaled and said, "Does the team think they are planning something?"

"The consensus of the group is, yes, they are. What, they don't know. They haven't been able to monitor the conversations between the Imam and the men. Too short of notice on what he was going to do."

"I don't like the proximity to Cooper being discovered."

"Alan, that's why I'm calling. Make sure our friend has this information, unofficially of course."

Seltzer nodded and said, "I'll head to the office and take care of it."

"Alan, if our friend can confirm there is a relationship to Cooper, I'll take it to the director. If he doesn't want to hear it, I will take it straight to the President."

"I'm sure our friend will be willing to look into it."

"Thanks, Alan. Sorry I had to bother you on Sunday."

Seltzer ended the call, his headache now pounding behinds his eyes. With his anticipated day off now impossible, he walked to the kitchen cabinet where his wife kept the Extra Strength Excedrin. Taking two, he chased them with the now-cold coffee.

His thoughts turned back to the current problem as he emptied the coffee into the sink and poured a fresh cup. What could an Imam in northern California visiting young men have to do with Thomas Cooper? A sudden thought occurred to him. His eyes widened. He poured the fresh cup of coffee into the sink and rushed upstairs to wake his wife. He had to get to the office as quickly as possible.

THE FED EX package was on the doorstep of Charlie Craft's modest ranch-style home in Montgomery, AL, when he returned home late Saturday night. Tired and dirty from sifting through the remains of Cooper's house for two days, the last thing on his mind was opening it. A quick shower and the comfort of his own bed were his priorities.

Late Sunday morning, he took the box into the kitchen and pulled at the tape designed to open the FedEx container. He ripped the remaining end of the box off and emptied the contents. Two bundles of bubble wrap and an envelope slid onto the kitchen table. One of the bundles had a handwritten sticky note attached with the words "Call Me – JR" in bold letters.

Charlie removed the bubble wrap and found the damaged hard drive he had handed to Kruger on Thursday. The other bundle contained a cell phone. Finally he opened the envelope and found a sheet of paper with instructions on how to contact JR.

Glancing at this watch, he noted the time was almost 9 a.m. Sunday morning. It might be too early to contact JR, but then, JR could always call him back whenever he was ready. He found his cell phone, sent the message to the number on the sheet of paper, and waited.

Exactly one minute later his cell phone vibrated. Charlie checked the caller ID, "Unknown," and smiled as he answered.

"Hello."

"Charlie Craft. How in the world are you?"

It had been a long time since Charlie had heard from JR, and it was good to hear his voice. "I'm fine, JR, yourself?"

"I take it you got my presents."

"It came yesterday, but I got back late last night and just now opened it. Did you find anything?"

"Lots of cool stuff on both objects, but the stuff's hard to find."

Charlie noted JR did not refer to the contents, so he didn't either. Instead he said, "Okay, how do I find it?"

"Give me your personal email address and I'll send you a roadmap. It'll guide you to the pertinent stuff."

After telling JR his personal email address, Charlie said, "I know you're very good with this type of computer work, JR. Will this be something above my abilities? You know it might draw attention we really don't need right now."

JR didn't answer for a few seconds. Finally he said, "No, it really isn't, Charlie. Besides, once you've know how to do it, you'll understand the process, and guess what? It isn't above your abilities anymore."

"Thanks, JR, I owe you and Kruger a lot."

"Don't mention it. Besides, as my business continues to grow, I'll be looking for an associate someday. Who knows, as good as you are, I might have to give you a call. See ya, Charlie."

The call ended at one minute and fifty-seven seconds. Charlie smiled. Amazing. JR was always consistent with his phone calls, less than two minutes.

Charlie went to the desk were he kept his personal laptop. By the time it booted up and his email program was running, a new message was in his inbox. The sender's address was a series of random letters and numbers, once again demonstrating JR was in a league of his own when it came to computers.

After reading the directions, Charlie smiled. The process wasn't that hard, but it wasn't something he would have intuitively known how to do. The process would need more computer horsepower than his laptop possessed. Besides, it would not look good for him to work on this at home. He needed to be at his lab. He took a quick shower and headed to his office.

Two hours later, he was making progress. Data on the cell phone and hard drive revealed more than one person was involved, several more. At the crime scene, he had told Franklin Dollar there wasn't enough information available to declare the case closed. But, according to Dollar, his position as Special Agent in Charge gave him the authority. Charlie, as a lowly forensic technician, wasn't going to determine if the case was closed or not. It would be interesting to see how Dollar tried to explain his way out of this mistake.

Charlie waited until after 3 p.m. to call Pam Haworth, his boss in Washington, D.C. She answered on the second ring, "Charlie, I hope this is about the Cooper investigation."

"It is. I've found evidence that Cooper wasn't acting alone. In fact, I found a distinct possibility of five additional accomplices."

Pam Haworth remained silent for a few seconds and said, "Agent Dollar declared there were no other suspects. What evidence do you have indicating more individuals are involved, Charlie?"

"Agent Dollar made his statement before consulting with any of the investigators at the scene. If he had consulted with us, we would have told him there was evidence Cooper had accomplices."

"I see. That's a serious accusation, Charlie. Can you back up your statement with the other techs?"

"Yes, I can. I found evidence on Cooper's cell phone and his computer's hard drive. It's solid, Pam."

"Very well, I have to report this directly to Deputy Director Stumpf. He's become personally involved. Put all of your findings in your report and email it to me as quickly as possible."

"I will."

He ended the call and tried to decide if he needed to call Kruger. Might as well, the day was shot anyway.

Chapter Twenty-Six

KANSAS CITY, MO

Sunday

KRUGER HAD JUST RETURNED from his morning run and getting ready to join Stephanie in the shower when his cell phone vibrated. The caller ID showed "Unknown." Strange. Only a call from JR would have a similar ID. But JR never called unless he was called first. He pressed the receive icon and said, "Kruger."

"Sean, something big's in the works," JR said without hesitation.

"Slow down, JR. What is the something and how big?"

JR took a deep breath and let it out slowly.

"The traps I set on the email addresses paid off. Lots of communications over the past twelve hours. One refers to the C4 and wanted to know what happened. Then the person sending the message wants it replaced immediately. After this initial exchange, there are several exchanges with three other individuals."

"Okay, back up just a second. You said emails. How many are you talking about?"

"At least twenty."

Kruger thought for a second then said, "Summarize the messages."

"Of the six known computers, two have been silent, Cooper's and one that hasn't accessed the internet since I identified it. Previous messages from this individual seem to be in the Baltimore area, but I need it to access the internet to be sure. There is one in Dallas, one in the St. Louis area, and the others are accessing the internet on military bases in the south. One of those computers was unknown before last night."

"Huh. There's the possible source of the C4. Go on."

"The computer in St. Louis seems to be the central organizer. This guy talks to everyone. The Dallas computer is the commander of the group. But his only contact is St. Louis, who, by the way, was in Memphis earlier this week."

"He's mobile, moving from city to city to avoid detection," Kruger said.

"I agree, the other computers are more stationary. But the dialogue suggests they're planning to hit a big target, soon."

"Was the new target identified?"

"No, not in these emails," JR was quiet for a moment. "There's some tension in the group. The guy in St. Louis is frustrated about not getting a response from Baltimore. The Dallas member wants more C4. Lots of it. The three contacts on military bases are saying no way, too much heat from CID."

"What do you think?"

"I'm convinced these guys are ex-military and current military."

Kruger was quiet for several moments. "Yeah that makes sense. I need you to dig into Cooper's military history and find out who he served with. Who his commanders were, who his sergeants were, and finally who among those individuals are no longer in the military."

JR didn't respond right away, and Kruger could tell he was thinking through the problem. "Well, I haven't been in the Pentagon's computer for a while. They get pissy when people hack into their system. Guess I'll just have to make sure they don't know I'm there."

"Thanks, JR, let me know what you find."

"Okay, gotta run, I'm way over my time limit."

After the call ended, Kruger looked at his phone and noticed the time duration was almost ten minutes. JR violated two of his rules. He initiated the call and stayed on the phone for more than two minutes. Apparently JR was as involved as he was. The thought made him smile.

Stephanie came out of the bedroom in a bathrobe and her hair wrapped in a towel. "Thought you were going to join me?"

He held the cell phone up. "JR called. There's another incident being planned." He paused for a moment, shook his head, and continued, "Why is the director listening to Dollar? The agency needs to be using all its resources to find these guys, not just one ready-to-retire agent. It just doesn't make any sense to me, Stef."

Stephanie hugged him and said, "Sean, think it through. You've told me numerous times, you work better by yourself. No meetings to attend, or wasted hours waiting on others to approve your next move. Find these guys, Sean, then walk away with your head held high. Afterward, we can move on with our lives."

He nodded and hugged her tighter. "Yeah, you're right.

I'm starting to feel sorry for myself, another reason to get out."

After his shower, he went back to his desk and called Seltzer's cell phone. Alan answered quickly, "Sean, I was going to call you when I got to the office."

"Alan, there's a lot of chatter on the internet. My source tells me there are at least six other individuals still involved, maybe more. Plus, there's another target."

Seltzer was quiet. Finally he said, "There's something else."

"What?"

"An Imam in the San Francisco area received a phone call late Thursday night. The call was from a Dallas payphone." Kruger didn't respond, but a piece of the puzzle fell into place as Alan talked. "The next day, this normally reclusive holy man started making house calls. He's been visiting members of his mosque."

"Who's he visiting, or should I guess?"

"Young adult men, ages 19 to 24."

"I was afraid you were going to say that."

"Paul doesn't like the coincidence of this happening immediately after the Cooper affair. He's thinks there's a connection."

"He's probably right. One of the members of Cooper's group is in Dallas."

"That's not good."

"Nope."

Seltzer didn't respond for several seconds. "Okay, once again, I'm not going to ask how you know all of this, but I'm going to need specific information on the additional members before I take this to Paul."

"Talk to Charlie Craft. He was the lead tech at the Cooper farm. He'll know what I know today or tomorrow."

"Okay, Sean. We asked you to pursue this on your own, so I won't ask for details."

"Yes, you did, and you're right, don't ask."

"I can live with that. Things are going to get hot around here when Charlie gives us this information."

"Alan, the only person who needs to take the heat is Dollar. Everybody else is just doing their job. And, I might add, a lot more professionally."

"I know. The director is listening to Dollar and no one else; there's a lot of politics involved."

Kruger couldn't believe what Seltzer had said. "Then the director is a fool. What about the innocent victims here in Kansas City? Should we just tell them politics is more important than catching the people responsible for the explosion? That's wrong, Alan, and you know it."

Seltzer was quiet for a long time. Finally he said, "I know. Paul is aware it's wrong as well. He's a good man, Sean, and he's trying to make changes, but it takes time."

Kruger was now totally disgusted with the conversation. "He needs to try harder. I'll talk to you later." He pressed the end call icon and tossed the cell phone on his desk.

Kruger leaned back in his desk chair and pressed his palms against his eyes. Was there a connection between the Imam suddenly visiting young male members of his mosque and the incident on the Cooper farm? His instinct told him there was.

He left his office and found Stephanie reading the Sunday Kansas City Times on the sofa.

"Let's take a walk," he said.

They were a few minutes into the walk and he was holding her hand. "Let's suppose the incident on Cooper's farm started a chain reaction within the group."

She looked up at him. "Okay, what kind of chain reaction?"

Shaking his head, Kruger took a deep breath. "This is a stretch, but let's suppose the C4 we found was designated for a huge terrorist attack. One they had planned for later."

Stephanie nodded, but said nothing.

"The group leader is pissed, really pissed, and is pushing the group to find more explosives. But the group says it can't be done in his timeline. Are you following me?"

"Yes." She stared ahead, "What if this group's leader decides he needs to move in another direction? What would be his next move?"

"Depends on if this is a domestic group, or a group from another country."

"Sean, you know something, what is it?"

"There was a call from a Dallas payphone to an Imam in San Francisco. Did I mention one of the email computers is in Dallas?"

She shook her head.

"Well, it is. Now this Imam is visiting young single men from his mosque. About what, we don't know, but I can guess."

She took a deep breath. "Sean, they're trying to find martyrs, aren't they?"

Kruger nodded, but did not answer right away. "We've no proof or even a hint that's what the Imam is doing. But higher ups in the agency don't like the coincidence. Neither do I."

"What if there is no connection?"

"There may not be."

"Don't you think you need to find out?"

Kruger walked in silence for several minutes contemplating. Finally he said, "I knew there was a reason I married you. That's exactly what I need to do."

They looked at each other and both started laughing. Suddenly to Kruger, the weight of the investigation was lifted from his shoulders and the only thing in the world was Stephanie holding his hand.

The feeling wouldn't last very long.

Chapter Twenty-Seven

Monday

"I FAIL to understand why we are still committing resources against this investigation. It has been closed," FBI Director Phillip Wagner said, standing next to the coffee service in his office. He had just poured himself a cup without offering one to Deputy Director Paul Stumpf or Alan Seltzer.

Director Wagner was a political appointee from the previous administration. He was unfamiliar with the internal workings of the FBI. He knew how to get funds and keep Congress at bay, but investigations were handled by others.

"Yes sir, that's the conclusion of Agent Dollar," Stumpf said. "Unfortunately, he may have been premature in declaring the case resolved. We have evidence discovered last night of at least six more individuals involved."

"Paul, do you realize how much damage will be done to the agency's image if we retract our conclusions of last Friday?'"

"Sir, I understand there may be a few eyebrows raised. But if a network of domestic terrorists is targeting U.S. citizens, shouldn't we keep the case open?"

Wagner walked back to the ceiling-to-floor window behind his desk. He gazed out the window slowly sipping his coffee. He kept his back to them as he spoke.

"There will be more than a few eyebrows raised. There will be congressional hearings and the media will have a feeding frenzy. We have no proof this man belonged to a group of domestic terrorists." He turned slightly back toward them. "Gentlemen, I do not want those words used with the media, it will raise questions that do not need to be asked. Congress will demand to know why we dropped the ball. No, I don't believe we can go that direction. The case is closed."

He returned to staring out the window.

"What if the killings continue?" Seltzer said, expecting another lecture on agency image.

The director turned to look at them again. "Then you deal with it, Mr. Seltzer. You deal with it. But it is not to be associated with the Cooper incident. Do I make myself clear?"

He turned back toward the window and sipped his coffee.

Paul Stumpf motioned for Alan to remain quiet and said, "Yes, sir, we understand. Thank you for your time this morning."

He and Alan stood and left the office as the director continued facing the window as they left.

Stumpf walked quickly down the hall toward his office, Seltzer barely managing to keep up. After they were in Stumpf's office, he closed the door and with a trembling voice said, "What an idiot. I cannot believe I just witnessed a director of the FBI more worried about his public image than the safety of the public. Unbelievable."

Seltzer leaned against the closed door, listening to his friend vent.

"How in the hell are we supposed to conduct an investigation when the director is blind to the facts? All he can see are the political consequences. Trust me, this incident will blow up in his face, and the rest of us will have to clean up the mess."

After a few seconds of silence, Seltzer said, "Thanks for keeping me quiet. I was about to say something unproductive."

Stumpf nodded, "You were going to say the same thing I wanted to. We'll need to keep Kruger's activities quiet. Is he making progress?"

"Yes, in fact he's the one that told Charlie Craft how to find the information on the cell phone and hard drive from Cooper's farm," Seltzer said.

"Okay, keep Charlie's involvement quiet, he's a good man. I don't want him in the crossfire when the bullets start flying. I'm surprised we keep any competent people with the likes of Wagner and Dollar in management."

"When I spoke to Kruger yesterday, he wasn't pleased with the situation. It's just my opinion, but I think he'll retire when this is over."

"I wouldn't blame him. If things don't improve around here, I might follow him."

The room was silent for a few moments, until finally Stumpf said, "Alan, you have to make sure Kruger has as much support as we can provide. I know he trusts you, let him know I'm trying to make changes around here."

"Yes sir, I will."

Seltzer headed back to his office hoping Kruger still trusted him.

———

CHARLIE CRAFT WAS DISCUSSING evidence found at the Cooper site with two of his team members when the phone rang. It was his boss, Pam.

"I need to take this, let's take a break and be back in my office in five minutes."

He answered the call as they walked out of his office.

"Charlie, I hate to tell you this, but the director wants the investigation into the Cooper incident stopped immediately. All the evidence needs to be sent to Quantico as soon as you can box it up. I'm sorry. You did excellent work on this."

Charlie was stunned. "How in the world can they justify shutting down the investigation. My team just spent two days gathering and cataloging evidence. There's so much material it's overwhelming."

He took a deep breath and exhaled slowly. "Pam, I don't understand. Most of the evidence hasn't even been given a cursory look. What's going on?"

Silence was his answer. Finally Pam said, "Politics, nothing more, nothing less. Mint Dollar declared it closed and the director is following his lead. He doesn't want to embarrass the agency with a retraction. Sorry, I wish I had a better answer."

"This is wrong, Pam."

"I know, Charlie. But my hands are tied."

"No they're not."

"Charlie, be careful."

Charlie was silent. He knew his position in the agency was not high enough to effectively fight the decision. He closed his eyes, sighed and said, "I'll have everything sent as soon as we can get it packed. Anything else I need to know?"

"Alan Seltzer said he would call you later today and explain. I'm not sure why he's involved, but he asked me to tell you."

Charlie understood immediately, but said, "I have no idea. Guess I'll find out when he calls."

"Thank you for your cooperation, Charlie. Let's put this behind us and get back to work."

"Yes, ma'am."

After the call ended, he sat back in his chair. Seltzer would be honest with him, or at least Charlie hoped he would be. He got up and went into the lab to tell his team the bad news.

THE CALL CAME two hours later.

"Lab, Charlie Craft."

"Charlie, Alan Seltzer. How are you today?"

"I've been better. I'd like to understand why my investigation of the Cooper property was shut down."

"Good question. Wish I had a good answer, but I don't. The fact is the director doesn't want the agency embarrassed by retracting a statement made by Agent Dollar. Regardless of the accuracy of the statement."

"Sir, I respectfully disagree with this decision. There is ample evidence Cooper did not act alone."

"A mutual friend of ours agrees with you. In fact, he is conducting a separate and unofficial investigation into this matter."

Charlie now understood the purpose for the call. "Good."

"Do you have any vacation time left, Charlie?"

"Not really. I had to use all of it when my father passed away."

"I'm sorry to hear of your loss. My condolences. Perhaps a personal leave of absence to attend a forensics conference would be in order?"

Curious about where this was going, Charlie said, "I could use a refresh. Do you know of any conferences currently accepting applications?"

"Actually I do. There's one at Missouri State University in Springfield, Missouri, and it starts this Wednesday. Could you leave early in the morning?"

Charlie finally got it. JR was in Springfield. He frowned. How many people knew about JR? He'd have to ask Kruger later. The cover about the conference would hold. He'd learn more in one day working with JR than he would during several conferences. He finally said, "Will you handle my registration?"

"I would be more than happy to take care of it. In fact I'll have Deputy Director Stumpf clear it with your boss and make sure all of your expenses are reimbursed."

Smiling, Charlie said, "Guess I'll pack tonight and leave in the morning. I'll book my flight as soon as we're off the phone."

"Excellent, I'm sure our friend will be pleased to hear you're going to attend."

After booking his flight, he decided to call it a day and left the office. He was almost to his apartment when he received a call on his cell phone. The caller ID read "Unknown." Puzzled, he answered the call.

"Charlie, it's JR. When do you arrive tomorrow?"

"Around noon."

"After the plane lands, retrieve your bag, then stand outside the terminal on the west side. I'll pick you up. What's the flight number?"

Charlie told him. JR said, "Great, see you then." The call ended abruptly. He smiled, only thirty seconds long. Same old JR.

———

PAPPY'S BAR and Grill was a small out-of-the-way place in a strip center located near a blue collar neighborhood in Arlington County. Because of its location, very few of Washington's elite patronized the establishment. This was one of the reasons Alan Seltzer relied on it for a quiet beer. Plus they made the best pulled pork sandwich in the district. He was sitting at the bar when Paul Stumpf pulled out the stool next to him and sat down.

"Everything is cleared for Charlie," Stumpf said. "Did you make contact with the individual you mentioned?"

Seltzer nodded. "Yes, he was very glad to have the help. However, I haven't called Kruger yet. I'm not sure what to tell him."

"Tell him the truth; he deserves it. We haven't been exactly truthful with him lately, have we?"

"No. It bothers me, too."

"Alan, this could be the opportunity we need to make real changes around here. But we have to let Kruger do what he does best."

"I know." Seltzer took a deep breath. "What if he needs back up, what do we do then?"

"What is the name of the detective Kruger knows in

Alexandria? Lark or Stark, something like that. He called for Kruger to come out to the Rousch murder."

"Ryan Clark, good man." Seltzer paused for a moment and nodded his head, "You know, that might work. Could we unofficially borrow him from the Alexandria Police Department?"

The deputy director stood. "That's what I had in mind. I'll call the Chief of Police."

He retrieved his cell phone from the inside pocket of his suit coat, scrolled through the list of contacts and pressed the send icon. He held the phone to his ear as he walked outside away from the din of the restaurant.

It was ten minutes before he returned. He sat down and took a sip of his beer. "Clark is available whenever and wherever we need him. The Chief and I go back a few years. I explained to him we needed someone to work with one of our agents on a special assignment. I also mentioned how the director swept the Rousch murder under the rug. He understood and agreed to the lend-lease program." He smiled when he said the last part.

Seltzer took a sip of his beer and relaxed a little. "Good, I'll call Kruger tonight and let him know he has backup."

"Alan, I want to make sure you understand the ramifications if our conspiracy becomes known."

Nodding, Seltzer said, "I'm very much aware of what could happen. I'm starting to agree with Kruger. Retirement might look pretty good if things don't change around the agency."

Chapter Twenty-Eight

HOUSTON, TX

Monday Evening

THE SHORT FLIGHT from Dallas to Houston landed a little after 7 p.m. Before leaving the airport, he called the Imam on a payphone.

"As-salamu alaykum."

"Wa-alaykum salaam. I have good news for you, my brother."

"Good, please tell me."

"The help you requested is ready to assist you. When do you need them?"

Abbas was quiet for a few moments.

"Within the next two weeks. I will have to finalize the project and let you know. Their assistance will come at the end, when I need them the most."

"Excellent, that will give us time to prepare them for their journey. Do you know where yet?"

"Yes, but I will let you know the location later."

"Very well."

Their conversation lasted a few more minutes, and after their goodbyes, Abbas walked to the rental car area.

The La Quinta Inn he chose was in La Porte, TX, north of the import warehouses situated around the Port of Houston. This would give him time to wait for the containers due to arrive at the Port the next day. On paper, Eduardo Acosta was identified as one of the principal owners of a Spanish olive oil company. A company who regularly imported oil grown and packed in Tunisia. He had no ownership at all, but it gave him a legitimate reason to be at the Port and to manage the transportation of the containers after clearing customs, a process he knew could last as long as ten days. Because the business did a lot of traffic through the warehouse, their wait was now down to just a few days.

After checking into his room, he left and walked over to a seafood restaurant next to the hotel. While sitting at the bar nursing a beer, Abbas thought about the restraints of his religion. He enjoyed the occasional beer and it helped him blend into the local culture. While he sat, a tall dark man sat down on the stool next to him and ordered a beer.

After the bartender sat the beer down and walked away, the newcomer said, "The ship arrived a day early. Your containers have already off-loaded and are in a holding facility."

"Any issues?"

"No, not at this time and I don't see any issues arising."

Abbas nodded, stared ahead and sipped his beer. "Once they clear customs, your money will be wired to the account you requested."

The newcomer stood, drained his beer in one long gulp, and walked out of the bar area of the restaurant. Neither man had looked at the other. Their conversation was short and quiet. No one heard it, or even thought twice about the encounter. After the man left, Abbas ordered a meal and spent the next hour sitting at the bar.

———

California
Wednesday evening

FUNERALS DEPRESSED HIM. But this one had been a fitting tribute to his mother-in-law. Roy Griffin respected her, and more importantly, he loved her like a mother, and she loved him like a son. Now his task was to help his wife get through the grief and settle the estate.

He wondered how much time he could spend in his home district without generating issues with his staff and the media. He couldn't even decide if he wanted to run again. The atmosphere in Washington was toxic, unproductive and uncooperative. He spent more time being told by lobbyists how much money they would spend against him in the next election than he did trying to do his job.

His wife was refusing to return with him. Her excuse was the amount of work needed to settle her mother's estate and keep all of her charitable institutions functioning. This added more pressure for him to just finish out his term. But he had overwhelming support in his district, the poll numbers were good, and a legitimate challenger had yet to emerge, even though the election was just six months away. Anything could happen in that length of time, so he would wait a few weeks before making his decision.

The vibration of his cell phone broke his thoughts.

Glancing at the caller ID, he sighed and accepted the call. "Hello."

"Good evening, Congressman, it's Bob. Is this a good time to talk?"

Bob Thomas was his Chief of Staff, the one person in Washington Griffin trusted and depended on. "Yes, Bob, it's fine. Good to hear from you. What's going on back there?"

"It's been quiet since you left. You have a lot of messages, but nothing that can't wait for your return. Uh, sir, do you have a return date we can announce on your website?"

Griffin hesitated, "No, not yet. I need to help my wife with the estate. My mother-in-law appointed me executor of her will, so I have a few more official duties I need to perform."

"I see. Sir, could I at least get an approximate date? The emails requesting appointments are mounting up."

"I'll be back after Memorial Day."

"Yes, sir. You realize that's more than two weeks away."

"Yes. I am very much aware of how long it is, Bob." Griffin rarely raised his voice with his support team, but Bob was pushing him tonight. "Just put out a press release stating I'm dealing with family matters and will return after Memorial Day."

His assistant sounded distant when he said, "Yes, sir, I will update your website. Thank you, Congressman."

The call ended and Griffin felt terrible. He had never kept anything from Bob. Perhaps in a few days he could give an exact date, but not right now.

Bob Thomas set the handset back in the desk phone's cradle, sighed and accessed the congressman's website as the administrator. He updated the link on the Home page which informed every one of the congressman's availability. It simply stated he would return to Washington after Memorial Day. Satisfied, he closed the site and shut down his laptop.

Glancing at his watch, he smiled. There were some advantages in having the congressman out of town. His fiancée had found a trendy new restaurant and it was still early enough that they would have plenty of time to try it tonight. As he walked down the now dark and abandoned halls of the House of Representatives, he called her with the good news.

KRUGER'S CELL PHONE VIBRATED. He checked the caller ID and smiled, "I was planning to call you a little later."

"Were you going to call and quit?" Seltzer asked with a note of seriousness.

Kruger chuckled and said, "No, not yet."

"Good, I've got several things you need to know. First, the director shut Charlie's investigation down."

"What?"

"He wants the Cooper case closed and wants nothing else associated with it."

Kruger remained silent.

"I spoke to Joseph," Seltzer continued.

"And?"

"He worked it out with JR, Charlie is flying to Springfield in the morning to help."

"Is JR comfortable with this arrangement?"

"From what Joseph said, he jumped at the opportunity. He likes Charlie and plans to hire him one day. Anyway, you now have an underground forensics team working on the investigation. Charlie will be available to travel if needed. Secondly, we have Ryan Clark on loan from the Alexandria police department. He will be your partner and backup. Just tell us when and where you need him and he'll be there."

"I'm impressed, Alan."

"Don't thank me yet. We're trying to give you as much support as possible. We have to be careful with the current political situation."

Remaining silent for a few moments, Kruger thought about making a comment on the politics, but decided against it. "I'm heading to St. Louis tomorrow. It's the last location we have for the guy organizing this group. Can Clark meet me there?"

"Are you going as an FBI agent?"

"Hell yes. Do you have a problem with that?"

Seltzer didn't answer.

"Alan, if you want me to continue this investigation, I can't do it with one hand tied behind my back."

"Okay, but be careful. We can't afford to alert the director."

"Alan, if I have to worry about the director every time I do something, I might as well just stay home."

"Point made. I'll try not to micromanage. You're the guy in the field."

"That's right, I seem to be the only guy putting his neck on the line right now."

"Calm down, Sean. Paul and I are walking a tightrope on this as well. We're getting you resources and assistance. If the director finds out, all of us will have our necks stuck out. Besides, we believe your theory. As soon as you have positive proof, get it to us. Paul has a plan. He just needs you to prove there are others involved."

Kruger took a deep breath. Seltzer was right, but it wasn't time to tell him so.

"We'll have Clark fly to St. Louis. Can you pick him up?"

"Yes, have him send me his itinerary as soon as possible."

"Keep us posted, Sean. We need positive proof more than one individual is involved."

"I'll talk to you when I know more tomorrow." He ended the call.

Standing, he paced his small office area for a few seconds before deciding to make coffee. As he walked to the kitchen, a plan for St. Louis started to come together. If JR could determine the locations used by the Traveler, the name he was using for the suspect in St. Louis, he and Clark could stake out various locations and wait for the man to access the internet. It would be time consuming and they stood a good chance of missing the individual. But even with the small odds of matching someone with the pictures JR had retrieved from the Army's computers, the effort might be worth their time.

After drafting an email to JR, he revised it several times until satisfied. As soon as it was sent, he glanced at the time on his computer. It was after 6 p.m. and Stephanie wasn't home from the office. When she did work late, she normally called. Mildly concerned, he called her. The call went straight to voicemail.

Thirty minutes later, she walked into the condo and went straight to their bedroom without saying a word. Kruger was sitting at his desk when he heard her come in. He walked out of the office and to their bedroom, where she was standing in front of the closet and taking out clothes. An open suitcase was on the bed. He said, "I heard you come in."

She turned, looked at him, but didn't say a word. She went back to getting clothes out before saying, "I have to drive to Arkansas tonight."

"Why?"

"I got a call from Linda, our District Manager in Bentonville, at five. Apparently Walmart is demanding a top-to-top meeting with our senior management at eight tomorrow morning. Neil is still in the hospital and since Frank..." She hesitated for a brief second, her voice shaky, "I'm it. I'm leaving as soon as I get packed. Not sure what this is about and neither does Linda. But with this short of notice, it's probably not good news."

"Do you have a hotel room?"

She shook her head.

"I can make the reservation for you. I'm platinum with Marriot, they have to give me a room. Even this late." He smiled as he said it.

She stopped, turned to him, and her frown melted. She chuckled and walked to him. They hugged and he kissed the top of her head.

"I have to go to St. Louis in the morning," Kruger said. "Not sure how long I'll be gone at this point."

Looking up at him, she sighed. "I thought when we got married, this hectic pace would stop. It isn't, is it?"

"Nope."

"What are we going to do?

"We... No, that's not correct, I need to make some changes." He suddenly realized his mistake of not walking away from the case as soon as the director shut it down. "This is my last case, Stef, I'm done."

Silence was his answer. Finally she said, "I heard from the adoption agency today. They think they may have found an expectant mother for us. They want us to come in on Friday. Can you be here?"

"I'll make sure I am."

Chapter Twenty-Nine

ST. LOUIS, MO

Thursday

KRUGER'S DRIVE TO ST. Louis started early. With Stephanie out of town, he'd slept poorly and was on the road by 4:30 a.m. Clark's plane arrived at Lambert International Airport a little after 9 a.m. and by 10:30, their surveillance had started.

Centering their search on the busy Westport Plaza area of St. Louis, they were watching two coffee shops. Both identified by JR as frequent Wi-Fi access points for the Traveler. Clark's location was a Starbucks and Kruger's a St. Louis Bread Company location several blocks away. Clark sat at a table by the main entrance, which permitted an unobstructed view of the remaining tables. Kruger had chosen a similar spot at his location.

Paul Stumpf had arranged for Clark to be sworn in as a US Marshall on Tuesday. This provided jurisdiction in St. Louis, should they need to arrest the Traveler. Plus it permitted Clark to carry his service weapon on an airline flight.

"Exactly who are we looking for?" said Clark during the drive from the airport.

"We don't know exactly," said Kruger, "This may be a fool's errand, but it's a starting point. We gave him a code name, Traveler. The evidence we have so far points to him as the leader of a group responsible for the Washington and Kansas City murders. If he isn't, he might lead us to the individual who is responsible. I think it's important we find him."

Clark nodded. "Makes sense. Tell me about the picture files you sent. Are they all suspects?"

Kruger shook his head. "No, they're individuals Thomas Cooper served with while in the military. We eliminated the ones currently overseas or ones we determined weren't involved. Which left ten men, and we suspect the Traveler is one of those ten."

Clark was silent for a minute. "I brought the communication gear you requested, it's in my backpack. Cool stuff, tiny ear buds, tiny mikes and the wireless receivers can be hidden anywhere. Not items you'd find at Best Buy, are they?"

Kruger chuckled, "Nope, I don't suppose they are. Hopefully we can use the gear to communicate discretely."

"Alan Seltzer mentioned we had help. Who is it?"

"A very bright and talented forensic technician from the Bureau is assisting an old friend of mine. The friend is very handy with a computer."

"Seltzer warned me about asking too many questions concerning your friend."

"You can ask," Kruger grinned, "I just won't answer."

"Okay, I get it. I won't ask."

Kruger glanced over at his friend. Clark was concentrating on the road more intently than a driver. His jaw muscles clenched and his brow furrowed. Kruger said, "Don't be nervous, Ryan."

Clark shook his head. "I'm not. I just don't want to screw up."

"You won't."

Thinking back on the first time he'd met Ryan Clark, Kruger remembered a young detective with drive and determination. The Beltway Sniper was terrorizing the Washington, D.C., area during the fall of 2002. Clark had just been promoted to detective, and Kruger was one of several FBI profilers working the case. Clark was married, but the relationship was stressed due to the hours he spent away from home.

One evening, while they were on a dinner break together, Clark said, "How do you deal with being away from your wife?"

"I'm not married. Divorced, actually."

"I'm sorry."

"Don't be. It happened a long time ago."

Clark was quiet. They both ate in silence for several minutes. Finally Kruger said, "It hurts at first. It makes you feel like a failure. But once a little time goes by, you realize it wasn't completely your fault. There was another person involved. They also had some responsibility in the marriage collapsing."

Clark nodded. "I just can't put my finger on when things started going downhill."

"Don't try to figure it out, it will drive you nuts. It happens. I saw the warning signs in my marriage didn't acknowledge them until it was over. While I was married, I blissfully ignored them."

"I'm wondering if I even want to save the marriage."

Taking a sip of coffee, Kruger smiled grimly. "You probably don't. Motivations are a tricky part of the human psyche. Our true motivations are sometimes masked by contrary behavior."

Clark looked at Kruger with a frown. "How so?"

Shrugging, Kruger took another sip of his coffee. "Various ways. What have you done to save the marriage?"

"Counseling."

Kruger nodded. "But you haven't stopped working long hours."

Clark stared at him for a long time. "You know how the job works."

Remaining quiet, Kruger sat and looked at his new friend. Clark's shoulders slumped and he looked down at the table. His only response was to shake his head.

"Ryan, it takes two people working together to keep a marriage alive. If you're not willing to put the effort in, let it go."

A decade later, Clark was still single and sitting in the passenger seat of Kruger's Mustang. He said, "What's our first step, Sean?"

"After we get in position, our friends will monitor the Traveler's computer. If he accesses the internet, we'll be notified. If one of us is in the correct location, you'll receive a simple text message, 'Your Location.' If it's where you are, use your radio and call me immediately. I'll come to you. Same process if I'm in the right spot."

"Okay, what if he accesses the internet from a completely different location?"

"Our friend will send the GPS location in a text message to my cell phone. We'll move as quickly as possible."

Clark was quiet. Finally he said, "Sean, do you honestly think this will work?"

Kruger shrugged. "If he's still in St. Louis, it might. He's been offline for two days, so he might have moved. But my friend doesn't think so."

TIME PASTED SLOWLY. Kruger ordered a sandwich around noon to blend into the now crowded restaurant. By 2 p.m., he was thinking about suspending the operation when he got a text message giving a GPS location and the words, 2 blocks west. He activated his radio and said quietly, "Get to the car, they found him."

Ten minutes later, they were ready to enter the Bean Counter Coffee Shop. It was large by coffee shop standards and fairly crowded for midafternoon. Kruger entered first and found an empty table in the middle of the room against a wall. With the ten pictures of suspects on his cell phone, he was just another patron staring at a phone. Clark entered several minutes later and found an empty table near the shop's front entrance. He too consulted the pictures on his phone and surveyed the room.

Kruger received a text message, *Accessing net now*, so he nonchalantly scanned the room as if looking for someone to take his order. There were several men typing away on their computers, but only one of them matched a picture on his cell phone.

The picture identified the man on the computer as Norman Ortega. He was a former sergeant of Cooper's. He was older than the picture, wore glasses, shaved head, and had grown a mustache and goatee. But the eyes were the same, cold and unemotional. It was him.

He replied to JR's text with Ortega's name and the

words *need more data* Clark was copied on the text. Standing to go to the bar for coffee, he casually surveyed the room. After paying for the coffee, Clark headed back to his seat, looked at Kruger and slightly nodded. He had a visual on Ortega.

Now the tricky part. Kruger sent Clark a text message: *Going to car will wait for T to exit. You follow. I'll back up.* If Ortega became suspicious, Kruger was sure the man would disappear.

While sitting in the car waiting, Kruger called JR. Surprisingly, he answered, "Yeah?"

Kruger said, "Get me all you can on Ortega."

"We're on it. Traveler made contact with the computer in the Baltimore area. Their target is out of town until June. They're now trading messages about contingency plans."

"Interesting. Was the target identified?"

"Not yet."

"As soon as you can, check to see if he's in a hotel around here under his real name."

The call ended just as Ortega exited the coffee shop. The man walked toward the parking lot, paused, lit a cigarette, looked around, and then headed toward an area packed with cars. Clark appeared at the door of the shop, trying to keep his eye on Ortega. Kruger couldn't tell if Clark had a visual on the suspect, so he opened the car door and stood. Quickly scanning the parking lot, he saw no one. The man had disappeared.

———

AT FIRST HE didn't think there was a problem, but Norman Ortega watched as a man entered the Starbucks around 10:30 a.m. There was nothing suspicious about the guy, other than that neon sign above his head flashing *COP*. Ortega shut his computer off and studied the new arrival. The man was about five-feet-ten, clean shaven, with a slender build and short brown hair. Not military short, but close. He wore Nike running shoes, blue jeans, a light blue polo shirt, and a black Nike windbreaker. A slight bulge in the windbreaker on his right hip gave him away—a holstered weapon.

He watched as the cop ordered a coffee from one of the baristas. So far it was innocent, just an off-duty cop getting a coffee. After sitting down at a table, the guy pulled a smart phone out, glanced at the screen, and then surveyed the room. When the cop did this for the third time, Ortega had seen enough. He packed his computer into his backpack and looked for a way to leave without getting too close to the man. An opportunity presented itself as a large group finished their meeting and started to leave. He joined the crowd, kept his head down and managed to exit the building without drawing any attention. Returning to his car, he drove to another coffee shop he liked. No point in taking any chances. He doubted it was anything other than an off duty cop getting a coffee. But why be careless.

After several hours of writing, he had enough messages prepared to access the internet and start the tedious communications process. Finally, Billy was back online. The first message from Billy reported the target was not scheduled to return to Washington, D.C., until June. Two more weeks. A delay of that duration was too long for their timetable. It had to be sooner. After an internet search, Ortega discovered the target's mother-in-law had passed away. His return to Washington was being delayed by family matters in his home district.

Glancing up from the computer, his heart almost

stopped. The cop from Starbucks was sitting at the front of the coffee shop. He was following the same procedure from the morning, glancing at his phone and surveying the room. This was not a coincidence. Somehow, he was being tracked. He watched as the cop stood and walked to the coffee bar. As he returned to his table, Ortega noticed his head turned slightly and barely nodded at another man sitting in the middle of the room.

Ortega thought the new guy looked familiar, but he couldn't place him. Finally, remembering, he opened a video file on the computer and checked several news clips made during the media coverage at Cooper's farm. The video he was searching for was a long-range camera shot of two men standing next to the barn where Cooper had stored the C4.

Ortega remembered the clip, having viewed it dozens of times. It was the moment he realized all the C4 had been found. The news announcer had identified one of the men as the local county sheriff and the other as an FBI agent. Pausing the video, Ortega stared at the profile of the FBI agent and then at the guy sitting in the middle of the coffee shop. It was hard to make an exact match, considering the distance of the camera shot, but there was a strong resemblance. This was no coincidence. They'd found him.

It was time to leave. Ortega started considering his options for the best way to exit the shop. After ten more minutes, the FBI man got up and left, leaving the other cop sitting next to the front door. There were no other exits visible except the front door. He got up and walked to the restroom in the back. The rear exit door was for emergencies only and an alarm would sound if opened. Leaving this way would draw too much attention. The front door was his only option.

Returning to his table, he closed the laptop, placed it in his backpack, threw a $5 bill on the table, and casually walked through the shop toward the front door. Turning his head as he approached the door, his face was away from the cop as he reached for a pack of cigarettes in the backpack. Outside the shop, he paused to light a cigarette and quickly scanned the area. Not seeing the FBI agent anywhere, he started walking toward the parking lot. Once among the cars in the tightly packed parking spaces, he bent over below the roof lines and hurried toward his car. Once there, he carefully opened the door, slid behind the wheel, hunched down in the seat, and waited.

———

KRUGER SAT BACK DOWN in the car while Clark hurriedly walked to the Mustang and got in. He said, "Damn, he must have made me. Sorry, Sean, I think I blew it."

Shaking his head, Kruger said, "No, I should have realized, a lot of video was being shot by the news media at Cooper's farm. I'm positive the cameras were trained on the barn when the Hummers showed up. I was outside with the sheriff during that time. I guarantee you I'm in those shots, and Ortega probably scrutinized them very carefully. More than likely he recognized me, not you."

"Now what?"

"Charlie's trying to locate Ortega's hotel. I'll call and see if he's made any progress."

Charlie answered JR's phone and said, "Just found him at the Hampton Inn Westport, registered under Norman Ortega. Been there almost a week."

"Nice work, Charlie." Kruger ended the call and started

the Mustang. "He's at the Hampton Inn Westport. I saw it this morning when we drove in from the airport. Let's find out if he's still there."

Kruger parked under the canopy directly outside the front entrance. Each clipped their badges to their belts and got out of the car. Kruger went straight to the front desk and asked for the manager while Clark stayed by the car to watch the parking lot.

An overweight middle-aged man with a receding hairline and a bushy mustache emerged from an office behind the front desk. He smiled. "Can I help you, sir?"

Kruger showed his identification and said, "Agent Sean Kruger, FBI. Is there some place private we can talk?"

The manager's eyes widened and stared at the ID. He looked up, paused briefly, and then motioned Kruger back to his office. After closing the door, he said, "May I ask what this is about, agent?"

"Sorry to startle you back there. A man by the name of Norman Ortega is registered here. Can you tell me if he's checked out?"

The manager sat down at his desk and consulted his computer. "No, he hasn't." He glanced at his watch, "It's past check out time. What's this about?"

Kruger smiled and ignored the question. "Sir, I need you to show me his room, open it, and make sure he hasn't left yet."

The manager looked at Kruger with a disapproving expression. "Before I can do that, I need to know what this is about."

Kruger nodded and said, "Mr. Ortega is a suspect in a murder. That's all I can tell you right now."

The manager's eyes grew wide and he started quickly searching through the papers and objects on his desk. He found his pass card and held it so Kruger could see. "His room is in the back on the first floor. You won't tell the other guests, will you? It might be bad for business."

Kruger grinned. "No, sir. We won't tell the other guests."

As they entered the lobby, Kruger motioned for Clark to follow. Ortega's room was situated next to the rear exit door with easy access to the back parking area. He turned to the manager and said, "Give me the pass card. Please stand back away from the door, sir."

Clark held his SIG Sauer P226 with both hands, pointed it down, and stood on the left side of the door. Kruger held his Glock in his right hand, looked at Clark who nodded, and then opened the door. Both rushed in as Kruger yelled "FBI."

It took less than ten seconds to secure the room. It was empty, except for Ortega's luggage and personal items. Kruger said, "His stuff's still here." He went back out to the hall and asked the manager, "Are any of these adjacent rooms occupied?"

The manager reached for a radio attached to his belt, pressed the transmit button and said, "Stella, I'm at 148, are any of the rooms around it empty?"

After a few seconds, a voice said, "Only 147 and 144. The rest are occupied."

Kruger looked across the hall at a door with the numbers 147. "We'll take that room." He pointed at the door. "Please let the front desk know."

The manager hesitated, looked at Kruger and then at Clark, started to say something, and decided against it. He opened the door to 147 and left. Kruger turned to Clark, "You needed a room for the night anyway."

Clark chuckled. "Perfect, a room across from a murderer. Thanks, Sean, I like you too."

———

ORTEGA WAITED fifteen minutes before starting his car and backing out of the parking slot. He had to go back to the hotel. There were too many essential items in the room he needed to retrieve before leaving town. It would take time, but time well spent. Pulling into the parking lot of the Hampton Inn, he saw a Mustang parked under the canopy. Leaning against the car, talking on a cell phone, was the cop from Starbucks. The FBI agent was probably inside.

Driving slowly around the hotel, he parked near the entrance door next to his room. Ortega sat in the car, thinking. Was it worth the risk to go in, or just drive off and leave everything? Finally, after ten minutes of careful debating, he decided to take the chance and get in the room.

The entrance door was glass, allowing a visual of the hallway outside his room. The hall was empty. Slowly and quietly, he used his card key to unlock the door. Standing in the exit with the door half open, Ortega could see his room ten feet down the hall on the right. The door was open, and he could hear someone in the room, apparently on a phone describing the contents. No need to go farther. He quickly closed the outside door and walked back to the car. He sat there a few seconds, trying to determine how incriminating the remaining contents would be. Finally realizing there was nothing to be done at this point, he started the car and drove toward the exit. Replacing the luggage and clothes would be simple. He had his backpack, which contained his computer, notes and money. But as Ortega pulled out of the hotel parking lot, he hit the steering wheel with the palm of his hand and yelled, "Shit."

———

"ALAN, I need a search warrant for this room and I need it yesterday. This is the guy. I'm standing in his room and I see something pretty incriminating. I just can't use it until I have that search warrant."

"Tell me what you see," Seltzer said.

"I see a notebook, it's open, with handwritten pages. Do the words Cooper and C4 mean anything to you?"

"Calm down, Sean, we'll get it. But I have to have some probable cause, that's all."

He closed his eyes and forced himself to breathe slowly. "I'm not sure about hotel law, but if one of us is staying in the room across the hall and smells smoke, can we have management open the door to check for fire?"

"That's an interesting question. I'm not sure. Let me call Legal and find out."

"Hurry, Alan, the guy might come back and try to get the notebook. If he does, it might get ugly."

The call ended and Kruger pulled on surgical gloves Clark had bought at the Walgreen's next door. He leafed through the handwritten pages of the five-by-seven spiral notebook. The information inside described how to steal and get C4 off military bases. There was a list of Army bases where C4 was stored, who to contact at each location and how much it would cost to bribe those individuals. Quickly scanning the remaining pages of the notebook, Kruger found references on how to communicate through the internet, friendly gun shops and summaries of the Wheeler and Rousch murders. Finally here was the proof they needed to convince the director of a conspiracy.

His cell phone vibrated, and Kruger answered, "Talk to me Alan."

"Yes, it is considered probable cause for an agent to enter a hotel room to search for a fire. The rooms are not really private property since they're owned by the hotel. Danger to the other guests is taken into consideration. Evidence found during the search for a fire is admissible."

Kruger smiled and said, "Then you'd better get Paul on the phone, because we now have evidence Norman Ortega was involved with Cooper."

"Describe it."

"I'm holding a notebook in my hand outlining how the group operates. The relationships, how they communicate, where to get C4, and where to get weapons. Do I need to go on?"

"I'll get Paul."

AFTER EXITING the hotel parking lot, Ortega found I-270 and drove north toward I-70 west. A new ID was now essential. Denver was 850 miles to the west, and Ortega knew someone there who could provide one. As St. Louis and the surrounding communities receded in the car's rearview mirror, he relaxed and thought through his current situation.

They would not know what type of vehicle he was driving. The information on the hotel registry was false. But as soon as possible, he would switch license plates with a similar car. Next he reviewed the contents of his backpack. He still had his laptop, which contained files and details of the operation. A CZ 75 9mm pistol, 200 rounds of hollow point ammunition, three clips, his K-Bar serrated knife, several credit cards both real and fake, and almost $50,000 in cash.

Nothing he had left behind was critical, except the notebook. When they found it, the supply team would be compromised. Tommy and their banker would be harder to determine from its contents. Their names were never used in his notes. His clothes were gone, but easily replaced.

Finishing the final stage of the operation before Memorial Day would be up to him. He was the only one even remotely close to California. With luck, he could be in Denver tomorrow, meet his contact, buy a new driver's license and passport, and then switch cars. California was another twenty-hour drive from Denver. After a stop in Utah for a day or two, San Francisco was only a hard day's drive away. Once in California, he would be in place to complete the mission.

Satisfied with the plan, the rest of the team needed to know they were compromised. Hopefully he would be in time to give them plenty of notice. It was getting close to midnight when he stopped at a Day's Inn just outside of Topeka, KS. Once in the hotel room, he accessed the internet, and sent text messages to all the remaining team members to check for a message in their email accounts.

Chapter Thirty

Thursday Evening

"I NEED ALL the evidence brought to Washington immediately," said Paul Stumpf over the phone. "It's critical we shut down the supply lines tonight. I'm sure Ortega will warn them at his first opportunity."

"Yes, sir." Kruger glanced at his watch. It was after 5 p.m., and he needed to get back to Kansas City for the meeting with the adoption agency in the morning. "We're certain he's fled. He was last seen around two this afternoon and so far has not returned to the hotel. I'll have Clark summarize what we have in St. Louis, and Charlie Craft will provide details on the computer evidence. They'll have preliminary reports to you tonight and fly into Washington early tomorrow."

"No, I need you to handle this, Sean. You're the agent in charge of this investigation."

"With all due respect, Deputy Director, I am unofficially investigating this case. Remember? Besides, I have a commitment in Kansas City first thing in the morning, one I refuse to miss."

There was silence on the phone for fifteen seconds, until finally Stumpf said, "Sean, I need you to take charge of this thing right now. As soon as you can get the information to me, we can start making arrests. I'm taking it to the Attorney General early tomorrow morning, who will take it to the President. Once that's done, we can make some changes around here."

Kruger closed his eyes, thinking how he could do both. Finally he said, "I'll be in Washington late tomorrow. Meanwhile, Ryan and Charlie will get everything to you. Will that work?"

"What's going on, Sean?"

Hesitating, Kruger finally said, "It's personal, Paul. I'll tell you tomorrow when I see you."

"Very well, let Alan know your itinerary. I'll arrange a meeting with the director. And Sean... your team did a great job on this."

Kruger should have felt a sense of satisfaction when the call ended, but the feeling eluded him. His team had accomplished a lot in less than a week. He was proud of them. But he personally had made several mistakes, ultimately leading to the escape of Ortega. Was he losing his edge? Or did he just not care anymore? Probably the latter. Leaning against the wall across from Ortega's room, he watched the forensics team from the St. Louis FBI office carefully searching the room for more evidence. He closed his eyes and tilted his head back.

Clark came out of the room holding the notebook from Ortega's suitcase. "Have you read any of this?"

Kruger opened his eyes, stood up off the wall and shook his head. "No, just skimmed it."

"This is the Rosetta Stone. There's enough evidence in here for a multitude of arrests."

Kruger nodded silently.

Clark looked at him, frowned, and said, "What's wrong? You should be pumped. We've broken this thing wide open."

"I just got off the phone with the deputy director. I need you to gather all the important evidence after they catalogue it and fly back to Washington early tomorrow. I'm sending Charlie there with the computer evidence. Both of you will present it to Alan when you get there."

"What about you, aren't you going?"

"Yes, but I have an important meeting in Kansas City first thing in the morning."

It was 6:10 p.m., four hours to Kruger's condo. If he left immediately, it would be at least 10:30 before he could arrive. With the meeting scheduled for 8 a.m., he would have plenty of time to catch a flight and arrive in Washington by early evening. Kruger looked up at Clark and said, "I'll be there tomorrow evening. Meanwhile, gather the evidence you need for the meeting and have the rest sent Fed Ex tomorrow. I'll call the Bureau's travel agency after I leave and arrange a flight for you. They'll call you with the details."

"Okay, I'll take care of it. See you tomorrow. Oh, and Sean," he paused briefly, "I hope everything is okay at home."

Kruger smiled. "It is, Ryan, it is. I just have a lot on my mind right now." He left the hotel and started the drive to Kansas City.

KRUGER WAS twenty miles east of Columbia when his phone rang. After glancing at the caller ID, he quickly accepted the call.

"Hi, I was just about to call you."

Stephanie said, "How long before you get home?"

"I should be there by ten thirty, why?"

"Just nervous about tomorrow and wanted to hear your voice." She took a deep breath and let it out slowly. "I miss you."

Kruger smiled. "I miss you too. Why are you nervous about tomorrow?"

"I don't know what to expect and don't want to be disappointed."

"Then let's go to the meeting not expecting much. That way, we won't be disappointed."

She didn't answer right away. Finally she said, "You always know the right words to say, Sean. After our meeting this morning at Walmart, I realize all I want is to get our family started."

Kruger was concerned. "Why, what happened?"

"Just more frustrations. I'll tell you more when you get here."

The call ended ten minutes later after he told her about his schedule. Kruger was also frustrated with the pending trip to Washington, a trip he really didn't want to make.

———

THEY ARRIVED fifteen minutes early for their appointment. The agency's door was locked, so Stephanie stood by the door while Kruger paced. At exactly 8 a.m., the door opened. Terri Fischer shook both of their hands and said,

"It's nice to see you again, Mr. and Mrs. Kruger. Please come in."

At five feet tall, Terri Fischer was a petite woman in her late 40s. Her hair was prematurely gray, which she wore to her shoulders. Her face was narrow and her eyes an intense green. Dressed in a navy pants suit, she had the appearance of someone who took their job seriously.

As they sat down in her office, she said, "I have exciting news for you."

Stephanie's eyes grew wide, and Kruger smiled.

Fischer continued, "A young girl, actually a teenager, from a small town south of Salina contacted us this week. She's pregnant and, at this time, wants to give the child up for adoption."

Stephanie said, "What do you mean, at this time?"

"Well, sometimes they change their mind. Sometimes the father convinces them to keep the child, and sometimes it's the mother's parents. Depends on the circumstance. But in this case, I believe she will give the child up."

Kruger cocked his head to the side. "What makes you say that?"

Fischer sighed. "The girl doesn't know who the father is, plus she was raised by a single mother. Their financial situation is dire. The young woman told me she personally doesn't want her child raised like she was, poor and neglected."

Wiping a tear from her eye, Stephanie said, "How far along is she?"

"She just started her third trimester. The child will be here before the end of the summer."

The rest of the meeting was a blur. Papers needed to be signed, emotions had to be addressed, and the expectant parents had to be cautioned about the potential for disappointment.

It was several minutes past nine when they were back in Kruger car. He said, "You realize this could all fall apart, Stef."

"I know." She was silent for a few moments. "I'm trying not to get too excited, but I can't help it. I've wanted this for a long time, Sean. I just didn't realize how much."

"It is kind of exciting, isn't it? Our lives will change completely, you know."

She nodded. "Yes, they will, and yesterday's silly meeting will be forgotten. Yes, I'm ready for a change."

Kruger thought about yesterday's events and his own disappointing performance, and realized he also was ready for a change.

"When does your plane leave today?"

"I don't know," he said.

Since he was driving, Kruger handed his iPhone to her. "Check my messages, it vibrated a couple of times while we were in the meeting."

She read the messages and said, "Delta at one-forty p.m. Arriving Reagan at seven, one stop in Detroit. That doesn't sound too bad. At least we have time for an early lunch."

He nodded. "You're right, that does sound good."

———

KRUGER'S PLANE landed on time at Reagan International. He called Clark as he walked through the terminal to find out when to expect his ride. Clark was already waiting for him in the passenger pick-up lane outside the terminal.

As Kruger slid into the passenger seat, Clark said, "Paul's having a meeting at his house. Alan and Charlie are already there. He wants to prepare us for the meeting with Director Wagner in the morning."

"What time is the meeting with Wagner?"

Clark said, "Nine. Paul won't be with us, it'll just be the four of us."

Kruger was quiet for a few moments, contemplating why Paul wouldn't be there. "Did Paul say why?"

Shaking his head, Clark glanced at Kruger. "No, he didn't. He just said there was a prior commitment."

Kruger suddenly remembered his conversation with Seltzer. "Did Paul meet with the Attorney General this morning?"

"I believe so. Charlie and I didn't get in until afternoon. Someone mentioned the meeting, but nothing else. Why?"

Kruger stared out the passenger window." Just curious. Guess we'll know more after we meet with Paul tonight."

Chapter Thirty-One

WASHINGTON, D.C.

Saturday Morning

DIRECTOR WAGNER SAT behind his desk, arms flat on the surface and hands clasped with fingers intertwined. As a practiced politician, his face was a mask of neutrality. He listened quietly as Seltzer summarized the evidence discovered in Ortega's hotel room and through Charlie Craft's computer forensics. Kruger watched the director closely, noting a tiny sheen of perspiration developing on Wagner's upper lip and an increased respiration rate.

Seltzer paused at the end of his presentation. Wagner did not comment, so Seltzer continued, "Last night, military police arrested two individuals, each at separate bases. Preliminary audits of those facilities indicate inventory discrepancies with specific weapons and ordinances mentioned in the Ortega notebook."

Wagner stared at a spot on his desk. When he raised his head, he stared at Seltzer.

"I was under the impression Agent Kruger was no longer involved with this case," he finally said. "Why are we discussing his involvement, and why is this agency still investigating a closed case?"

"Director," Seltzer said, "Agent Kruger was doing a follow-up investigation on what was originally thought to be an unrelated case. This investigation led Agent Kruger to the suspect in St. Louis. Agent Kruger was unaware of the suspect's involvement with Cooper until specific evidence was discovered during the lawful search of the suspect's hotel room."

Smiling, Wagner shook his head.

"Mr. Seltzer, I've been a politician for over two decades and my built-in BS meter is finely tuned. It just pinged. Please do not insult my intelligence with this fictitious account. You were specifically instructed to remove Agent Kruger from this investigation. Now I find these instructions were not carried out."

Seltzer stared at the director, not believing what he was hearing. Before he could comment, Kruger said, "Alan, I'll answer this. Director Wagner, you were misled with unsubstantiated information about this case. Agent Dollar has a history of declaring cases prematurely closed, he ignores facts, and he refuses to listen when evidence is presented that contradicts his conclusions. He's a lazy, undisciplined FBI agent and totally unfit to be in charge of a major investigation."

The director stared at Kruger and cleared his throat.

"Agent Dollar made that announcement after consulting with me," he said.

Kruger shook his head and chuckled. "Then you are the bigger fool for following the fool."

Wagner jumped from his chair, leaned forward and slapped his palms on his desk. His face had turned a bright crimson. He stared at Kruger.

"How dare you accuse me of collusion? Consider yourself suspended, pending an internal investigation. And you, Mr. Seltzer, will consider yourself suspended for disobeying a direct order from the director. Do I make myself clear?"

Kruger started to say something when the director's intercom interrupted him. "Excuse me, Director, line one. It's the President."

Wagner's face turned ashen. He sat back down, snatched the handset from the phone, hesitated briefly, took a deep breath, and said, "Yes, Mr. President."

He was quiet as he listened. "Yes, sir, they're sitting here in my office."

Another pause.

"Yes sir, I have been briefed."

Wagner closed his eyes and covered them with his free hand.

"Yes, sir, I will inform them after our conversation."

He listened for more than a minute, the perspiration above his lips more pronounced. Even though he was sitting across the desk from the director, Kruger could hear the angry garbled voice on the other end of the call.

"I understand, sir... My apologies... Yes, I understand."

Wagner stared at the top of his desk for several more moments as he listened to the President.

Finally, he said, "I will have it on your desk within the hour."

Wagner returned the handset to the phone's cradle. He looked at Seltzer and Kruger, and placed his arms once again on the desk with his fingers intertwined.

"It appears you two have a guardian angel watching over you. I apparently resigned ten minutes ago. You are to report immediately to Acting Director Stumpf. Meanwhile, I have a letter to write."

Wagner turned his back to them, opened the laptop on the credenza behind him and started typing. Seltzer stood and motioned for Kruger to follow. The two left the ex-director's office and hurried down the hall to Stumpf's office. His assistant smiled and motioned for them to go in immediately.

Stumpf was listening on the phone. He smiled as he pointed at two chairs in front of his desk. After a minute, Stumpf said, "Yes, sir, I will handle it immediately. I appreciate your confidence."

He returned the handset to the phone and said, "I wish I could have been there to see Wagner's reaction. How was it?"

Seltzer said, "Interesting. One second he's suspending Kruger and me, and the next, he was apologizing to the President. What did you do?"

"I merely presented Kruger's evidence to the Attorney General at breakfast yesterday. He presented it to the President this morning, who promptly fired Wagner. The President just informed me you two did him a huge favor. Wagner was a holdover from the previous administration and the President didn't like him or trust him. But, he didn't have a solid reason to fire him—until today."

Kruger said, "Excuse me, Paul, but it wasn't my evidence; it was the team's evidence. I didn't do it alone."

Smiling, Stumpf said, "I know, Sean, it's just a figure of speech. Your team did an excellent job on this. We already have the supply chain shut down. I'm told those individuals are cooperating and giving us details on how the C4 was obtained by Cooper."

"How do you want us to move forward?" Seltzer asked.

"First, as of now, Kruger is totally in charge of the investigation. Franklin Dollar, even though he is currently unaware of it, has been demoted and transferred to the branch office in Fargo, North Dakota. Sorry about the BS we put you through, Sean. You officially have FBI resources at your disposal as of this moment."

"Thank you, Paul," said Kruger. "I'm sorry if I don't jump up and down with excitement. Ortega's in the wind and two additional conspirators are currently unidentified."

Stumpf nodded. "Understood. I have one more point to discuss, your pending retirement. With Wagner gone, the President has authorized changes around here, good changes. The agency will be stronger and more responsive. I need people like you and our new Deputy Director, Alan Seltzer here, working with me to make those changes."

Seltzer apparently had not been informed of his promotion. He said, "Thank you, Paul. Are you sure I'm the best candidate?"

Smiling, Stumpf nodded. "Yes, Alan, you are. The President agreed with my recommendations this morning. I've been working behind the scenes preparing for this change of administration for several months." He turned to Kruger and continued, "Sean, I know you want to stop traveling, and I don't blame you. My plans call for naming you the new Special Agent in Charge of our Kansas City office."

Kruger eyes grew wide. For the first time this morning, he did not possess any idea how to respond. Finally after what seemed like hours, he said, "Thank you, sir, I appreciate your confidence. But this is a decision I need to discuss with Stephanie. Besides, I have an investigation that needs to be resolved. Afterwards we can discuss it."

Stumpf said, "That's the reason I need you on my team Sean, good decision-making skills. I can wait."

"Good. In the meantime," Kruger said, "I need to keep my team together. They're familiar with the case, plus we're making progress. While Charlie's here in Washington, he needs to brief a local team before flying back. They can start accessing his information and searching for the shooter located in this area."

"You two handle the details. Alan, you have the authority to use whatever resources are necessary. Meanwhile, if you will excuse me, I have to undo a lot of damage caused by my predecessor."

Seltzer and Kruger left the office and found Charlie Craft and Ryan Clark waiting in the hall outside Stumpf's office. Charlie said, "Rumors are flying around here. Is Wagner out?"

Seltzer nodded and said, "Let's find a conference room, and we'll bring you both up to speed."

The next two hours were spent organizing how the investigation would move forward. Charlie was assigned to Kruger until further notice and relieved of all other duties. Later in the afternoon, a new task force would be assigned to the East Coast search and Charlie would review the evidence with them. Clark was given the option of staying on the team, or going back to the Alexandria Police Department. He chose to stay on the team.

Once the meeting broke up, Clark and Charlie left, leaving Seltzer and Kruger alone for the first time.

"I told you Paul had a plan, Sean. I didn't know all the details, but he hinted it would be big."

Kruger nodded. "First positive change around here for a long time."

"I know your plans are to retire after this is over. But Paul wanted me to assure you the traveling would be minimal if you accept the Kansas City position. Besides, you've spent your entire career in the field. It's time you take a promotion."

Kruger looked out one of the windows in the conference room as Seltzer spoke. He was silent for several moments.

"The offer is tempting, Alan. I have to discuss it with Stephanie before I can give you an answer. There was a reason I didn't return immediately to Washington."

Seltzer nodded. "Paul told me you had something on your mind, but wouldn't tell him."

"Stephanie and I had a meeting with an adoption agency yesterday morning. There's a good chance they've found a child for us. Looks like it could be as early as late summer. Stephanie wants this and so do I. She deserves the opportunity to experience the joys and heartbreak of being a mother."

"Congratulations to you both. I'm happy for you, Sean. But that doesn't keep you from taking the new position. In fact, it's a great opportunity for you."

"I know, but I missed a lot when Brian was growing up. I don't want to repeat that mistake. Besides, it may be time for me to hang it up any way. Clark and I had Ortega." He made a fist as he spoke. "We had him in our hands, Alan. All we had to do was arrest him, but I made the wrong call and he got away. Not sure that's Special Agent in Charge material."

"Nonsense. You're still one of the best Sean. You deserve this promotion, more than anyone I know. It'll keep you in Kansas City where you can focus on local issues. You'll have less travelling and time for your new family. It's perfect for you."

Kruger was silent as he nodded. Finally he said, "Yes it is perfect, but I'm still not sure. I really need to discuss it with Stephanie." A grim smile appeared as he stood up to leave the conference room.

Chapter Thirty-Two

WESTERN UNITED STATES

THE SUN WAS BARELY PEAKING over the horizon as he left Topeka, Kansas driving west. By 1 p.m., Ortega was parked outside a warehouse next to the railroad yards in Denver. The building was on the outer rim of a large industrial park, surrounded by old abandoned structures. After checking to make sure the CZ's safety was on and there was a bullet in the chamber, he tucked it in his belt and pulled his sweatshirt down to cover the gun. The KA-BAR was strapped to his right calf, covered by his pant leg. Stepping out of the car, he scanned the dock area. Except for an old red Toyota pickup, the place was deserted. Satisfied no one else was around, he entered the warehouse through a side door next to the loading dock.

Except for rows of shelving stacked with crates along the far back wall, the interior was empty. His contact was in a glassed-in office area located on the west wall approximately fifteen feet from the door he had entered. The man sitting at the desk was in his mid-50s, unnaturally skinny, with wispy salt and pepper hair. His eyes squinted behind thick black-rimmed glasses and it appeared he hadn't shaved in a week. When he saw Ortega, he frowned and stood up. He walked to the office door, unlocked it and waved Ortega in. "You're late."

"Traffic," replied Ortega.

"Yeah, whatever. You mentioned on the phone something about new IDs. What do you need exactly?"

"A driver's license and passport."

"Any credit cards?"

"Maybe an American Express. How much?"

"I don't know, man. You're a hot commodity right now."

Ortega frowned. "What do you mean, hot commodity?"

"You been sleeping under a rock, man? Your military ID picture's all over the news. FBI's calling you a person of interest in two murders in New York."

Ortega was silent. Finally he said, "How much for the stuff?"

"Fifty thousand, half up front, and you can have them in the morning."

"Seventy if you can have them in an hour."

The man took his glasses off and wiped the lenses with the tail of his untucked shirt. He stared at Ortega and smiled. "My, my, my... You are in a hurry, aren't you? Make it a hundred and you can come back in an hour."

Tilting his head, Ortega paused and narrowed his eyes. "No, I'll wait."

The man shrugged. "Suit yourself. What state?"

"Utah... Yeah, make it Utah."

The man started spreading the legs of a heavy duty tripod. He reached for a camera on his cluttered desk and secured it to the top. A wooden straight-back chair sat in front of a blank wall painted an off-white. Pointing to the chair, he said, "Sit there, I need a picture."

Before Ortega sat down, he handed the man an envelope with cash. The man fanned the bills in the envelope and nodded. After the picture was taken, the man disappeared into another room behind the office.

Exactly ninety minutes later, Ortega was presented with a new Utah driver's license, passport and a Gold American Express card in the name of Duane Horton. Ortega examined them and said, "Nice work. I'll get you the balance."

He reached around, pulled the CZ from his belt, pointed it at his contact's head and said as he pulled the trigger, "Sorry, man. Can't let you talk to the Feds." The shot reverberated in the empty warehouse.

Ortega retrieved his initial deposit and found an additional sixty thousand dollars in another desk drawer. He smiled and glanced at the dead body. "Don't think you'll be needing this—man."

After wiping down all the surfaces he might have touched, he spent another ten minutes searching for the ejected casing from the CZ. He found it lodged behind a filing cabinet and placed it in his jean pocket. Finally he stepped into the room where the man had been for an hour and a half.

The computer was still on. He searched for any files containing information he didn't want the FBI to know. Not knowing where to look didn't help. After several minutes of searching he gave up and deleted the entire My Document file on the computer. It was getting late and he needed to get on the road toward Utah. After looking around the rooms one last time, he exited the warehouse and made sure both the office and outside warehouse doors were locked.

Sitting behind the wheel of his car, he examined Duane Horton's new driver's license and passport. The man did excellent work. Too bad he was collateral damage. He drove out of the parking lot and started the long drive to Provo, Utah.

The next morning, shortly after eleven, Ortega pulled into the Discount Sporting Goods and Gun Shop's parking lot in southern Provo. The place was busy, which was good. With a lot of customers in the shop, there was less possibility someone would remember him if the FBI showed up and started asking questions.

Once inside the store, he was pleased to see every salesperson occupied. A rack of long guns was behind the counter on the right side of the store. It extended the entire length of the wall. In the middle he found a Remington 700 SPS Tactical. Combined with the Bushnell Elite Scope laying on a glassed-in shelf beneath the counter, he would have a formidable combination for the task ahead.

It took fifteen minutes before a busy salesperson walked over and said, "Did you find anything you need?"

"Yeah, let me see the Remington 700 SPS."

The salesperson handed it to him and said, "Great rifle, last one in the store, too."

"I'll take it and the Bushnell Elite," he said, pointing at the scope on the shelf.

The salesman nodded and said, "Great combination. Goin' for elk?"

Ortega nodded and said, "Yeah. I need to sight it in; do you know of any local ranges?"

The salesperson said, "Sure do, I'll give you one of their cards. It has directions. If you'll follow me, I need you to fill out some paperwork."

Thirty minutes later, Ortega walked out of the gun shop with the Remington 700 SPS, Scope and 400 rounds of ammo legally purchased under the name of Duane Horton.

In the afternoon, he paid cash for a 2007 Jeep Wrangler

with 81,112 miles. Thirty minutes after walking onto the car lot, Ortega had paperwork showing Duane Horton as the new owner. He drove back to the hotel, removed the license plates from his car and placed them on the Jeep. Next he drove the car to a local Walmart Supercenter and parked it among the employee's cars on the west side of the store. He locked the car, threw the keys into a trash receptacle and walked into the store.

It took forty-five minutes to find everything he needed: a suitcase, underwear, socks, jeans, shirts, hooded sweatshirt, hiking boots, toothpaste, deodorant, shaving cream, razors, a cell phone with two hours of prepaid time, and a small electric screwdriver. After paying cash for his purchases, he used the new cell phone to call a taxi for a ride back to his hotel.

Sunday was spent at a rifle range in the foothills east of town zeroing in the Remington 700 SPS and Bushnell scope. It took 150 rounds of ammunition, but Ortega was centering shots at 500 yards with regularity. Pleased with the rifle and scope combination, he felt ready to get back to his mission.

Early Monday morning, after loading the Jeep, he drove north toward Salt Lake City and I-80 west. Before heading west on the highway, he cruised through one of the long term parking lots at Salt Lake City International Airport, searching for a similar color and model year Jeep. Locating several was not difficult in this part of the country. One in particular met his needs. It was in the most isolated section of the lot and was next to a large van. Parking his own Jeep several rows away, he checked to make sure he knew where all the security cameras were located. Satisfied he could accomplish his goal without being recorded, he walked to the target Jeep and using his newly purchased electric screwdriver, removed the license plates. He returned to his Jeep and left the parking lot.

Once outside the airport complex, he stopped, changed the license plates, and then followed his GPS to I-80 West. San Francisco was now only twelve hours away to the west.

———

Houston, TX

ABBAS STOOD on a wooden deck outside of a popular night spot on the northern side of the Port of Houston. He leaned forward against the handrails. His gaze was on the tranquil water of the harbor, but his thoughts were on the coming two weeks.

He sensed rather than saw someone walk up next to him and lean against the handrail.

"The lights are pleasing to view, yes?"

Abbas nodded. "Yes, they are pleasing. How are you, my brother?"

The newcomer stared out over the harbor. "I am well."

"Thank you for avoiding our traditional greeting. It might draw unwanted attention."

The man next to Abbas chuckled. "I have been in this country too long, Aazim, I know what to say and what not to say."

"Soon, my brother, we will go home. The Americans will then know jihad has reached their land."

"How is your diversion going?"

"I did not choose wisely, Naadir. It was discovered too early."

"The Americans are undisciplined. They are distracted by too many electronic toys."

Abbas nodded. "Yes, this is true. But the one I chose is not. I am not sure how he was discovered, but he was. There is one more task he must accomplish, then he will be useless to us."

"Have you changed our plan?"

Silence was Naadir's answer.

The two brothers did not say anything for several minutes. Finally Aazim stood up straight. "We have been blessed by Allah to bring this upon the infidels. Our plans have to be flexible, to follow his will. My ultimate goal has not changed. The path however, is subject to change."

Naadir nodded.

"I need you to arrange for the containers to be delivered to the warehouse in Tulsa." Aazim looked at his brother. "Have them picked up on Tuesday and delivered on Wednesday. You will need to meet them and make sure they are secure. I will correct my mistake when I meet Ortega there. Until then, secure the containers. We will have help arriving by the end of the week."

Smiling, Naadir stood straight and glanced at his brother. He nodded and walked quickly to the interior of the restaurant. Aazim watched him exit the building, get into a Ford pickup and drive away. He turned and leaned against the railing again. A slight grin came to his face as he watched the lights of the harbor.

Chapter Thirty-Three

Saturday Evening

UPGRADING to first class had been easy; Kruger's frequent flyer miles had accumulated to a point he could fly anywhere in the world first class. As the plane chased daylight across the country toward Kansas City, Kruger sat in his window seat and stared out into the early evening sky.

Before leaving FBI Headquarters, he had been briefed on interviews conducted with the supply sergeants now in custody. The one in Florida identified Ortega as the driving force behind the group. The other sergeant in Georgia told interviewers a similar story and corroborated what was known about the organization. Ortega had recruited both men in Iraq before the withdrawal. Neither of them knew the other members or where they lived. The recruiting process had been carefully done. Each man had lost close friends in the war due to poorly designed equipment. Equipment that should have protected them, but had not.

Both men were bitter and returned stateside vowing to

make things right for their fallen comrades. Kruger understood their motives, and was sure they felt they were being patriotic. What he didn't understand was why the specific targets were chosen. There was something else more sinister underlying the misplaced patriotism of the sergeants. Unless they were lying, which was a possibility, he would need to interview them personally.

He awoke just as the plane touched down in Kansas City. Realizing what was going on, he glanced at his watch and was glad to know it wasn't too late; he called Stephanie as the plane taxied to the terminal.

———

THE SOUNDS of The Plaza winding down after a busy Saturday night served as the background to their late dinner at the breakfast bar. Kruger ate sparsely, concentrating more on several glasses of wine than his plate of pasta. Stephanie noticed and said, "You want to talk about it, or just drink a couple bottles of wine tonight?"

He smiled and looked at her. "Talk about it—and drink more wine."

The frustration on her face was apparent as she said, "Sean, I can't help you if you keep everything inside. Talk to me."

"Paul Stumpf will be the new director, Alan will be the new deputy director, and they offered me the SAC position in Kansas City."

"What? You're kidding! How wonderful. When did all this happen?"

"Today." He chuckled. "Wagner was fired while Alan and I sat in front of his desk. The president named Paul the acting director, pending congressional approval, but

Paul has lots of contact in Congress. It's just a matter of time."

"This is perfect, Sean, you accepted didn't you?"

He shook his head. "No, I wanted to discuss it with you first."

She put her fork down and looked at her husband, her head tilted slightly, her eyes sad. "I've worked all my career for the next promotion. Things are different now aren't they? Any decision you or I make affects both of us." Her melancholy vanished as she smiled and took a sip from her glass of wine. "What do you want to do?

"Not sure." He held his glass at eye level. "I was getting used to the idea of retiring soon." He swirled the remaining liquid in his glass watched the fingers of wine run down the side. He took another sip and continued, "If we get this baby, I really don't want to be tied down to a management job and I certainly don't want to travel any more. Besides, being the Special Agent in Charge is time-consuming and you deal with personnel matters more than investigative matters. Not sure that's what I want."

She got off the bar stool, stepped over, hugged him and put her head on his shoulder. "Lately, I've had doubts about my job too. Do you think it's time to make a change?"

He nodded. "Yes, I do."

He hugged her, kissed her forehead and said, "You always help me put things in perspective. Whatever we decide, we do it together. I like that part, doing it together."

"So do I."

———

LATER, as they lay in bed together, Kruger's arm was around her shoulders and her head on his chest, their conversation concerned the adoption and what to do about the condos. Neither one felt comfortable raising a child just off The Plaza. So the decision was made to sell hers and start looking for a house. After the conversation, they both fell into a long silence, but neither one slept.

"Stef, let me ask you a question. The men they arrested on the army bases said they joined Ortega to make changes. They wanted to bring attention to contractors putting profit ahead of the safety for the soldiers. If this is your goal, how would you go about accomplishing it?"

She was quiet for a few moments, considering. "Work within the system, suggest the changes, get support from others to make the changes happen. Why?"

"Exactly. These guys said their goal was to draw attention to poorly manufactured equipment being used in Iraq and Afghanistan."

She rose up on one elbow and stared at him. "These guys are killing people."

"Yes, they are. Why?"

She was silent, a look of understanding crossed her face. "It's not their true motive."

"Exactly. There's something else going on here. I understand how the military guys believe they're helping their buddies. But someone else is using them for another purpose."

They were quiet again. Stephanie said, "What if this is just a distraction. You mentioned an Imam in California suddenly visiting young men who attend his mosque. Is that related?"

"Don't know." Suddenly his weariness faded, pieces of the puzzle started falling into place. "JR keeps talking about how the contact he found in Dallas was the information provider and financier of the group. What if that person is the one manipulating the rest of them? It would make sense."

Stephanie nodded. "All this person has to do is provide just what they wanted the team to know. Ortega wouldn't realize they were being manipulated."

Kruger threw the sheets back, found his cell phone and sent JR a text. The call came thirty seconds later.

"Question for you," Kruger said, "Can you zero in on the guy in Dallas?"

"Yeah. He's in Houston right now."

Frowning, Kruger paused for just a heartbeat, "Where exactly in Houston?"

"He keeps accessing the internet around the Port of Houston."

"Damn."

"What am I missing here, Scan?"

"He's waiting on a container."

"Uh, oh."

"Yeah, uh, oh. Can you find what he's looking for?"

"We don't know his name, how would I be able to find the container? Do you know how many containers go through the Port of Houston on a daily basis?"

"No."

"Roughly twenty five to thirty ships arrive daily. Each ship has at minimum of one thousand containers on it, and by the way, that's a low estimate. So all of a sudden, we have, at minimum, twenty-five thousand containers arriving daily. If we narrow our search to just containers arriving from Europe and the Mediterranean area, we could narrow the number of containers, to oh, let's say seventy-five hundred containers—a day. I don't have the computer power or the manpower to even do that kind of a search.

Plus, limiting our search to just that part of the world means we could still miss something."

Kruger was silent, waiting for JR's next rant.

"Even if I had the manpower, which I don't, and had the computer power, which I don't, who would we be looking for? Answer that question?"

"JR, take a deep breath."

"You're not listening to me."

"Yes, I am. Find out who the contact is. Then finding the container becomes easy."

Kruger could hear heavy breathing on the other end of the call. After two minutes, JR said, "Yeah… Okay, that's how Charlie and I need to approach this. Find out who this contact is. Got it."

The call ended abruptly. Kruger smiled, JR was on the job with a purpose. If the name could be found, he would do it.

———

THE ALARM CLOCK on his nightstand showed 9:05. He had slept in. He reached for Stephanie and found her side of the bed empty. He heard music coming from the living room and smelled coffee and a fabulous combination of peppers and onions. Realizing she was probably fixing brunch, he threw the bedcovers back and grabbed a pair of boxers, a t-shirt, and sweat pants. After dressing, he brushed his teeth and headed to the kitchen.

Stephanie was pouring coffee when she saw him.

"Good morning. Do you realize this is the first morning since we've been married you slept longer than I did?" Smiling, she added, "I marked it on my calendar."

He walked over to her and said, "Ha, ha, I was tired."

"You drank a bottle of wine."

He shrugged and kissed her. "What're you doing?"

"Making us a fantastic Sunday brunch, like the ones I used to make before we got married, remember those?" she said with a grin.

He smiled and said, "Oh, yeah..."

Before he could finished the comment, his cell phone vibrated. Glancing at the caller ID, he recognized only a Kansas City area code. He frowned. "It's local, but I'm not familiar with it." He accepted the call.

"What did I ever do to you?" the voice said, slurring the first and last words.

Kruger looked at the ID again and said, "Who is this?"

"Of course you don't know! You don't care..." The words continued to be slurred. "You're the one that ruined my career..."

Finally recognizing the voice, Kruger said, "What do you want, Dollar?"

"What do I want? I want my career back."

"I didn't take it from you. You lost it."

"Asshole."

"Franklin, you're drunk."

"No shit."

"Why are you calling?"

"I've been transferred to Fargo, North Dakota as an agent. For gawd sake, I was a Special Agent in Charge, and now..." There was silence on the call. "I'm just an agent again. Because of you!"

"Franklin, the only reason you're an agent again is because you're incompetent."

His cell phone was silent. Kruger almost ended the call when Dollar spoke again.

"You've always had it in for me Kruger. Always... Why?"

"Because you won't do the work, and you always take the easy way out. Franklin, I really don't have time for this conversation."

After a long pause, Kruger heard, "Not my fault... The work was complicated, no one ever told me it would be complicated."

Disgusted with the conversation, Kruger said, "How the hell did you ever get through the academy?"

His words slurred, Dollar said, "My dad pulled some strings."

Kruger shook his head and ended the call, his good mood shattered.

"I take it he was not a happy person this morning," Stephanie said.

"No, he's drunk, feeling sorry for himself and blaming others for his own screw-ups."

She handed him a cup of coffee and said, "Here, take this, go take a shower and I'll have brunch ready when you're done."

Chapter Thirty-Four

Monday

"NOW THAT I'M HERE, tell me why we couldn't discuss this on the phone," Kruger said as he removed several empty Hot Pocket wrappers from a desk chair.

The computer area was strewn with empty, crushed Mountain Dew cans, numerous Dr. Pepper bottles with varying amounts of liquid still in them and an assortment of discarded frozen food packaging. Dropping the wrappers into a nearby waste basket, he brushed crumbs from the chair before sitting down.

"What we found is too complicated to discuss over the phone, it would take too long," JR said. "Besides, I'd have to use too many words the NSA would tag."

"You're being paranoid JR. Trust me, no one is looking for you anymore."

"My rules."

Kruger held both hands up, palms toward JR. "Okay. What've you got?"

"Your assumption about the Dallas contact was essentially correct. We downloaded a program to his computer that allowed Charlie and me access to its hard drive. What we found at first surprised us, but then after digging further, it made sense."

Kruger was not in the mood to deal with JR's habit of dramatic pauses. He said, "Spit it out, JR. What did you find?"

"The computer used to communicate with Ortega was a cut-out. Its only task was to write emails to Ortega. But, somewhere along the line, the operator screwed up and left a link to his main computer, which we found."

"And?"

"I'm getting to it, stay with me. Once we knew about the other computer, it was easy to find it accessing the internet. After downloading one of my little programs to it, the information we obtained definitely confirms your suspicions. The Dallas contact is manipulating Ortega."

Nodding, Kruger said, "Not surprising. Did you learn who they are?"

JR smiled. "No, but we learned the answers to several other more important questions. You've had the suspicion these activities are a diversion from the real purpose? The answer is a definite yes. So far, the communications do not reveal the true reason. However, we do know the following. One, there is mention of help being sent to Tulsa. Two, references to Tulsa are included in several conversations about materials arriving at the Port of Houston. Third, the next diversion is the assassination of a member of Congress. Whoever it is, serves on the Subcommittee on the Middle East and Africa."

"Do they mention any names?"

JR shook his head. Charlie was sitting at another

computer across from JR. His eyes were bloodshot with dark circles under them. He said, "I've checked on who is currently serving on this committee."

With his patience gone Kruger snapped at Charlie, "Spit it out."

"All but two of the members live east of the Mississippi River. One is from Oregon and the other from California. Ortega accessed the internet in Topeka on Friday and again Saturday in Denver. He's heading west."

Kruger stood and began pacing. He accidentally kicked an empty Mountain Dew can and watched as it tumbled across the carpet.

JR said, "We're cross-referencing shipments from the Port to Tulsa. Over the past week there were over three hundred containers transported by truck to Tulsa. It's going to take time, Sean, and we may never pinpoint the right containers."

"Shit." Kruger kept pacing. "Who are the congress members?"

"Roy Griffin in San Francisco and Marlene Osborne in Portland."

Kruger walked toward the conference room, "I have to make some phone calls."

———

KRUGER DIALED Alan Seltzer's cell phone. The call was answered immediately.

"Alan, we think the next target is located on the west coast. It's possibly one of two congress members."

"What do you mean, 'you think' and 'possibly'? You're not sure?"

"At this stage, we aren't. But everything we know so far points toward them. Let me explain."

Seltzer listened carefully, interrupting only once to ask a question. Finally he said, "Your reasoning is sound. What's your next step?"

"I need you to brief the Portland and San Francisco offices. We'll need to get a team out to both members of congress for protection and surveillance. I'm going to Oregon and sending Clark to San Francisco. We're the only two individuals who can recognize Ortega on sight. We have to split up."

"Okay, I'll call you back."

Kruger ended the call and walked back to the cubicles where JR and Charlie were hunched over keyboards. JR said, "Sean, come here, this is interesting."

Kruger crouched over to see what JR was staring at and said, "Yeah?"

Pointing to one of the screens on his desk, JR said, "This police report in Denver. A man named Goodman was found murdered in his warehouse. I know about this guy; he was a hacker at one time. Not a very good one, but still. His other vocation was making fake IDs, which he was very good at. Expensive, if I remember correctly, I almost used him one time. Before meeting you."

Kruger stood back up and started pacing. "Are you suggesting?"

"Yeah, I am. Ortega.

"Does the report give the detective's name?"

JR looked back at the screen, found the answer, wrote it on a sticky note, and handed the paper to Kruger. After reading the name, Kruger used his cell phone to call an individual at FBI Headquarters. After confirming his ID number, he asked to be patched through to the Denver

Police Department. After five minutes of explaining who he was and what he needed, Detective Ray Newton finally came to the phone.

Kruger said, "Detective Newton, this is FBI Agent Sean Kruger. I'm with a special task force investigating a series of murders across the US. We have reason to believe the death of Walter Goodman may be connected."

After a long pause, Newton finally said, "How'd the FBI come up with that idea?"

"Detective, I'm not trying to interfere with your investigation, but we know our suspect was in Denver and needed the services of a man like Goodman. I would like your permission to stop on my way to Oregon and see if my information helps you solve the case."

"Well, right now we don't have a lot to go on, any information would be helpful. When are you planning on being here?"

"I'll have to get back to you after I schedule my flight." He gave the detective his cell phone number and ended the call.

Chapter Thirty-Five

SAN FRANCISCO, CA

Tuesday

"I'M STILL NOT sure I understand why the FBI believes someone is planning to harm me, Agent Clark." Congressman Roy Griffin stood in the foyer of his San Mateo, California home, his arms crossed over his chest and his head slightly tilted to one side.

"Sir, we feel our evidence is credible and prefer to error on the side of caution. As I said earlier, the threat may be directed toward Congresswoman Marlene Osborne and not you. Our evidence doesn't specify which one of you is the target."

Griffin nodded. "Marlene is a good person. We don't see eye to eye on a lot of issues, but she has the good of her constituents at heart."

"I'm sure she does. We're having the same conversation with her today."

"So, Agent Clark, how do you and the FBI plan to protect my family?"

ORTEGA FOUND the house just before sunset. After cruising past, he parked his Jeep a half mile away and walked back to a house diagonally across the street. With the deepening twilight and a ten-foot tall California laurel, he could observe the congressman's house without being seen. Considering the neighborhood and how rich Griffin was, the house was modest and tasteful. The structure was a two-story Colonial with a professionally landscaped yard of trees and foliage. Five minutes after he started watching the house, a black Chevrolet Suburban pulled into the driveway. Four men in suits emerged from the vehicle, two walked to the front door and the other two started walking around the house in opposite directions. The two men at the door entered the house after it opened.

Following their trek around the perimeter of the home, the two men in suits conferred with each other and took separate positions. Ortega watched as one man stood just outside the front door and made a cell phone call. The other stood behind the Suburban and directed his attention toward the street and the neighborhood.

Ortega frowned. How had the FBI discovered Griffin was a target? First they tracked him in St. Louis, now they were here even before he arrived. Had Billy been caught? Did he leave evidence behind in Denver? It was essential to find the leak and plug it immediately. He waited until it was completely dark before returning to the Jeep. Remembering a McDonalds advertising free Wi-Fi close to Griffin's neighborhood, he accessed the internet after buying a Big Mac and fries. He needed to contact Billy.

LATE TUESDAY NIGHT, Charlie was monitoring the computers alone. Earlier in the evening, JR started nodding off while working at his computer. Charlie watched as he stood up from the desk, switched off the screen and walked up the stairs to the third floor. As usual, he didn't say anything; he simply left.

His time spent with JR had been both stimulating and frustrating. JR was brilliant with computers, but not real patient with those of lesser abilities. Charlie was confident with his own skills, but once in a while, JR made him feel like a complete novice. So when JR was not around, Charlie was able to practice and review the techniques he was learning.

He was about to close everything down for the evening when one of their trip wires indicated Ortega was accessing the internet. Quickly following the steps outlined by JR, he identified the access point as the San Mateo area in California.

Kruger was in Portland, and Clark in San Mateo. He grabbed his phone and called Kruger. The call was answered immediately.

"Sean, Ortega just accessed the internet in San Mateo. He's after Griffin."

"Damn." He paused. "Let Ryan know. I'll head that way on the next shuttle. Thanks, Charlie, good work."

———

CLARK'S PHONE VIBRATED. He glanced at the caller ID while Griffin was explaining his itinerary to a San Francisco FBI agent. Excusing himself from the meeting, he answered the call as soon as he was out of Griffin's home office.

"Ryan, it's Charlie. Ortega just accessed the internet

there in San Mateo. I've called Sean, and he's catching a flight as quickly as he can."

Clark was silent for a few seconds.

"Okay, Charlie, pass the word to Seltzer. I'm going to ask for more teams on Griffin."

As soon as he ended the call with Charlie, his phone vibrated again. It was Kruger. He accepted the call. "I just heard. When does your plane land?"

"Around midnight. I've already contacted the SAC in San Francisco and told him the situation. He's an old friend of mine and agreed to send an additional team to your location. You'll have six agents to secure the property. Stay there and keep the congressman inside the house until I arrive."

"Got it. See you in a few hours."

———

ORTEGA WAS PUZZLED. Billy had responded faster than normal, he was still in Virginia, and his contact in Dallas was still online. He had not mentioned the presence of the FBI in his communications, just in case one of them had been compromised. Because neither asked him for details on his location or activities, he didn't believe either of them were the leak.

The big question now was how the FBI knew about Griffin. His supply contacts didn't know any details of the operation; they just supplied materials. They knew who he was, but not his location. Somehow the FBI was following his movements. One possibility might be his computer, but since he changed Wi-Fi locations all the time, it was not likely. But to be on the safe side, he would use his computer sparingly. If they were tracking his movements, it wouldn't matter in a few days. The mission would be completed.

He searched Congressman Griffin's website and found no references to any appearances scheduled for California. The only announcement was his return to Washington on June 1st. A Google search on the congressman produced the same results, with no references to any public appearances or events. On the third page of the search, Ortega found a link to the obituary of the congressman's mother-in-law. Within the obituary was the mention of a public memorial service. The notice gave the location, the date and the time of the service. It was the opportunity he needed.

———

THE CONGRESSMAN STOOD HIS GROUND.

"Agent Clark, I will not hide like a coward. I haven't been in Congress long enough for someone to get mad enough to try and kill me. I can't and will not crawl into a hole just to avoid being out in public. My wife and I have a commitment to attend the service on Wednesday, and we will not break that commitment. Besides, I'm delivering a tribute to a great lady. She believed in me and I will not betray her trust. There will be no further discussion."

"Yes, sir, I understand your commitment. If we can't convince you to cancel your appearance, then I would respectfully request your agreement for our teams to accompany you to the service. We'll provide as much protection as possible."

"You really believe there is a man out there trying to kill me, don't you?"

"Yes sir, I do. When my partner arrives, he'll give you more details.

Griffin was silent for several moments. Looking at Clark, finally he said, "Okay, I'll cancel all my appointments, except the memorial service. It's important to my wife and me."

"Thank you, sir. Hopefully we'll be able to locate this individual before the service and you can go on without us. But until then, we have a better chance of protecting you if you limit your outside activities."

The congressman stood, "I need to discuss this development with my wife. She hates Washington, D.C., with a passion and I'm sure this news will only reinforce her attitude."

Chapter Thirty-Six

SAN MATEO, CA

Tuesday

AS SOON AS Clark drove Kruger past Grace Cathedral, both men realized immediately they had a challenge facing them. The church was a traditional large metropolitan worship center surrounded by high rise apartments and office buildings. The cathedral's main floor was twenty-five feet above street level with four levels of concrete steps ascending to the sanctuary doors. There were at least seven tall buildings within 600 yards, providing ample opportunities for sniper hides. Kruger didn't have the manpower, time or authority to check each one. His only hope was Ortega didn't know about the memorial service.

After walking around the church several times, they decided on a strategy and left to meet with Charlie Brewer, the Special Agent in Charge of San Francisco, and an old friend of Kruger's. After introducing Ryan Clark to Brewer, Kruger said, "I haven't seen you since your promotion, congratulations."

Brewer shook Kruger's hand and said, "If I knew how busy I would be out here, I'm not sure I would have accepted. Understand you're in line for the KC position."

"A vicious rumor. Apparently Seltzer's let his promotion go to his head."

Brewer chuckled. "Yeah, he told me to encourage you to accept the promotion. Something about your new-found status as Director Stumpf's wonder boy. I stopped listening when he said that."

"Seltzer's delusional." They both laughed, then Kruger grew serious. "Charlie, I need a favor."

"I'll do what I can; what's up?"

"You're aware of the threat to Congressman Griffin, right?"

Brewer nodded.

"Well, he's the main speaker at a memorial service for his late mother-in-law tomorrow at Grace Cathedral. Even with the six agents you assigned us, I'm not sure we can protect him at such an exposed location. I could use a couple of snipers on the rooftops surrounding the church."

"Well, I normally wouldn't hesitate, but all my guys are training in San Diego this week. How about the locals? The San Francisco PD has several excellent sniper teams. My guys say they're some of the best on the west coast."

Kruger smiled. "I would really appreciate anything you could arrange. Getting him in and out of that church tomorrow will be tricky at best."

"Let me make a phone call. I've had lunch with the police chief several times since I've been here. He seems to be someone who will work with us when needed."

Brewer made the call while Kruger stepped out of Brewer's office and called JR. When he answered, Kruger said, "Any updates on Ortega?"

"We haven't seen any activity since last night, Sean. He accessed the internet three times around the San Mateo area utilizing a different Wi-Fi spot each time. He hasn't established a pattern Charlie and I can determine, so it's hard to guess where he's staying."

"I was afraid of that. He's being cautious after St. Louis. We may have a problem tomorrow. I need to have as much information on him as possible. I'll touch base with you later." Kruger ended the call and stepped back into Brewer's office just as he was returning the handset to the phone.

"My analysis of the Chief was correct," Brewer said. "He's assigning three teams to assist you tomorrow around Grace Cathedral. He said they've practiced this scenario at the cathedral several times and know where to set up. I gave him your contact information and told him you were the agent in charge."

Kruger nodded. "Thanks, Charlie. We might be taking unnecessary precautions, but I would rather be prepared." He paused briefly and frowned. "What can you tell me about this Imam you guys are watching?"

Brewer chuckled. "Which one? We have several in the bay area on our watch list."

"The recluse who all of a sudden started making house calls."

"Oh, that one. I beefed up surveillance on him immediately after he started doing it."

"Do you know what sparked his sudden interest in visitations?"

"We think it was a phone call he received last Thursday. The call was from a pay phone in Dallas."

Kruger nodded. "I was told about the call. One of our suspects was in Dallas at the time."

Brewer furrowed his brow. "Why wasn't I informed of this?"

"Politics. I wasn't officially on the investigation. Wagner had me taken off after Dollar said I was interfering."

Closing his eyes and shaking his head, Brewer leaned back in his desk chair. "I won't miss Wagner." He was quiet for a few seconds. "The phone call was cryptic. The caller asked the Imam to send three individuals to help him."

"Did he say when he needed them?"

Brewer straightened in his chair and started typing on his computer. "I can't remember exactly; let me review the report." He paused while he read something on the screen. "Looks like he said a week… which would be this Thursday. Why?"

Kruger didn't answer right away. Finally, he shook his head. "Not sure, but keep your eyes and ears on this guy. Something is going on; I just can't put a finger on it yet."

SEVERAL VACANT APARTMENTS in and around Grace Cathedral were available. After driving around the neighborhood and checking the angles of the various buildings to the church, he decided to check on the listing for an apartment building at Sacramento and Cushman. If the vacant room offered a view of the church, its location would be perfect.

After parking several blocks away, he walked back to the entrance and checked with the building manager. As they took the elevator to the fourth floor, the man told him about all the amenities available to tenants of the building. Ortega nodded, not listening to him. Once inside he found the sliding glass door in the bedroom offered a direct line of sight view of Grace Cathedral. He turned back to the manager and said, "I'll take it. When can I move in?"

"Well, I'll need your first and last month's rent, plus a $1,000 deposit. Once the background and credit check come back, you can move in."

Ortega pulled out a roll of cash and handed the manager $5,000 in hundred dollar bills, which was a thousand dollars more than was needed. Ortega smiled, "I'd like to start moving in tonight. Would that be a problem?"

The manager stared at the cash, then looked at Ortega, smiled, and said, "Not a problem at all. I need a few forms filled out and the place is yours."

By 9 p.m., Ortega had his equipment secured in the apartment. The view of Grace Cathedral with the sliding glass door open allowed him to place his Remington within the apartment without exposing the rifle to the outside. He scoped the distance at 457 yards, which was fine since he had sighted the Remington in at 500. Once the rifle was set up, he drove to a twenty-four-hour grocery store and bought beer, beef jerky, a frozen pizza, apples and a few bananas. No need for more. He'd be gone before noon tomorrow. He parked the Jeep several blocks away and positioned it so he could drive off as quickly as possible.

Once back in the apartment, he ate the pizza, drank two beers, settled down and catnapped until morning. His thoughts turned to the coming day's events. Would he be alive this time tomorrow? If his plan worked out, he had a good chance. If he miscalculated, he'd be dead in less than twenty-four hours. It was a concept he had lived with for the last five years.

WEDNESDAY

KRUGER STARED at the digital clock, 4 a.m. His body was still on Central Time, so it was 6 a.m. to him. Rolling over he tried to get back to sleep. Fifteen minutes later, he gave up. Sitting on the side of the bed, he pressed the palms of his hands against his eyes. How many more days before he retired? The weariness of constantly waking up in hotel rooms swept over him. He thought about calling Stephanie, but didn't want his dark mood to rub off on her.

After putting on a t-shirt and running pants, he walked down to the street outside the hotel and started his run. Hopefully the exercise would ease his mind and help him think. Running the hilly streets of San Francisco pushed Kruger to his limit. He ran until his legs felt like rubber, then staggered back to his hotel room. After a shower and several cups of coffee brewed in the room's coffee machine, he called Clark.

"What time is it?" said a groggy voice.

"It's late, if you must know it's almost nine your normal time."

"Why are you calling me? It's six here in California. My alarm isn't set to go off for another thirty minutes."

"Tough, get up and let's get going. We have a busy day ahead of us."

"I quit. Now let me go back to sleep."

Kruger chuckled and said, "Sorry, Ryan, put your suit on. We need to get going."

Three hours later, after a quick breakfast, they arrived at Roy Griffin's home. While Kruger met with Congressman Griffin in his study, Clark briefed the FBI team on the memorial service.

Griffin argued with Kruger for thirty minutes about how extra precautions were unnecessary. Finally his patience exhausted, Kruger said to the congressman, "Let's assume I'm wrong, then nothing will happen. Everybody goes home safe. If I'm right, and we prevent any harm coming to you or your wife, everybody goes home safe."

Griffin stared at Kruger, his head tilted slightly to the right. "I see your point, but it still seems like a waste of the FBI's time."

"I'll take the blame for wasting everybody's time."

The congressman smiled and said, "Okay, Agent, I'll cooperate."

Kruger placed the congressman and his wife in the lead Suburban with Clark and the driver. He, a driver and two other FBI agents rode in the trail Suburban. Upon arriving at to the church, Kruger and two agents exited their vehicle and surrounded the lead Suburban. Kruger surveyed the various buildings, making sure the three sniper teams were on alert. Each team was scanning the area with binoculars and rifle scopes.

Once he was satisfied with the situation, he nodded to an agent standing by the rear passenger door, who opened it to allow Clark and the Griffins to emerge. The agents immediately surrounded the husband and wife, and hustled them up the concrete stairs into the cathedral.

———

ORTEGA OBSERVED Griffin and his wife exit the Suburban through his rifle scope. As the group hurried up the steps, he centered the scope on the back of the congressman's head, allowed for a lead, and started squeezing the trigger. Suddenly one of the men in front of his target turned his head. It was the cop from St. Louis. Surprised, Ortega looked up from the scope. Before he could get back on target, the group disappeared through the sanctuary doors at the top of the steps. He raised his eye from the scope again and looked at the scene. Thinking through his options, Ortega decided the cleanest shot would be as they descended the steps after the ceremony.

How much did the FBI know? Rubbing the back of his neck, he stepped away from the rifle and stared at the cathedral door. Apparently the two agents from St. Louis were still tracking him. Unfortunate for them, if he had the opportunity, a few extra rounds would thank them for their diligence.

He glanced at his watch and decided he had at least an hour before he had to get back on the scope, maybe more. He almost drank one of the beers left from last night, but decided against it. He casually walked out onto the apartment's balcony eating an apple. There was a SWAT team on top of a building three blocks to the east surveying the taller buildings. Two more teams could be easily seen, one on the roof of the building next door, and another on the roof of a building one block to right. That made a total of three teams. He was impressed, but it didn't matter. He would still make the shot.

The presence of the sniper teams altered his escape plan however. He'd have to leave the rifle and use the fire escape situated on the opposite side of the building. The Jeep was a short walk from the apartment building. Five minutes after making the shot, he'd be driving to the airport. Not enough time for anyone to figure out where it came from.

Putting on surgical gloves, he wiped the room for prints,

including the Remington, scope and cartridges. Once that was done, it was time to settle behind the rifle and wait. The scope was centered on the stairs just below the entrance to the church. He had decided on the position while watching several other groups of people enter the church. The shot would be easier with the congressman walking down the stairs.

Fifteen minutes after noon, the doors of the cathedral opened and attendees started exiting the church. Twenty minutes later all was quiet as the last attendee's walked down the stairs. Finally he noticed one of the FBI agents from St. Louis open the door and step out to survey the area. Both black Suburbans pulled up and parked in front of the church steps. The driver of the lead vehicle jumped out and opened the passenger doors, then immediately returned to his driver's seat.

Once the vehicles were in position, the agent at the door nodded to someone behind him. The door opened further, and the congressman and his wife exited. One of the FBI agents from St. Louis was in front of Griffin and the other one was behind him. There were other agents on both sides. Ortega centered the crosshairs on the congressman's head, gave him a slight lead, took a breath, and applied pressure on the trigger as he exhaled.

The shot went low, hitting the agent in front of Griffin. Before Ortega could fire another shot, the congressman was smothered by the rest of the agents. Ortega thought briefly of taking more shots, but dismissed it as a waste of time. His opportunity to get the congressman was lost. Accepting the situation, he stood and walked out of the apartment. As he was running down the fire escape, he realized his error. Provo, Utah, was a city almost a mile in elevation, while San

Francisco was at sea level. The air was denser and the bullet dropped more than in Provo. A simple mistake, but a mistake that kept his mission from being completed.

WHEN CLARK OPENED the cathedral door; the steps were empty. The last of the loitering attendee's now gone. Satisfied no one else would be in danger, he radioed for the Suburbans to move into position at the bottom of the steps. Once the lead vehicle was in position with the passenger doors open, it was time to get the congressman and his wife out of the cathedral. Clark was in front and Kruger behind the congressman, with the two other agents on either side.

The bullet struck Clark in the upper right shoulder with the force of a sledge hammer, pushing him back into the congressman before he even realized what had happened. The other agents reacted immediately and practically carried Griffin and his wife to the waiting safety of the Suburban.

Clark sat on the steps, stunned. There was no pain, but he had no feeling in his right arm. Time stood still as he watched the other agents move in slow motion herding the Griffins into the Suburban. His trance was interrupted as the lead Suburban squealed its tires and sped away. Finally he glanced at his shoulder, where the blood flowed freely. The question of what had hit him started to form, but he grew dizzy and lost consciousness as his body slumped back onto the steps.

As the now departing Suburban moved rapidly away, Kruger rushed back up the steps to Clark. He was unconscious and losing blood rapidly. Kruger applied pressure to the wound, saying, "Ryan, hang on, buddy, the EMTs will be here soon."

Off in the distance, the sounds of a siren could be heard. The direction was undetectable as the sound echoed off the surrounding buildings.

While he held Clark's head off the concrete stairs and applied pressure to the wound, Kruger was overcome with a feeling of helplessness. Fearing the worst, he closed his eyes and said a silent prayer for his friend. Finally after what seemed like hours, the ambulance arrived. Two EMTs ran up the stairs and took over. Kruger stood, stepped back and stared unthinking as they worked on Clark.

Once stabilized, they gently placed Clark on a stretcher and prepared to transport him to the waiting ambulance. As they secured him to the gurney, one of the EMTs handed Kruger a card with the name of their destination hospital. The EMT smiled and said, "Don't worry, we've got him. He'll make it."

Kruger watched as they loaded his friend into the ambulance, closed the doors and started the run for the hospital with sirens screaming. More San Francisco police arrived and took control of the scene. Kruger walked down to the bottom of the steps toward several officers. He glanced at his hands and saw they were soaked in blood. Without hesitation, he wiped them on his suit coat and asked to speak with the commander of the SWAT teams. After Kruger was briefed, the commander handed Kruger a tube of baby wipes he kept in their command truck.

Charlie Brewer arrived twenty minutes later and joined Kruger in the apartment the SWAT team had located.

"What've we got, Sean?"

Kruger pointed to the Remington 700. "One shot was

all he got off. I have two of your agents interviewing the building manager. He's not being cooperative at this point."

Brewer nodded. "There's no way anybody could have seen the set up this far into the room. We're lucky he didn't take any more shots."

They were both quiet as they watched a forensics technician photograph and catalog the contents of the apartment.

"I underestimated this guy, Charlie. We had the area covered by sniper teams and he takes the shot anyway."

Brewer placed his hand on Kruger's shoulder. "Not sure what else you could have done, Sean. The Congressman's still alive."

"Let's hope Ryan makes it." He paused and surveyed the room again. "I have to get to the hospital. I'll call Seltzer and brief him when I get there. Keep me posted on what you find."

Brewer nodded.

At the hospital, Kruger was directed to the surgery waiting room. An elderly woman sitting at the information desk outside the surgery area was unable to provide him with any updates on Clark's condition. He paced for a while, sat for a while, drank several cups of coffee secured from a snack and beverage area next to the waiting room and then paced some more. Three hours later, a doctor emerged dressed in surgical scrubs. He spoke to the lady at the information desk, who pointed at Kruger. The surgeon introduced himself and said, "Your friend's out of surgery. He's stable, but lost a lot of blood. Were you the one who applied the pressure after he was shot?"

Kruger nodded.

The surgeon smiled, patted Kruger on the shoulder and said, "You saved his life. If he had lost any more blood, he would have died at the scene. The bullet ripped an artery, that's what took us so long to repair. There isn't a lot of muscular damage, just the artery. He'll be fine after some physical therapy."

"How long before I can talk to him?"

The surgeon smiled and said, "We're going to keep him sedated for now, so probably tomorrow morning."

Kruger nodded, thanked the doctor and walked to an isolated area of the waiting room. Pulling his cell phone out of his suit coat pocket, he dialed Seltzer's private number, who answered on the second ring.

"How's Clark?"

"Stable. I can talk to him in the morning."

"Okay, tell me what happened. Brewer briefed me, but indicated he wasn't there during the shooting."

Without hesitation, Kruger said, "My fault, I didn't take enough precautions."

"That's not the assessment of Brewer or the San Francisco Chief of Police. They both said Ortega had the hide set up deep inside an apartment. There was no way the teams on the roof could have spotted him. They both commented on how difficult the location was to secure. Considering all those stairs, you probably saved the congressman's life. A second shot was impossible."

"Yeah... Tell that to Clark. He's the one in the hospital. I wasn't able to convince the congressman about the danger. I hope he realizes his stubbornness resulted in a good man being injured."

"He's a politician, Sean. He'll spin it to his advantage."

Kruger smiled and said, "I'm sure he'll make himself look like a hero."

Seltzer was quiet for a few seconds, then said, "We all know the dangers of the job. Clark knew. It didn't stop him from helping us out, did it? He volunteered to do this because it was important. You need to recognize that and stop kicking yourself." He paused briefly. "You're still the lead on this investigation, Kruger. Stop acting like the victim. Get back out there and catch this guy."

The words stung. Seltzer was right; he was feeling sorry for himself. "I'll call you after I talk to Clark in the morning."

Chapter Thirty-Seven

Wednesday Afternoon

AFTER RUNNING down the apartment building fire escape stairs, Ortega paused at the exit door, took a breath, and walked casually to his Jeep. During the drive to the airport, he repeatedly checked the rearview mirror for police cars. He saw nothing suspicious. Forty-five minutes after leaving the apartment building, he was parking the Jeep in a long term lot at the airport.

Once inside the terminal, he checked the departure board, found a Delta flight to Tulsa, purchased his ticket and casually walked through security. No one stopped him and he arrived at the gate without incident.

Sitting in the last row of first class next to a window, Ortega wondered, as he watched mountains pass underneath the plane, how the FBI knew he was in San Mateo. What had he done to tip them off? He was traveling under the name Duane Horton, and the American Express card had not been used until purchasing the ticket for this flight. Paying cash at cheap hotels had allowed him to register under different names, so that wasn't the reason. It had to be something else. Billy. It was the only explanation.

But that didn't make sense either. Billy was still following communication protocol. Had the FBI discovered how they communicate? Cooper's computer and cell phone were destroyed in the blast and subsequent fire. Had the FBI caught Billy and offered him a deal? That seemed likely. Nothing else made sense; Billy had to be the leak. There were no other possibilities.

He glanced at his watch; the plane was forty minutes from landing in Minneapolis. If no one was waiting for him at the connecting flight gate, he'd be in Tulsa by 10 p.m. A surprise meeting with Acosta in the morning would probably tell him who the leak was. It would be time to clean up and start eliminating loose ends.

JR RARELY PACED, but he was pacing now. It was the first time Charlie had witnessed his new mentor agitated. After receiving the news of Ryan Clark being shot, JR started pacing. When he wasn't pacing, he was muttering to himself. Now he was pacing and muttering. Charlie didn't know if he should interrupt or just start doing what he knew to do.

His first task was starting a facial recognition routine at the airports surrounding San Mateo. Thirty minutes later, he had a hit from the TSI computer at San Francisco International. The file he opened showed Norman Ortega handing his ID to a TSI agent. He quickly accessed the airport's computers, but failed to get another hit. At this point, there was no way to know which flight Ortega took until they knew the name he was flying under.

Charlie had an idea. He called the San Francisco Crime Lab, identified himself and asked to speak to the head of the department. They had met six months ago at a conference in Washington, D.C. She had sat next to him at a dinner function the last night of the conference. After a week of meetings and work groups, they had laughed and enjoyed each other's company until the hotel staff kicked them out of the banquet room. He just hoped she remembered him. Finally after several minutes on hold he heard, "Hello, this is Michelle Young, may I help you?"

"Michelle, this is Charlie Craft, we met..."

"Charlie, how in the world are you? I heard you were promoted to head up the Montgomery Forensics team."

Charlie was surprised. Not only did she remember him, but she'd been keeping up with his career. He'd have to ask her about it later, right now he needed information.

"Yes, I was. But currently I'm working with a special task force. We're investigating a possible serial killer who may be involved in an incident out there in San Mateo."

"Are you referring to the attempted assassination of Congressman Griffin?"

"Yes, have you received the weapon at your lab yet?"

"About two hours ago. What do you need to know?"

"Have you identified the person who registered the rifle?"

"It was purchased at Discount Sporting Goods and Gun Shop in Provo, Utah, last Saturday. The name given was Duane Horton, with an address in Springville, Utah. We were just informed several minutes ago that the address is a vacant field on the southern end of town."

Charlie was silent. He had a name. "Michelle, can you hold the phone for a few minutes while I check something?"

Using one of JR's new computer routines, he entered the name Michelle gave him and the airport. Fifteen seconds later, he had Duane Horton's exact seat assignment on Delta flight 1246, destination Minneapolis. He got back on the phone and said, "Michelle, you're beautiful! Duane Horton is on a flight out of San Francisco International to Minneapolis-St. Paul."

"Wow... How did you find it so fast?"

Realizing his mistake, Charlie quickly said, "A team member's been working on a search routine for airline manifests. Seems to be working, doesn't it?"

"Sure does. I'd like to learn more about the program." She hesitated for a moment and said, "Uhh... I know this sounds forward, Charlie, but do you ever get out to California?"

This was a first for Charlie. He couldn't remember the last time a woman had showed interest in him. Usually his clumsy efforts to make a date ended in total disaster. "Well, I had plans to tour the wine country in a few weeks," he lied. "Why?"

"Really, were you coming with someone?"

"No, sounds weird, doesn't it?" he said, getting deeper into the lie.

"Oh no, not at all. I could show you around when you're out here. That is, if you don't have other plans."

"That would be wonderful, my own personal tour guide for the wine country. Sounds great."

"Kind of what I thought. When are you planning on being here?"

Charlie panicked. Quickly pulling out his cell phone, he accessed its calendar. The end of June was about a month away. Realizing he had used all of his vacation time, he shrugged. He'd figure out the details later. This opportunity wasn't going to slip away from him.

"My flight lands in San Francisco on the 22nd."

"I'll give you my email address, and you can send me the flight number and arrival time. I'll pick you up."

Listening to the conversation, JR shook his head and stared at Charlie. He couldn't believe he was making a date while the world was crashing down around them. Finally he cleared his throat and said, "Charlie, we have a lot of work to do."

Charlie looked over his shoulder at JR and said, "Michelle, I have to go. I'll email you the details; I'm looking forward to seeing you again. And thanks for the information."

He ended the call and turned around to face JR.

"Duane Horton is the name Ortega is traveling under. He's currently on a flight from San Francisco to Minneapolis. His flight is scheduled to arrive," he quickly looked at the screen and then the clock in the lower right corner of the computer, "in five minutes. He's booked on a connecting flight to Tulsa, which leaves at six-twenty-one. He arrives in Tulsa around ten."

JR cocked his head to the left. "How do you know all of this?"

Charlie summarized his steps. JR grinned and nodded several times.

"Tulsa's the key," he said. "All the players are converging on Tulsa."

Charlie smiled.

"You're making progress, Charlie. Now get this information to Kruger and Seltzer. Maybe they'll have time to intercept Ortega in Minneapolis. Oh, and Charlie, have a good time in wine country."

———

ORTEGA WAITED until half the passengers were off before getting his carry-on bag and joining the crowd exiting the plane. He blended into the multitude of other passengers around the gate and searched for anyone overly interested in exiting passengers. Not noticing anyone, he turned right and found a shop selling Minneapolis-St. Paul memorabilia. Entering the shop, he watched the crowd surrounding the gate for a few minutes. When he did not see anything out of the ordinary, he turned and started looking for what he needed.

Five minutes later, wearing a Minneapolis Twins baseball cap, wraparound sunglasses and a black Nike windbreaker, he exited the shop and started walking toward the connecting gate for his next flight.

———

"HE NEVER BOARDED his flight to Tulsa. We had three teams at Minneapolis-St. Paul International within thirty minutes of his flight arriving from San Francisco. Nothing after that. His boarding pass to Tulsa was never used. We even managed to get a US Marshal on the flight, she saw nothing."

Ryan Clark listened silently to Kruger's briefing. At the conclusion, he said, "They spooked him."

Kruger nodded, "We didn't have time to set it up properly. I'm not surprised."

"So now what?"

"I'm leaving for Washington later today. The Bureau is putting a top priority on this. We'll have all kinds of assets in Tulsa by the end of the day. They've even put a plane at my disposal."

Clark chuckled. "Wouldn't you know it, I get shot and you get chauffeured around in a private jet."

Kruger shrugged. "I was planning on leaving as soon as I knew you were okay. Your doctor said, under certain conditions, we could transfer you back to Baltimore in the morning. I've arranged for a Bureau jet to meet those conditions and fly you first thing tomorrow. An ambulance will be waiting to transfer you to Walter Reed Hospital where you'll start your rehab. Plus, the agency is picking up the tab."

Clark smiled, reached to shake Kruger's hand and grimaced as a spasm of pain spread across his chest and back. "I've never been shot before. It kind of sucks."

"I've never had a partner shot before, and it does suck."

He was silent for a few seconds as he watched his friend's pain subside.

"Ryan, I spoke to Seltzer this morning. The director retroactively made you a full-time agent yesterday. He wants you to officially join the agency after your recovery."

"I'll have to think about it. Not sure I want to give up my safe and lucrative job at APD," Clark said with a grin.

Kruger returned the grin. "It's there if you want it. Get your shoulder back to normal, then we'll discuss it further." He glanced at his watch and continued, "I have to go. My ride lands in an hour. I'll see you when you get to Walter Reed."

THE AGENCY JET provided a quick and less stressful flight back to Washington, D.C. Seltzer picked him up at the airport and by 7 p.m. Eastern Time, they were pulling into the parking lot at FBI headquarters. As soon as they entered the building, an agent escorted them directly to the director's office where Stumpf and a light dinner buffet were waiting.

Kruger fixed a small salad and picked at it. He remained quiet, waiting for someone else to start the conversation. Finally Director Stumpf said, "We've no idea where Ortega is. He's vanished. I'm open for any ideas, gentlemen."

"He's on his way to Tulsa," said Kruger. "My guess is he's driving. He probably ditched the Duane Horton ID after we spooked him in Minneapolis."

"Tulsa seems a stretch to me. All you have are a few sketchy hints."

Nodding, Kruger stirred the salad leaves for several seconds and put down his fork. He looked up, placed his elbows on the table, grasped his hands together and placed it against his chin. "What if they're communicating somehow besides the emails? What if they're using disposable cell phones? We can track them with the emails, but if cell phones are being used…"

Paul Stumpf nodded, "There is only one way to find out." He picked up his cell phone and punched in a number.

Chapter Thirty-Eight

FORT MEADE, MD

Friday Morning

AS A TWENTY-YEAR VETERAN of the navy, Nick Carroll had spent the last ten of those years in signals intelligence or in the alphabet soup of government, SIGINT. Now he worked for the NSA. He made more money, got to sleep in his own bed at night and had a regular eight-to-five job. He also got to work on his fluency in Farsi and Urdu.

His newly poured cup of coffee was still steaming as he sat down in his cubicle. Out of the corner of his eye, he noticed his immediate supervisor approaching. Holly O'Brien walked up and smiled. She said, "I've got a wild goose chase for you this morning."

Nick looked at her and sipped his coffee. "Yeah, what kind?"

"Right up your alley, Nick."

He sipped his coffee again and held his hand out for the memo.

She shook her head. "It's not on paper."

Frowning, Nick pulled his hand back. "Not on paper?"

"Nope. This is a special favor from our director. He's doing a favor for his counterpart over in the Hoover Building."

Nick's brow wrinkled and his eyes narrowed. "Holly, am I going to be comfortable with this request?"

"Probably not. But you don't have a choice. You're the victim of your own success."

"What's the request?"

"Nothing taxing, but we need you to write an algorithm to search domestic to foreign calls for a few new tag words. Run it on foreign to domestic calls also."

"What are the key words?"

She shook her head, "They seem silly, but who knows." She handed him a small five-by-seven sheet of paper from a yellow pad.

Nick glanced at it, read it twice and then looked up.

"Most of these are common key words," he said. "Do you know how many hits we will get with 'Tulsa,' 'container' and 'Port of Houston'?"

She shrugged. "Probably a lot. Just run the algorithm and we'll see what the results are. Maybe it will make sense then."

"How far back?"

"Let's try six months. If you get nothing go back a year. See what you get. I was told to key in on those three words first."

"Okay, I'll let you know."

By noon, Nick Carroll was seeing a pattern emerge, a troubling pattern. He stood and walked to Holly's office. He tapped on the door as he walked in. "You got a second?"

She looked up and smiled. "No, but I'll make time. What'd you find?"

"I went back a year. Not much until about five months ago."

"Okay. What happened then?"

"Lots of hits for two weeks. Then nothing for a few weeks, then the activity started again. It stopped until a week ago and now…"

She frowned. "What'd you find, Nick?"

"Now, mind you, there was a lot of clutter I had to filter out, but the troubling calls are in Farsi."

She was quiet as she waited for him to finish.

He swallowed and took a deep breath. "If I had to guess, there's going to be a major terrorist attack on the Friday after Memorial Day."

"Where?"

Shaking his head, "The target is never mentioned, but it will be in the center of the country."

She glanced at a calendar. "That's next Friday."

He nodded. "Yeah, it is."

She was quiet as she stared at the calendar. She stood, crossed her arms over her chest and walked closer to the calendar on the wall. "Keep searching. Expand if you have to, but find out where. I'll call the director."

The Hoover Building
Friday afternoon

"THE COMPUTER in Baltimore hasn't been online for several days." JR paused. "Ortega has been offline as well. If they figured out how we're tracking them and switched to new computers..."

Kruger had excused himself from the meeting and had found an unoccupied office to check in with JR. "What, JR?"

"We're screwed. I won't be able to track them."

Standing next to a window overlooking Pennsylvania Avenue and the National Archives, Kruger was silent as he as listened to JR.

"The computer in Dallas has been offline as well. What is it, Charlie?" There was a short pause, "Hold on, Sean, Charlie has something."

The phone was silent for almost five minutes. Kruger was getting ready to end the call and redial when JR said, "Charlie just got a hit on the Baltimore computer. It accessed the internet, left a message and signed off. Charlie is accessing the email account. Do you want to wait or call back?"

"I'll call you back in fifteen minutes." Kruger ended the call and sat down in the chair behind the desk. He closed his eyes and took a deep breath. Letting it out slowly, he suddenly felt weary. If he took the SAC position in Kansas City, there would have to be restrictions on his travel. He'd crisscrossed the country several times in the last two weeks. With a new marriage less than twenty-two days old, he'd been gone for half of it. Would anything really change? Probably not.

Other questions swirled in his mind. Could he still give one hundred percent? Did he even want to anymore? Would his marriage survive?

His answer to all three questions was, no. His first

marriage had been based on sex more than love. As time passed, he remembered it more like a long bad date, than a marriage. After she left, he completely forgot about her and moved on with his life. Still, it had taken him years to realize how shallow their relationship had been.

But now, with Stephanie, it was totally different. Their relationship was based on friendship, trust, respect for each other, and a shared longing for something other than their careers. He would not jeopardize their relationship; she was too important to him.

Suddenly realizing he was thinking of personal problems and not the investigation startled him. This was a first.

Kruger smiled in the dark room. His metamorphosis was complete. The devotion to the agency and the job had been a substitute for devoting himself to someone else. Someone like Stephanie who would, for lack of better words, be his partner in life.

The vibrating cell phone brought him back to reality. Glancing at the caller ID, he noticed almost half an hour had gone by. He answered it, "Kruger."

"Thought you were calling back in fifteen minutes?"

"Sorry, got tied up. What'd you find?"

"It's the Baltimore computer. He's asking Ortega if he should finish the contract on Griffin. Ortega's computer hasn't accessed the internet at this point."

"Where did he access the internet?"

"A Starbucks located on Cherry Hill Road in Baltimore."

"Has that location been used before?"

There was silence on the phone, he heard the phone muffled and voices in the background. Finally, JR said, "Uh... Sorry about that. I didn't think of it, but yes, he's used it several times."

Kruger thought for a second before saying, "Check his other access points and see if they triangulate."

"Charlie's already working on it. Your question cleared some cobwebs in our brains. Hold on." The phone was muffled again, but he heard, "I didn't think of that. Charlie, yeah it makes sense... Hey, Kruger, Charlie thinks the Baltimore contact lives around the Cherry Hill Road area, close to Patapsco Plaza. He's never used an access point outside of that general area."

"Well, it's more than we had thirty minutes ago. Have Charlie email me all of the locations used by that computer. I'll see if we can get several surveillance teams to stake them out."

The call ended and Kruger walked back to Stumpf's office. Opening the door, he saw Stumpf on the phone and Seltzer studying an open file at a conference table. He noted the presence of two stacks of files, one on his right and one on the left. Seltzer looked up and said, "Got anything?"

Kruger nodded. "We think he's in the Cherry Hill area of Baltimore. I need to set up surveillance teams on several locations in the morning. No guarantees, but at least it's a starting point."

Stumpf motioned for Kruger to sit down in one of the two chairs in front of his desk. He continued listening to the caller on the other end of the call, nodding occasionally and making notes. After several more minutes, he ended the call, replaced the handset in the cradle and said, "That was an interesting call."

Seltzer had walked over from the conference table and sat in the chair next to Kruger. He said, "How so?"

Looking at Kruger, Stumpf said, "It appears there's a growing interest in your career by the President, Sean. He was impressed with your contributions to the removal of my predecessor. He got a big chuckle when told about your 'fool following the fool' comment. When I mentioned you are planning to retire after this investigation is over, he expressed disappointment. That phone call was from his Chief of Staff. You and I are scheduled to meet with the President at fifteen till six tonight. He has fifteen minutes for us."

Kruger was quiet for a few seconds. "I'll try not to mention I didn't vote for him."

———

LIKE THE VAST majority of citizens in the United States, Kruger had never been in the Oval Office. He, Stumpf and a presidential assistant made small talk as they waited for the President to arrive from a meeting. Finally the President entered the office, walked up to Stumpf, shook his hand and said, "Thanks for coming, Paul." He turned, shook Kruger's hand and said, "Agent Kruger, I've been looking forward to meeting you. I also wanted to personally thank you for your service over the past twenty-five years. I understand you're scheduled to retire soon."

Kruger caught himself before stuttering. He cleared his throat. "That is correct, sir."

The President nodded and walked over to a coffee service. "Coffee, anyone?" Stumpf also went to the coffee service and poured one for himself. Kruger shook his head, not trusting himself to drink a cup of coffee in the Oval Office without spilling it. The President took a seat at his desk and motioned for the two other men to sit. Finally he said, "Sean, Paul has briefed me on your career. An impressive collection of successfully closed cases."

"Thank you, sir."

"I hate to see someone with your experience and talents leave the agency at such a young age. May I ask why you're retiring?"

"It's a personal decision, sir."

The President nodded. "Does it have something to do with traveling and your recent marriage?"

Embarrassed, Kruger looked at Stumpf, then back to the President. He said, "To be honest, sir, it has everything to do with it."

"What if we assured you there would be less traveling and a supervisory role?"

Kruger glanced at Paul Stumpf, shifted his position in the chair and cleared his throat.

"With all due respect, Mr. President, I'm not a supervisor. I'm an investigator. I have to go where the crime occurred, wherever the location. The fact is, to do this job properly takes a lot of travel to various locations and staying as long as it takes to get results. I'm just not willing to do that anymore. If I'm not willing to give one hundred percent to the agency, then it is time for me to retire and move on."

The President smiled. "The truth, something this town isn't known for. I respect your reasons, Sean, but I'm not used to people telling me no. I would really like for you to think about taking the SAC position in Kansas City. Please give it a lot of thought."

Kruger smiled and nodded, "I will, sir."

Before the President could say anything else, his Chief of Staff opened the door, walked quickly to his side and leaned over to speak into the President's ear. As he spoke, he handed the President a piece of paper, and the President's eyes grew wide. The Chief of Staff quickly walked out of the room.

"Paul, we have a serious development," the President said. "I was just informed the inquiry I authorized for you this morning has produced results."

Stumpf raised his eyebrows, "What did they learn, sir?"

"It appears there is a terrorist attack planned on an unnamed location in the center of the country. And," he paused and looked at Kruger, "it's planned for next Friday."

Chapter Thirty-Nine

ALEXANDRIA, VA

Friday Evening

KRUGER DETESTED DRIVING agency pool cars. First, they screamed law enforcement, and second, they were generally cars in their last few hours of service. Despite the rules against it, he always rented a car while in Washington, D.C. This time it was a new Mustang. Unlike his personal car, this was a six-cylinder model, but it had good acceleration and was definitely a major improvement over a pool car.

His first priority after the meeting at the White House was to drive by Congressman Griffin's residence. Once he had a chance to see the area, he would drive to the airport to meet the plane transporting Ryan Clark from San Francisco.

As he approached the house, nothing looked unusual or disturbed. After driving past, he noticed a motorcyclist taking a break on the side of the street and drinking what appeared to be a cup of coffee. It seemed a bit odd, but not enough to stop.

On his return pass, the motorcycle was gone. From the street, the congressman's house looked secure, nothing unusual. After the incident in San Francisco, Griffin had hired an outside security agency to improve security at the home. From what Kruger could tell, they had not started yet. Glancing at his watch, he noticed there was just enough time to get to the airport before Clark's flight landed.

Three hours later, he was sitting in a hospital room at Walter Reed and listening to Clark. He was talkative and his demeanor back to normal. Clark said, "Do you think the guy here in Baltimore knows anything about what's supposed to happen next Friday?"

"We won't know till we have a chance to talk to him. It was amazing how many agents were suddenly available once this new threat was uncovered. The Wi-Fi spots he frequents have round the clock surveillance."

Clark nodded. "What about Griffin's house? Anybody watching it?"

"Not yet. The congressman won't be back until tomorrow morning. I drove by before meeting you at the airport. Looked quiet. The only thing I saw when I cruised past was a motorcyclist taking a break on the side of the road drinking coffee."

Clark looked at him and tilted his head to the side. "You saw a motorcyclist drinking coffee? On the side of the road? You're kidding me. You didn't stop and ask him what the heck he was doing?"

"What? I thought it bit odd, but there's no crime against… Wait a minute." Kruger stood and started pacing. "Why do I have an uneasy feeling about this?"

Clark straightened up in his bed. "Did I ever tell you what we saw on the security tape at the Starbucks?"

Kruger stopped pacing and turned toward Clark. "No, you never did."

"We saw a motorcyclist pull up beside Rousch's Mercedes, point a pistol at the driver, fire twice and speed away. Two quick, clean shots, and he's gone."

"What was the color and make of the bike?"

"We couldn't tell color. It was an old grainy black and white security camera. The details of the bike were hard to determine, angle of the camera was bad. But one of the patrol officers who watched the video said it looked like a Yamaha."

Kruger was silent.

"Shit. The guy was parked and watching Griffin's house. I drove right by him."

"Sean, these guys aren't giving up and they don't mind taking chances. You need to find a backup. I mean it."

Nodding, Kruger gave his friend a grim smile. "I know, I just don't trust anybody out here. Only guy I trust is lying in a hospital bed telling me to be careful."

Clark smiled. "Can't help it."

Kruger glanced at his watch.

"I need to get going. Griffin is scheduled to arrive around noon tomorrow. The security company he hired will need to know about the motorcyclist. They're all ex-military, specialize in high profile clients. From what I've been told, they're very good at what they do."

"Watch your back and be careful."

SATURDAY MORNING

. . .

THE ONLY DIFFERENCE Kruger noticed at the Griffin residence from his earlier drive-by on Friday was the presence of three vehicles, a dark metallic gray GMC Yukon XL Denali and two black Range Rover Sports. All three SUVs had dark tinted windows to render the interiors unobservable. He parked the Mustang on the street next to the driveway, got out and surveyed the neighborhood. It was just after noon and quiet. He had not encountered another vehicle since driving into the gated community.

Kruger clipped his badge to his belt and turned his attention to the house. Standing by the front entrance, he noticed two men scrutinizing his arrival. Their closely cropped haircuts, dark Oakley sunglasses and gray business suits identified them as security. The taller of the two men started walking toward him as Kruger walked up the driveway. After identifying himself, he was escorted into the house and introduced to Lance Harpool.

Harpool was in his early 40s with short blond hair. The suit he wore was nice, but not expensive, with the coat slightly larger than needed for hiding the shoulder holster under his arm which held an H&K MP5 K. His deeply tanned slender face, non-descript nose, and steel blue eyes appraised Kruger as they shook hands.

"Nice to meet you Agent Kruger, I understand you saved the congressman's life in San Mateo. What can I do for you?

Kruger said, "Yesterday afternoon, around one, I drove by and saw a motorcyclist sitting across the street staring at this property. He was leaning against his bike drinking coffee."

Harpool's eyebrows rose as he stared at Kruger. "Unusual, but does it have anything to do with the congressman?"

Nodding, Kruger continued, "I believe so. I was informed yesterday afternoon that a motorcyclist was responsible for a murder connected to the threat against Congressman Griffin. I don't like coincidences, Mr. Harpool, do you?"

Harpool was quiet, his gaze never wavering from Kruger. "No, I don't, Agent Kruger. Follow me."

As Kruger followed Harpool he said, "Can we dispense with the 'agent' and 'mister' crap?"

Harpool turned back to look at Kruger with a grin on his face. "Agreed, too many wasted words."

At the back of Griffin's house, they entered a room converted into a high-tech communication and security center. The room's normal furnishings had been removed and replaced with two eight-feet folding tables, each against an adjacent wall. Two people, a man and a woman, occupied the room and were seated at the tables. Each wore a headset with microphone and ear piece and were watching numerous 40-inch flat-screen monitors. Each screen contained six split screen images from different security cameras positioned somewhere on the property. Harpool pointed at one screen and said, "These are the cameras monitoring the front of the house and the roads to the east and west. We should be able to watch any vehicle traveling the road. The cameras are good enough to record license plate numbers, should we need to check them."

Kruger gave a quick nod, pleased with what he was seeing. "Are there any cameras monitoring the back part of the property?"

Harpool pointed to other monitor and said, "These shots are from different cameras located about halfway to the property line, and these are on both corners of the house. They're sensitive to motion and have a one hundred-and-eighty-degree visual range. We should be able to detect anybody trying to access the house from the back."

Kruger smiled. "When did you do all this? I drove by earlier and didn't detect any preparation."

Harpool looked at Kruger without changing his expression. "That's what we do. You aren't supposed to detect any changes. Let me show you the rest of it."

They were in the backyard when Harpool stopped, listened to his ear bud for ten seconds, and said, "Griffin's limo is heading this way, ETA five minutes. If you'll excuse me, I need to make sure everything is ready."

Kruger returned to the security room to watch the arrival of the congressman and check the street monitors. The congressman's limo was met by four security agents, who hustled him into the house. Another agent retrieved the luggage from the trunk, and the limo backed out of the driveway. Just as Kruger was getting ready to leave the room and talk to Griffin, he noticed a motorcycle heading toward the camera facing the east. He tapped the screen and said to the woman monitoring it, "Can you record the motorcycle?"

The agent quickly started typing on her keyboard and said, "No problem, we can record it coming and going."

They watched as the bike passed the limo, slowed slightly as it came adjacent to the house, then sped back up after it passed the driveway. Kruger said, "I need a shot of the license plate and bike. Can you email from this station?"

She smiled and said, "Sure can, where do you need the file sent?"

Kruger wrote Charlie Craft's email address on a note pad and handed it to the agent. He excused himself and stepped out of the room to call Charlie.

He answered on the fourth ring, "Sean, just heard the congressman is returning to D.C early."

"Yeah, he just got here. Charlie, you're going to receive an email with a video showing a motorcycle. I need the license plate traced and I need it yesterday."

"Okay, where's the picture coming from?"

"I'm at the congressman's house. The security team here has some sophisticated cameras and just recorded a bike in front of the house. I suspect the motorcycle may have been involved in the murder of Kyle Rousch."

Charlie was silent for a few seconds, then said, "Just got something. Let me open the attachment." Kruger heard Charlie muttering to himself, and then he said, "Good quality video, but the license plate is partially obscured. Let me work with JR and see what we can do. I'll call you back."

Thinking there might be a better picture available, Kruger returned to the security room, opened the door and said, "Is there a better view of the license plate?"

The agent monitoring the road turned and shook her head, "Not at the moment. Looks like he obscured it on purpose. He'll have to return this way since the road is a dead-end two miles to the west. We'll try again."

"Thanks, keep me posted."

Kruger shut the door and headed to the front of the house where the congressman was being briefed by his security team. When he saw Kruger, he raised his hand to stop Harpool, walked quickly to Kruger, and shook his hand. "Agent Kruger, I never got the opportunity to thank you for protecting my wife and me. We're in your debt." Griffin paused, and said, "How is the agent who was shot?"

"He's doing well, Congressman, thank you for asking. You've hired a good team here. From what I've observed, they're taking every precaution. However, I must insist that you refrain from stepping outside unless they are aware of it."

Nodding, Griffin said, "I failed to heed your warning in San Mateo. I won't make that mistake again. I'll do as they instruct."

Harpool stepped over and said, "Congressman, we will need your schedule so we can plan any trips."

"Very well, I'll have that to you by evening. In the meantime, I need to make some calls. Will you both excuse me?" He retreated to his study and closed the door.

Kruger's cell phone vibrated. He glanced at the "Unknown" caller ID and quickly accepted the call. "What'd you find?"

"We can't determine the last two digits of the license," JR said. "However, it's a Virginia plate and their Department of Motor Vehicles shows at least thirty-two possible matches. The motorcycle on this video is a Yamaha; only five of the plates belong to a bike of that type. Of those five, only three are in the Alexandria area, and the other two are in the western part of the state."

"Three is better than thirty-two. Send me the names and addresses and I'll start checking them."

THE FIRST ADDRESS was in a quiet neighborhood in the Huntington area. As Kruger drove past the house, he noted two bicycles leaning against the side of a detached garage with a basketball hoop above the garage door. The house had been built in the '50s and appeared well maintained. Two mature oak trees shaded the front porch. On his second pass, he watched as a Chevy Equinox pulled into the driveway. When the SUV parked, two boys on the verge of being teenagers, jumped out and ran into the house. Kruger pulled into the driveway, blocking the Chevy from escaping.

A woman in her mid-to-late 30s was unloading a cargo bay full of grocery sacks. She turned toward the street when she heard his car stop. She smiled, but he noticed it appeared forced, her face reflecting a slight concern. Kruger stood outside the car with his arm on the door and in a non-threatening voice said, "Excuse me. Is this Phillip Morgan's residence?"

The woman said, "Yes, I'm Beverley Morgan, can I help you?"

"Is your husband here, Mrs. Morgan?"

The woman glanced toward the house. Kruger could tell she was feeling nervous as she said, "No, he's at work, but I expect him any second. Excuse me, what is this about?"

Kruger reached into his sport coat and retrieved his ID.

"My name is Sean Kruger, I'm with the FBI," he said as he held his ID and badge case so she could see them. "Does your husband own a Yamaha motorcycle?"

She relaxed slightly, but was still hesitant. "Yes, but he had an accident with it this winter. He parked it and hasn't ridden it since."

Disappointed, Kruger said, "Mrs. Morgan, I apologize for the intrusion, but it's critical I see the motorcycle."

"It's in the garage. What's this about, Mr. Kruger?"

He closed the Mustang's door, approached her and offered his ID again. She looked closer at it and noticeably relaxed. He said, "A bike similar to your husband's was identified at a crime scene. I really need to see the motorcycle, Mrs. Morgan. If it's damaged, then I can clear it."

She opened the garage with the remote and showed him

the motorcycle. It was definitively not the bike they were looking for. The front wheel was bent and the rear tire flat. He then noticed that the bike was missing its license plate. He said, "Mrs. Morgan, did your husband remove the license plate?"

She looked at the bike and said, "I don't know; he didn't mention it. Is that important?"

He said, "It could be. Would you call him and ask?"

She nodded, went back to the driver's side of the SUV, reached in for her purse, found her cell phone and made a call. While she was talking, Kruger used his cell phone to take several pictures of the wreaked motorcycle.

As he was reviewing the pictures, she returned to the garage and handed Kruger the phone, "Phillip wants to speak to you."

Kruger took the phone and said, "Agent Kruger."

———

AFTER CHECKING the other two motorcycles on his list, Kruger was confident the Morgan bike was the one he needed. It was almost 6 p.m. when he returned. Phillip Morgan was waiting for him in the garage when Kruger parked his car in the drive way.

Kruger introduced himself and said, "I appreciate you taking time to tell me about the bike, Mr. Morgan. What happened to it?"

"I used to really enjoy riding it, you know. But as the boys got involved in more activities, not so much. The last time I rode it was last March. I hit a patch of wet pavement, lost control and hit a curb. That bent the front wheel, scraped the paint and blew the rear tire."

Kruger looked closer at where paint had been scraped

away in the accident. He noticed some of the metal parts were starting to rust. He said, "Where would you have lost the license plate?"

"I'm afraid I don't really know. It's been here since my accident, except for the short time it was at a repair shop by Reagan National. They wanted too much to fix it, so I brought it home last weekend. I'll probably sell it before I fix it."

Nodding, Kruger said, "Could you give me the address of the repair shop?"

Thirty minutes later, Kruger parked his rental in front of the repair shop. It was almost seven on a Friday night, and he was concerned the shop would be closed. To his surprise, someone was still there, doing paperwork. He knocked on the office door and said, "Are you the owner?"

"Yep, name's Doug Sanders, owner, mechanic, janitor, you name it, I do it here. What can I do for you?"

Kruger showed his ID and said, "I'm Sean Kruger with the FBI. Can I ask you a few questions?"

"If it's about the bikes that were stolen, yeah, you can. Not sure what I could help you with if it's about something else."

"What do you mean, stolen bikes?"

"Already talked to the police. They weren't much help, haven't seen a detective yet."

Kruger tapped his foot and took a deep breath. "What about the bikes?"

"Last Friday night, someone broke in here and stole three bikes, two Hondas and a Yamaha. Broke the lock on the back door, pushed them out the door and loaded them onto a pickup. At least that's what the cop said. Haven't spoken to a detective yet. That part of it kind of pisses me off. I can't file an insurance claim until they do their report. Can you file the report for me?"

Smiling, Kruger said, "No, I'm here for a different reason, but they may be related. Could you look at your records and see if Phillip Morgan's Yamaha was still here when the other bikes were stolen?"

"Don't have to look it up. I can tell you it was. I was tired of it taking up space. I finally told him I was going to sell it for storage fees if he didn't pick it up. He did last Monday. Why?"

"Was the bike functional?"

"Hell, no, he hadn't taken care of it for years. The bike had mechanical issues, not including the bent front wheel."

"His license plate is missing. Do you remember if it was on the bike when he picked it up?"

Sanders chuckled. "Son, I've got a good memory, but it's not that good. No, I wouldn't be able to tell you. I was just glad the bike was gone."

"Mr. Sanders, I'm going to do you a favor. A bunch of really good FBI investigators will be coming here to check out your robbery. That should help you get the paperwork to your insurance company."

"Hallelujah. I can get three owners off my back."

An hour later, Seltzer and five forensic techs arrived and went to work. While waiting for them to arrive, Kruger had contacted the owner of the stolen Yamaha and asked her to come to the repair shop with pictures of her bike.

When she arrived, Kruger took the best picture of the Yamaha and photographed it with his cell phone. He immediately sent the picture in a text message to JR for comparison with the security video from Griffin's house.

Thirty minutes after their arrival, one of the techs

walked up to Seltzer and said, "Sir, I think I found something in the back."

Seltzer said, "Sean, this is Julie Bergman. She specializes in vehicle tracking. What'd you find, Julie?"

"Well, sir, I found distinct tire tracks back there. I can see where the three bikes were loaded into a van. The width of the rear axle is consistent with an older model Ford Econovan. Tire tread and type indicate it was more than likely a U-Haul. I've seen enough of them to recognize the pattern."

Seltzer pulled out his cell phone. "I'll make a call. We'll start contacting local rental locations and see which ones had a van out that night." He walked away, the phone against his ear.

At the same time, Kruger received a text message from Charlie. It read: "Stolen Yamaha is the same make and model as bike in security photo." Kruger looked at Julie and said, "If we find the right U-Haul van, can you match it to the tracks back there?"

"Yes, sir, I can."

Kruger smiled.

Chapter Forty

TULSA, OK

Saturday

THE DRIVE to Tulsa had taken over fourteen hours. Ortega had spotted the surveillance teams at the Minneapolis airport just before he entered the gate area for his flight to Tulsa. Realizing what they were, he left the airport and took a taxi to the Mall of America. There he wandered around trying to decide how to get out of Minneapolis.

Most of the mall stores closed around 9 p.m. After determining the only way to secure a car was to steal one, he settled on an elderly man who he had eavesdropped on earlier in the evening. The man worked in the suit department at JC Penney. He lived alone and was planning on going straight home after work.

Ortega waited outside the employee entrance and followed, at a discreet distance, the man to his car. As the elderly man fumbled with his keys to the ten-year-old Honda Accord, Ortega came up from behind, grabbed him by the neck and swiftly broke it. He lowered the limp figure to the pavement and unlocked the door. He then opened the back door and lifted the dead man into the floor of the back seat.

An hour after leaving Minneapolis, just north of Faribault, he stopped the car on the bridge over a tributary of Wells Lake. I-35 was deserted at this time of night, so he waited until no headlights could be seen in either direction. Opening the passenger side back door, he lifted the body out of the back floor and eased it over the short railing into the water below. After hearing the splash, he quickly shut the door and returned to the driver's side.

The remaining part of the drive was uneventful.

Guided by the GPS function on his cell phone, Ortega arrived at the address texted to him several days ago by the man he knew as Acosta. Its location was just north of I-244 and south of the airport. The building looked abandoned, as did the rest of the warehouses in the industrial park. He parked the Honda next to the loading dock and got out. The only sounds he could hear were birds chirping and the muffled roar of jet engines in the distance.

He walked around the building until he found a door to what looked like office space. Turning the handle of the door, it opened. Weaponless, he cautiously opened the door. The interior was dark and smelled of dust and rotting paper. He closed the door and walked back to the Honda. When he got back to the car, the man he knew as Acosta was leaning against it with a Glock in his hand. He said, "You're late. About two days late. Where have you been?

"Couldn't help it."

"Why?"

Ortega shrugged. "The FBI found me, somehow."

Abbas' expression stayed neutral and he continued to

glare at Ortega. "What do you mean, 'The FBI found me, somehow'?"

"Just that. They had the airport staked out. I couldn't get on my flight in Minneapolis. I had to drive."

Abbas was quiet. His eyes narrowed and he stopped leaning against the car. "Where did you get this car?"

"Let's just say I borrowed it. The owner didn't need it any longer."

Abbas was on Ortega in a flash. He grabbed him by the collar and put the barrel of the gun under his chin. He said through clinched teeth, "You fool. Have you led them here?"

Ortega pushed Abbas away. "No. I'm not stupid, Acosta. Apparently they've been tracking me through the computer. I haven't used it since I was in San Francisco." He paused and watched a passenger jet flying low on its approach to the airport. "My guess is they found Cooper's computer."

"Get the car into the warehouse. There are not many people around here, but I do not need attention from the ones that are."

He turned and walked toward the now open freight door. Ortega got into the Honda and thought about leaving. He stared at the open warehouse door for several long moments. Finally, he started the car and drove into the warehouse.

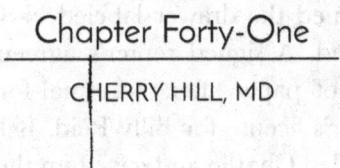

Chapter Forty-One

CHERRY HILL, MD

Saturday Morning

THE OWNERS and managers of the rental facilities were not happy about having to meet the FBI at their facilities this late on a Friday night and, in some cases, very early Saturday morning. Most took their time arriving. Finally at four a.m. at a location in Takoma Park, MD, they found the van. Julie was able to match the tread marks and found several traces of motorcycle oil in the back cargo area. Seltzer arrived at 5:30 a.m. with a search warrant after the owner refused to provide the identity of the renter.

Even with the search warrant, the owner refused to turn on his computer. Seltzer turned to Kruger and said, "Place him under arrest, Sean. I'm tired of fucking with him."

After the owner was in the back of a local police car, Seltzer turned to Julie and said, "Can you get that computer working?"

She smiled and nodded. Ten minutes later, she said, "Found the rental agreements. Hmmm... No wonder this guy didn't want us on his computer. He's been filing false insurance claims for already existing damage."

Kruger chuckled. "Go for it, Julie, you can have the bust. I want the guy who rented the van."

"Here it is." She paused as she read the information. "There's a reference to a paper file. Check one of the file drawers under Reid, Billy."

Kruger opened the drawer labeled N-S and found the file she identified. A signed renter's agreement was there. The first piece of paper after the rental form was a paper copy of a driver's license for Billy Reid, Beltsville, MD. He immediately called Charlie and gave him the driver's license number.

Charlie said, "Do you want me to call you back or wait?"

"I'll wait."

Two minutes later, Charlie was back on the phone. "Sean, the guy's ex-military. Didn't serve under Ortega, but was in the same locations in Iraq. Here's the clincher. He's a decorated marksman. Pistols and rifles. He's won a bunch of inter-service competitions and has all the citations to prove it. He went through sniper training, but was injured in an IED explosion on his first mission."

"Good work, Charlie, keep digging."

He turned to Seltzer and held the paper up.

"This is our guy. He was a certified marksman in the army, trained as a sniper and served in the same area of Iraq as Ortega. We need to find him. Now."

———

THE APARTMENT WAS STRATEGICALLY SURROUNDED by FBI tactical agents and the Baltimore SWAT Team by 7 a.m. Kruger was suited up just like the rest of the assault team, Kevlar Tact Vest and helmet. He would be the fifth agent to enter the apartment. With his Glock out and ready, he gave the order to breach the door.

The two agents in front swung the breaching bar. With a loud crack, the door jamb splintered, and the door flew open crashing against an inside wall. Two FBI tactical agents entered first, AR-15s in ready position, yelling "FBI...FBI..." The agents who popped the door dropped the breaching bar and immediately followed. As Kruger entered the apartment he heard the words, "Drop the weapon—now." There was more shouting, and finally, "All clear. Suspect in custody."

He holstered his Glock and watched as a thin man with burn scars on his face, hands cuffed behind him, was escorted down the narrow hall. Kruger stood in the middle of the living area, arms crossed, as the two FBI agents stopped the prisoner in front of him.

Kruger said, "Are you William Reid?"

The man just glared at Kruger, his brown eyes staring straight ahead.

An FBI agent stuck his head out of a bedroom further down the hall and said, "Sean, you'd better see this."

Before walking down the hall toward the bedroom, he was struck by the austere furnishings of the place. A worn sofa with sagging cushions, a cheap pressboard stand with a high-end flat-screen TV and a single bar stool scooted under a breakfast bar were the only furnishings of the living area. Not a single picture hung on the dingy walls, and the paint was so old that it appeared discolored in various locations. Stacks of gaming magazines littered the corners of the room. Fast food wrappers were scattered on the kitchen cabinet top. Dirty dishes were stacked so high in the sink, they touched the faucet. Kruger even detected a faint residual odor of marijuana.

As he entered the room, he immediately saw why the agent called him. A large cork bulletin board was nailed to one of the walls. Pictures of Congressman Roy Griffin and his house were pinned to every square inch of the surface. Kruger examined the pictures. Each had been taken from different angles and locations. Every picture had a clear view of the front door and had handwritten notes notating direction and a number. Kruger stared at the numbers and realized what they were.

"He was scoping the house, measuring distances from each location," he said. A grim smile appeared, and he tapped the one picture with a circle drawn around it. "Good thing we found him. He had a sniper hide picked out."

———

KRUGER RETURNED TO THE STREET. In the command car, Seltzer's cell phone was pressed to his ear by his shoulder. After the call was completed, Seltzer looked up at Kruger, his eyebrows raised. "Well?"

Kruger said, "Reid's got a wall full of pictures of Griffin's house. All of them have distances marked. One has a circle around it."

Seltzer nodded. "I'm heading back. Are you staying, or do you want a ride?"

"I'll ride with you. There are too many agents up there. Besides, I want to watch the interrogation."

BILLY REID SAT with his head down, staring at the top of the table. Two FBI agents, neither of whom Kruger knew, were firing questions at the young man. So far Billy had not answered any of them. One of the agents stood and walked out of the room. He looked around and spotted Kruger. He walked over, turned and glanced at Billy through the one-way mirror. He said, "The guy's stubborn. He's not talking."

Kruger nodded and continued to watch Reid. After a few moments, he said, "He knows all we have on him is the motorcycle theft and taking pictures of Griffin's house. Let me try something."

The agent nodded and both men walked to the interrogation room door. Kruger entered and sat in the empty chair across from Billy.

Billy looked up, a small smile came to his lips. "Who are you?"

"Agent Sean Kruger, Billy. I've come to ask for your cooperation."

Snorting, Billy shook his head. "You want my cooperation, that's funny."

Kruger smiled ever so slightly. "Why do you find it funny, Billy?"

"You guys bust into my place, tear shit up, drag me down here, and you want me to cooperate. That's what's funny. No way I'm cooperating. I want my lawyer."

"I understand and I agree, you do need a lawyer. He'll be here soon. But until he gets here, I need you to tell me something. Where's Ortega?"

Billy's eyes widened, but he quickly recovered and sat further back in his chair. "I don't know anyone called Ortega."

"Sure you do, Billy. He's the one who told you to shoot Kyle Rousch in his Mercedes at the Starbucks."

Billy's eyes grew scared, but he remained quiet.

"You see, Billy, the Starbucks had a security camera that took a perfect picture of you pointing the gun at Rousch's head and pulling the trigger twice."

Billy looked away from Kruger, his eyes darting around from the other agent in the room to the door and then back at Kruger. "No way, I had my helmet on…" Realizing what he had said, Billy slumped in his chair.

Kruger turned to the other agent and said, "Could you excuse us for a few minutes?"

The agent nodded and left the room. When they were alone, Kruger said, "I need your help Billy. I need to find Norman Ortega."

"I don't know where he is. I never talk to him."

"We know how you communicate, Billy. The unsent emails."

"Shit."

"Yeah, you're in it deep, Billy."

Billy nodded.

"If you help us find him, it will go easier on you. Ortega's got something planned, and I need to know what it is, where it will occur and when."

"Ortega takes his orders from someone else. We're paid to do what that guy says. Ortega thinks he's avenging our fallen brothers over in the sandbox. He's so full of shit. I was in it for the money. Look at me, who's going to hire a scarred-up guy like me. The only thing I was ever good at was firing a rifle."

Kruger placed his arms on the table and leaned over. "Billy, you have the means to find him. I have a friend who, with your help, can locate Ortega."

"Are we talking deal here, agent?"

Kruger shrugged. "I can't offer you a deal. That's up to

the prosecutor. But, I'm not above having a friendly chat with him."

Billy stared at Kruger for a very long time. "Griffin was the last one. Why, I don't know. But after we did him, we'd get the rest of our money."

Kruger was quiet as he continued to look at Billy. After a few moments, a bead of sweat ran down Billy's forehead. Finally Kruger shook his head.

"If you're going to lie to me, this isn't going to work."

Billy's voice rose an octave. "I'm not lying. Griffin was the last one. I was supposed to do it here in Washington, but he left for California."

Kruger said nothing.

Billy blinked several times, looked at the mirror, then back at Kruger. "I'm not lying. That was the plan: do Griffin, shut down and disappear. I swear, honest."

Kruger put his elbow on the table, rested his chin on the palm of his hand and sighed. "Not buying it, Billy. Something big is in the works. I need to know what it is."

Reid rolled his eyes to the ceiling. "What do I have to say to make you understand I was a mushroom in this organization?"

"A mushroom?"

"Yeah. Kept in the dark and fed shit."

Kruger chuckled.

"I was nobody, agent. A hired gun, that's all. I wasn't privy to the master plan. If there even was one."

Kruger's cell phone vibrated. He glanced at the caller ID.

"I have to take this," he said, then smiled slightly. "Don't go away."

After leaving the room, he accepted the call. "Kruger."

"Sean, it's Charlie Brewer."

"Hey, Charlie, you got something for me?"

"Yeah, the Imam has disappeared, and so have three of the young men he visited."

"Disappeared?"

"Uh-huh. The three men arrived at the mosque around six last night. We had two teams on the place. One in the front, one in the back. There was no way they could have left and we not see them."

"But now they're gone."

"One of our agents is Muslim. He wasn't on the surveillance teams, but was ready to go into the mosque if needed. Mornings are busy around the place, but not this morning. By noon, the watchers got nervous and sent him in. The place was deserted. Nobody, nothing."

Kruger didn't immediately reply. "Did they search the place?"

"Yeah."

Taking a deep breath, Kruger closed his eyes. "What did they find?"

"A tunnel. A tunnel that leads to another building across the street. We didn't know it, but that building is owned by the mosque."

"They knew they were being watched."

"Yeah, I'd say they did. We don't know when they left, but we think it was after sunset. This neighborhood is pretty dark, not a lot of street lights. Between the time it got completely dark and when we entered the building, sixteen hours elapsed. They could be anywhere."

"Did your surveillance team take pictures of the three men?"

"Yes."

"Send them to Charlie Craft's email."

Chapter Forty-Two

WASHINGTON, D.C.

Saturday Evening

APPROACHING forty-eight hours with little sleep, Kruger struggled to stay awake during a hastily assembled conference call. Even after four cups of coffee, he kept nodding off. Plus, he now had a bad case of indigestion. Seltzer was using the meeting to update the director and, via secure video conferencing, the President.

Seltzer started the meeting. "We are now in possession of Billy Reid's computers. Charlie Craft will return to Washington later today as lead on the forensic investigation of this device.

"Agent Kruger's team has traced the three Muslim men that we had under surveillance to three separate airports. One flew out of San Francisco International, one out of Oakland International and the third out of San Jose International. Destination unknown."

The President looked grim. "Can't we check the airlines to see where they went? Surely you have their names."

Seltzer looked at Kruger, who shook his head.

"Yes sir, we do have their names," Seltzer said. "However, they're flying under false identities. We have no idea of the airline or the flight they took. We just know they entered the airport and went through security. No TSA images were found past security."

The President slowly shook his head. "Gentlemen, I can't emphasize enough how critical it is to stop whatever it is they are planning."

"We understand, Mr. President." It was the first words Stumpf had uttered since the meeting began. "We will stop it, you have my word."

"I sure hope so, Paul. I sure hope so."

The meeting ended and the video screen went dark. Stumpf looked at Seltzer and then at Kruger. "Gentlemen, I do hope I wasn't too optimistic telling that to the president?"

Everyone in the room turned their attention to Kruger, who frowned and shook his head.

"I'm not making any progress sitting here on my ass," he said. "I need to get back to Kansas City as soon as possible."

"You didn't answer my question, Sean. Was I too optimistic?"

"I'm not prepared to answer that question right now, Paul."

————

THE TRIP HOME on a Bureau jet gave Kruger a chance to relax for the first time in days. His thoughts turned to his next steps. Everything they knew about the three men from San Francisco was now in the hands of the Tulsa FBI office.

Kruger felt a moment of guilt about not going straight to Tulsa, but quickly dismissed it. The field office knew what to do. They could get along nicely without him. He was also positive Charlie would make progress with Reid's computer having spent two intense weeks with JR. If Charlie couldn't stand on his own now, he never would.

He opened his eyes just as the plane touched down in Kansas City. The short nap only intensified his weariness. An hour and a half later, he was asleep in his own bed. It was 2:05 a.m. Sunday morning.

The digital clock on his nightstand changed from 11:09 to 11:10 as he stared at it. Where was he? A gentle hand touched his shoulder. Stephanie was sitting on the side of his bed, sipping coffee, and said, "Want some?"

"Depends on what 'some' you're taking about."

She grinned. "Coffee. You have a dirty mind."

"I've been away from my wife for a while. Dirty thoughts are a natural product of separation."

"Brush your teeth; you have morning breath. While you're doing that, I'll get you some coffee."

"SO WHAT'S the interesting news you refused to discuss with me yesterday?" Kruger said after dumping a little Sweet N Low in his coffee and stirring.

Stephanie smiled. "It wasn't something I wanted to discuss on the phone. I heard from the agency Friday. We've been accepted by the mother. As soon as she gives birth, we're parents."

Kruger was silent for several minutes, thinking through the possibilities. "Wow. Didn't realize it would be so soon. How do you feel about it?"

"As soon as we have the baby, I'm taking maternity leave and after that, I'm giving notice. I'm done with the job, Sean. I want to be a full-time mother."

He hugged her. "Good decision. Should we go ahead and put both condos up for sale? This isn't really a good place to raise a kid, no place to play outside."

She placed her head against his chest and said, "I agree. I spoke to a real estate agent while you were gone. She put my condo on the market and we can see how she does before we have her look for us a house."

"What about my place?"

"Not yet, let's see how this goes first."

She pushed away from him and looked straight into his eyes. "I think you should take the promotion."

He let her go, turned away and walked to the kitchen. He pulled a bottle of water out of the refrigerator. "Not sure I want to."

She crossed her arms against her chest. "Why?"

"Not sure I have it in me anymore, Stef. I found myself hesitate several times this past week. That's dangerous. I might hesitate at the wrong moment and then..." The implication of the unfinished sentence was left unspoken.

She walked over to him, put her arms around him and said, "You need to do what's best for you."

He shook his head. "No, I need to do what's best for us."

She nodded. "Guess I was being selfish with my last statement. We both need to do what's best for us." They hugged for a few moments, then she pulled away. "I have to be out of town this coming Thursday and Friday."

"Okay, what's going on?"

"Walmart shareholders meeting is this Friday. One of the issues we discussed at the last top-to-top was the lack of our senior management taking a serious interest in their business. I spoke to Neil, he's still recovering from his injuries and can't go. He's sending me."

"Have fun."

———

THE REST of Sunday was spent talking, making love and having dinner at Houston's. But later that night, Kruger was having trouble sleeping. His mind kept returning to all the possibilities of Tulsa as the destination of the Dallas contact, Ortega and the three Muslim men. After finally drifting off to sleep just after midnight, he woke from a dream and sat up in bed.

"Oh, shit." He stared at the draped window, street lights illuminating them dimly. "Could it be possible?"

Chapter Forty-Three

TULSA, OK

Tuesday

THE CONTAINERS ARRIVED early Tuesday morning. Three dark-skinned young men walked into the warehouse an hour later. They were barely out of their teens. The first one, whom Acosta called Barry, was five-feet-five and stocky, with a round face, curly black hair and a beard. He was also very quiet. He would not look at Ortega or engage in conversation.

The second man was a little older than Barry; Acosta introduced him as Chuck. He was taller than Acosta by several inches and spoke with a slight accent. Ortega recognized the distinct speech patterns of an Iraqi, something Ortega would never forget. The kid did not have a beard, only wispy facial hair. His face was thin and his eyes were a dark brown.

The third man was introduced as Darren. His demeanor was odd, and he seemed distracted when he spoke. His hair was lighter than the others and he was clean-shaven. The eyes were an intense green and he never smiled. Ortega guessed he was the oldest, 22, if that.

As soon as the new recruits arrived, Acosta had them unloading the containers. As they worked, Acosta walked over to Ortega and said, "I have a job for you."

Ortega accepted the folded sheet of paper, looked at Acosta and said, "Don't patronize me, Acosta. This is my operation."

Acosta stared at him, his eyes narrow and lips pressed together. Finally his face relaxed and he smiled. "I found three vans for sale. Each is in a different car lot. I need you to go to each one, pay for the vans and sign all the paperwork. After you're finished, return here and deliver each of our new friends to the car lots. They will drive the vans back here. Simple, right?"

Ortega nodded. "How am I paying for them?"

Acosta smiled and handed him an envelope. "I have negotiated the price of each van over the phone. There are three cashier's checks in the envelope. Each made out to the dealer for the negotiated price. All you have to do is deliver the checks and sign whatever paperwork they require."

"They'll want an ID."

"The vans are being bought under your false name, Duane Horton. You still have the driver's license, don't you?"

Ortega nodded.

"Good. I need the vans here before nightfall."

"Okay, when do we get our final payment?"

"Once the vans are bought and delivered back here, we will settle our account. I will no longer require your services."

"What about Griffin?"

"You tried." Acosta shrugged. "The attempt on his life will suit our purposes."

"Okay, I'll be back as soon as I can."

It took most of the afternoon to find the dealerships, pay for the vans and deliver the quiet dark skinned men to each car lot. After dropping off the last man, he started driving back to the warehouse. About a half mile from the building he pulled off into a parking lot and sat for a while. Nothing was adding up. Why had Griffin all of a sudden become unimportant? The original plan was to build up to Griffin and then shut down. He pulled his cell phone out and texted Billy's phone. Instead of a series of numbers he wrote, *Plan abandoned, no Griffin, break off, will get money to you soon. O.* He hit the send icon and sat for a few more minutes before starting the car. He had a stop to make, then he would return to the warehouse.

CHARLIE CRAFT WAS FRUSTRATED. The time spent with JR had been surreal. He'd learned more in two weeks than he had over the past few years. JR was so much more accomplished at what needed to be done, Charlie felt lost. As he sat in front of Billy Reid's computer, he stared at the screen. He wasn't finding anything they didn't already know. He was about to call JR when Billy's cell phone chirped. Picking it up, he saw there was a text message waiting to be viewed. He opened the message and read it. He immediately called JR.

"SLOW DOWN, Charlie. Take a deep breath and tell me the number that sent the text message?" JR held the cell phone against his ear with his shoulder and waited to write the number down.

Charlie told him. He paused for less than two seconds. "Can we trace that number to a cell tower?"

"That's what I'm doing. But it's going to take time. Call Kruger and let him know what's going on. As soon as I have something, I'll call him."

"How long?"

"I don't know, just tell him I'll call." JR ended the call and started methodically doing what he did best, hacking into secure servers and getting the information he needed—all without leaving a trace an intrusion had occurred.

Three hours later, he punched in a number on his computer and sent a call. It was answered on the third ring.

"Kruger."

"Sean, it's JR."

"Charlie briefed me. What'd you find?

"The location of the cell phone."

Kruger was quiet for a few moments. "Tulsa."

"Yeah, Tulsa. Just like we thought."

"Do you have a location?"

"General area only. The tower was close to the airport."

"Good work, JR. Call Charlie back and tell him. I'm calling Seltzer."

———

ORTEGA WAITED in the Honda as the doors to the warehouse opened. As soon as it was wide enough, he drove into the building, parked and got out. The man he knew as

Acosta was walking rapidly toward him. The three vans were parked next to the unloaded containers.

Acosta got up within a foot of Ortega and yelled, "Where the hell have you been? The vans were back hours ago."

"I stopped and got something to eat."

"For three hours? Are you kidding me?"

Ortega was tired of being ordered around. He started to walk away, but Acosta grabbed his arm.

"Let go of my arm, Acosta."

"Where were you?"

Ortega glared at him. They were eye to eye, less than a foot apart. "I told you, I got something to eat. Now let go of me."

The man released his arm and stood back a few paces. "As you wish. But you haven't answered my question."

"Give me my money and I'll get out of here. I'm tired of your shit."

Abbas reached behind him, pulled out a Glock 19 and pointed it at Ortega. Without a second thought, he pulled the trigger twice.

As he felt his body hit the warehouse floor, Ortega's last emotion before everything went black was relief.

Chapter Forty-Four

TULSA, OK

Wednesday

THE BUREAU PLANE landed at Tulsa International Airport a little after 9:30 a.m. Wednesday. One of the local FBI agents met Kruger in the VIP lounge; Kruger knew him from another case several years back. Kruger offered his hand and said, "How are you, Tom ? What's it been, five years?"

Thomas Stark was taller than Kruger's six feet by three inches. He was high school skinny, with an angular face and closely cropped brown hair. He shook Kruger's hand and smiled, "At least. I've been out of the academy six years and that was one of my first assignments."

Kruger and Stark had worked together on an investigation of a serial killer who used school buses as his shooting platform. "Where was the body found?"

"In an abandoned warehouse about a mile south of the airport. It's still there. The ME believes it happened less than twenty-four hours ago."

"I've seen the guy. Let's go make a positive ID."

Stark nodded and led Kruger out of the airport to a black Chevy Suburban parked at the curb, it's engine idling. Ten minutes later, Kruger was kneeling next to the body of Norman Ortega.

"How was he found so quickly? There doesn't seem to be a lot of traffic around here."

"The owner came by to check on his property. He got an anonymous call. The caller told him something was going on here. The place has been abandoned for almost a year and he doesn't come out very often."

Kruger stood up. "Where is the owner?"

Stark pointed to a small, elderly man about fifty feet away, talking to several police officers. Kruger walked over introduced himself.

"FBI Agent Sean Kruger. Are you the owner of this warehouse?"

The man nodded. "The name's Burt Collins. I own most of these buildings in the complex. Bought them for pennies on the dollar, thought I'd struck it rich. I understand why they were cheap, I can't give them away." He shook his head. "Now I find out some asshole's been using it without paying rent. Worst investment I've ever made."

Kruger rolled his eyes slightly and cleared his throat. "Mr. Collins, there will be some FBI forensic technicians here within the hour. I need you to tell me what's different from the last time you inspected this building?"

Collins snorted and pointed at the two large shipping containers situated one hundred feet further into the building. "Those are different. They weren't here last time I checked on the place."

WEDNESDAY EVENING

"WHAT DO YOU THINK, JULIE?"

Julie Bergman had accompanied Charlie to the warehouse. She was walking back and forth between three marked off areas. "I'm pretty sure we have three distinct vehicles, Sean." She pointed to one spot. "This one was leaking transmission fluid and the distance between tires is consistent with a Ford Econoline, late '90s or early 2000 model." She nodded toward the two other spaces she had marked off. "Those, I'm sure, are two Chevy Express Cargo vans. Probably early 2000s as well. Don't see any leaking fluid from them." She looked at Kruger. "Three vans, all capable of hauling heavy weight."

Frowning, Kruger walked slowly by each marked location. He looked up and noted their proximity to the shipping containers. "They off-loaded something from the containers into the vans, didn't they?"

Julie nodded. "I would say that's correct."

Charlie Craft hurried out of one of the containers and practically ran to where Kruger and Julie stood. "Holy shit, Sean, you have to see this."

They hurried after Charlie and walked into one of the now open containers. Numerous halogen lamps illuminated the interior. Charlie walked to a spot he had marked and knelt down.

"You see this spot?"

Kruger nodded.

"I just did a quick chemical analysis."

"What, Charlie, what is it?"

"It's ANFO."

"Speak English, Charlie."

"Sorry, ammonium nitrate fuel oil, Sean. It's highly explosive."

Kruger cocked his head to the side and blinked several times. "Are you saying they've got three fertilizer bombs?"

"No, no, that's an imprecise description. This is the stuff they use in coal mines, quarries and construction. It's perfectly legal, if you have the right permits."

Thomas Stark, slightly out of breath, joined them in the container and said, "I just got off the phone with Port Authority in Houston. These containers were used by a company that produces olive oil. Guess where they're from?"

Kruger rolled his eyes. "Dammit, Tom, quit playing games. Where, for gawd sake?"

"Tunisia."

"Shit…" Kruger took a deep breath and walked out of the container. As soon as he was out of the warehouse, he punched a number into his cell phone.

"Seltzer."

"Alan, we've got three truck bombs somewhere in Oklahoma."

There was silence on the other end of the call. Finally, Kruger heard, "What do you think the target is?"

"I have no facts to support this, but the proximity of northwest Arkansas to Tulsa is too much of a coincidence, and Friday is the day after tomorrow."

"What's in northwest Arkansas on Friday?"

"The annual Walmart shareholders meeting."

"Ah, shit." There was silence for several moments. "Lay out your theory and I'll run it past Stumpf."

"Alan, I don't have time for another damn meeting. We have exactly a day to find these vans. Local law enforcement needs to be involved now. If I'm wrong about the target, fire me. But I'm not wrong. We know there are three vans. Best guess, one will go up I-44 to Joplin and turn south toward Arkansas on I-49. Another will travel to Fort Smith and head north on I-49, and the third will go straight east on 412. It's a guess, but it's the way I would do it."

"Isn't driving the interstates taking a big risk?"

"They don't know we know about them, Alan."

There was a long silence, which Kruger found annoying.

"Alan, wake up. Don't turn into a bureaucratic asshole now that you're the deputy director. We need to act on this now."

Seltzer cleared his throat. "You're right. I'll get the wheels turning on my end. What do you need?"

"I need the director to contact local, county and state law enforcement in the four-state area. Kansas, Oklahoma, Missouri and, most of all, Arkansas all have to be involved. I also need as many agents as you can get into Fayetteville and Tulsa as fast as you can. We have a manhunt to wage, and we don't even know who we're looking for."

"Anything else?"

"Yeah, lots of prayers."

Chapter Forty-Five

Thursday

AAZIM ABBAS STROLLED the grounds of Razorback Gardens watching with interest the activity around Bud Walton Arena. There was a heavier presence of law enforcement and more security than in prior years. Four years ago, he had purchased shares in Walmart stock and had attended the meetings ever since, each year making notes of security and access points. This year the security preparations for the meeting seemed more intense.

Despite the increased security, he would not abandon his dream. Too much had gone into the preparation and execution. Too many men had given their lives so he could realize his goal of striking at the heartland of America. He would know in twenty-four hours if all of the years of devising tactics, securing the needed funding, formulating contingency plans and recruiting would pay off. Abbas wanted the sleepy, unconcerned, naive middle of America to feel the wrath of jihad.

As he approached the parking lot where his rental car was located, he turned back toward the arena and smiled. Regardless of the outcome, the United States would soon realize no part of their country was safe.

Sitting in the car and watching the activity around the arena, a nagging concern returned. Of the three men the Imam had sent, he was certain two would carry out their assignments. The man he had introduced as Darren was staged in a town called Miami, OK. The man called Chuck was south of Fayetteville in the small town of Van Buren, AR. Both were at small privately owned motels, places used to the coming and going of anonymous men. Each man knew when to leave their hotel on Friday morning. Abbas had made the drive several times from each motel and knew exactly how long it took.

He did not know their real names, nor did he care. They were tools, nothing more. Tools to use as weapons. But he was confident each of these two men were committed.

The man he called Barry was an unknown. Stoic and quiet, Abbas did not believe he had the nerve or the will to go through with his instructions. With each passing moment, Abbas grew more concerned about the third driver. Leaving the parking lot, he headed toward a town on the Oklahoma border. Siloam Springs, AR.

Barry was there with his van, waiting like the others.

———

JR STARED at the computer screen. Sweat formed on his lip. The server in Spain was resisting his efforts to hack into its operating system and files. The computer had an unusually well-designed firewall, easily defeating his efforts to get subtly past the safeguards. At 9:22 p.m. on Thursday, he said to hell with it and crashed through. He was out of time.

As he suspected, the server was a central routing location for the communications between Ortega and the man they had first found in Dallas. Charlie had been able to provide JR with several IP addresses discovered on Ortega's computer.

He figured it was 4:22 a.m. in Barcelona, so he had at least thirty to forty minutes to find the files he needed. He would be gone by 5 a.m. Spain time.

At 4:54 a.m., he found the data he needed and copied it. Before exiting the server, he downloaded a virus. It was one of his more malicious programs and would cause the entire system to crash as soon as he was gone. If he couldn't be subtle with his intrusion, there was no point leaving evidence he had been there.

Now with the data from Spain residing on a laptop hard drive, he started dissecting the file. He discovered a series of emails to the person in Dallas coming from a computer located somewhere in Iran. All were in Pashto and were quickly run through a translation program he liked.

After reading through the emails, he sat back in his chair. As he read through them a second time, he took a deep breath and said, "Oh shit."

He grabbed his cell phone, found the number he needed and hit the call icon. His call was answered on the second ring.

"What's wrong, JR?"

"Sean… Oh man, I think I found the information you need."

IT WAS midnight before Kruger finished making the calls. When he finished, he sat in his hotel room in Fayetteville and took a deep breath. Maybe, just maybe, JR's discovery would help them get through tomorrow without the loss of thousands of lives.

ABBAS KNOCKED on the door to room 161. It was on the back side of the hotel facing away from Highway 412 in Siloam Springs. No response. Frowning, he knocked again. Silence. He took the second key card he had asked for when he rented the room and opened the door. It was empty. The man he knew as Barry was gone. His duffel bag, clothes and toiletries were also gone.

He rushed out of the room and paused. The van was still in its parking spot, exactly where it had been since checking Barry into the room. He checked the doors on the vehicle; they were locked. Returning to the room, he searched for the keys and found them on the nightstand under a folded piece of paper. There was no writing on the paper, just folded and laid on top of the keys.

Taking a deep breath, he sat down on the bed and slowly exhaled. So be it, he would drive the van in the morning. It was too late to back down. He knew he would not see the aftermath of his plan, but Allah willing, it would be glorious.

Chapter Forty-Six

FAYETTEVILLE, AR

Friday Morning

IT WAS 5 a.m. when Kruger arrived at Bud Walton Arena. Sleep had eluded him even though Stephanie had agreed not to attend the shareholders meeting. After repeated attempts to have the meeting cancelled, Walmart management refused, stating they had faith in law enforcement to prevent anything tragic from occurring. Kruger was starting to understand Stephanie's frustration with Walmart management. Reality was not their strong suit.

He was dressed in khakis, blue polo shirt with an FBI emblem on the left breast, black Reeboks, and dark aviator sunglasses. An FBI windbreaker concealed the Glock on his right hip. Three extra magazines were clipped to his belt above his left leg for quick access.

Kruger had just completed walking around the perimeter of Bud Walton arena when Tom Stark approached him. "When do the shareholders start arriving?"

Glancing at his wrist watch, Kruger said, "Meeting starts at seven, it's a little past six now. We should see the bulk of the crowd start arriving in thirty minutes or so."

"Sean, I know we discussed this last night, but what are we looking for?"

"Well, Tom, I hope we don't see anything. With luck, the vans will be stopped before they get here. We have both the Arkansas and Missouri Highway Patrol looking for them, plus all the county sheriffs' departments between Van Buren, Arkansas, and Joplin, Missouri. If our plan works, the vans will be intercepted a long time before they get here."

Stark looked toward the west and said, "What if they don't stop them?"

Kruger took a deep breath. "Then it's up to us."

"I was afraid you would say that."

"Get back to your post. I'll walk the perimeter one more time to check on everyone. Don't worry, Tom, with as many law enforcement personnel looking for these guys as we have, there's little chance these vans will get through to our location."

"Where will you be?"

"I'll be here at the west entrance."

Stark nodded, turned and walked back to his post on the south side of the complex.

As he rubbed the back of his neck, he jumped when his cell phone vibrated. He accepted the call on the forth ring.

"Kruger."

"Everything in place?" It was Alan Seltzer.

"Yes, Alan."

"The director is with the President this morning. He wants regular updates."

"Who do you want to provide these regular updates Alan?"

"You, of course. You're our eyes and ears on the scene."

Kruger shook his head, not believing what he was hearing. "Alan, I'm in the middle of a potential catastrophic terrorist attack. You want me to stop every five minutes and give you an update?"

"Yes."

"Geez, Alan. When did you turn to the dark side?"

Kruger took the phone from his ear, pressed the end call icon and took a deep breath. His decision to retire from the agency after this was over was correct. It was correct, if he survived.

ABBAS STARED out the front windshield of the Chevy van as he started the engine. The sun was just peeking over the horizon. As the engine idled and warmed, his thoughts turned to the other men. He was confident they would fulfill their destiny this morning. He praised Allah and released the parking brake. As he pulled forward, a thought occurred to him. He stopped the van and took out his cell phone. Utilizing Google Maps, he checked alternate routes and smiled. No point in taking chances. There would be plenty of time to meet the deadline.

BY 7 A.M., the number of people filing into the arena was too many to count. Kruger stood several feet south of the sidewalk leading to the west entrance. He scrutinized each individual. Some stared back, but most totally ignored him.

At ten after 7, his cell phone vibrated. He accepted the call and placed the phone to his ear as he walked farther from the sidewalk.

"Kruger."

"Sean, this is Charlie."

"Hey."

"Just got a report from the Missouri Highway Patrol, they've been following a vehicle matching our description for the past twenty minutes. Right now it's six miles south of Anderson near Pineville. They think it's one of the vans. They have a roadblock set up two miles from the van's location with tire spikes stretched across the road."

"Good, are you listening to them live?"

"Yes, so is JR. He's here with me."

Kruger smiled slightly. "Keep me posted."

"Hold on, we're getting a lot of radio traffic." The line went dead for at least a minute.

"Sean, the van tried to run the barricade and ran over the tire spikes. Ten seconds later, it exploded. Early reports are the highway has a huge crater in it."

"Charlie, keep monitoring. The attack is real." He ended the call and glanced at the clock on his cell phone. At 7:15, he decided to call Seltzer.

The call was answered on the second ring.

"Thought you weren't going to call us?"

"Whatever, Alan. The Missouri Highway Patrol has apparently stopped one of the vans north of the Arkansas border. That leaves two to find."

Silence was his answer. Eventually, he heard, "Find the other two, Sean."

Kruger closed his eyes and shook his head. He wanted to say something, but decided the time was not appropriate. "When I know, I'll call."

Placing his attention back to his surroundings, he watched as more and more attendees filed into the building. If this was the scene at each entrance, the casualty count would be horrendous if any of the vans got through.

Five minutes later, Charlie called again.

"Sean, the van out of Van Buren was spotted and chased by the Arkansas Highway Police."

"And?"

Charlie hesitated. "It detonated inside the Bobby Hopper Tunnel."

Kruger pressed his free hand against his forehead. "How many civilian casualties?"

"They're not sure. There was one patrol car right behind him when the tunnel collapsed, and several vehicles were spotted heading south. It could be days before they know."

"Shit. Any word on the one in Siloam Springs?"

"Nothing so far. The Benton and Washington County sheriffs' departments have Highway 412 covered, but there hasn't been any radio traffic from them about a sighting."

"The van should have been spotted by now." Kruger was quiet for several moments. "Call them and make sure they have the alternate routes covered."

"What if we're wrong and he comes from a different direction?"

"Pray we aren't wrong, Charlie. It's too late to change tactics."

The call ended. Stretching his neck by rolling it from side to side, Kruger took a deep breath. With two vans accounted for, their odds of preventing this incident from happening increased. The third van bothered him. He took the cell phone and hit redial. Seltzer answered halfway through the first ring.

"Talk to me, Sean."

"They found the second van on the highway from Fort Smith. There was a high speed chase and…"

"What?"

"The van detonated inside a tunnel that cuts through one of the mountains in this area. One patrol car was caught in the collapse, possibly civilian traffic as well."

"Damn."

"Yeah."

"Any word on the third van?"

"No, Julie Bergman said she found transmission fluid on the floor of the warehouse. There could have been a mechanical issue, the guy backed out, or…" He paused as he noticed something toward the south on MLK Boulevard. "I'll have to call you back."

He glanced at his watch. It was now 7:31. The crowd flowing into the arena was down to a trickle, with only a few stragglers remaining outside. He figured the auditorium was probably packed at this point considering the number of people who had entered the building.

What had drawn his attention was a white van traveling at a high rate of speed heading toward Razorback Road. The distance did not allow him to see any details, but he watched as it made the turn north and accelerated toward his location.

He keyed his radio. "This is Kruger. Possible van sighted heading toward my position. Need back up…"

He dropped the radio and immediately reached for his Glock. The van had jumped the curb, purposely avoiding obstacles between his position and the street. Taking a Weaver stance, he raised the Glock and started firing at the oncoming vehicle. It continued coming.

When his slide locked open, he ejected the spent magazine and slammed another into the gun, all in one fluid motion. He aimed at the driver side of the van again and started pulling the trigger.

Just before the blinding flash of light and the concussion of the denotation hit him, his last thought was of Stephanie.

Chapter Forty-Seven

THE SENSATION of tumbling like a leaf in a strong wind was overwhelming. He wasn't sure how long he tumbled, but he ended up on his back. The surrounding blackness was more intense than any in his experience. Standing, he looked around. Off in the distance, he noticed a bright light. Instinctively, he turned toward the light and started walking. Or something that felt like walking.

As he got closer, the diameter of the light suddenly grew larger. It rushed toward him until he was engulfed by a blinding white. Squinting at the brightness, he continued to walk forward as the surrounding light changed to swirling shades of blues, yellows, reds and greens. Voices could be heard, although he did not understand the words.

As he walked, he heard his mother call his name. Then his father's voice could be heard, but what he said was unintelligible.

Then just as suddenly as they started, the voices stopped. He stood still and felt himself pulled backward, away from the light. His last thought before the darkness took him again was how disappointing it was not being able to talk to his parents.

———

Fayetteville, AR
Saturday morning

"MY NAME IS ALAN SELTZER. I am the Deputy Director of the Federal Bureau of Investigation. I will make a brief statement, then take a few questions."

Seltzer stood in front of the Washington Regional Medical Center in northern Fayetteville. The podium was littered with microphones, placed there by all of the national news organizations plus numerous local and regional outlets gathered in Fayetteville following the events of the previous day. He grasped the sides of the podium and spoke without notes. Facing him was an ever-increasing crowd of journalists. After Kruger's successful thwarting of the planned destruction of Bud Walton Arena, he needed to divert attention away from the investigation.

"On Friday, at approximately six fifty-two in the morning, the first of three vans, each containing approximately 500 kilograms of a combination of Ammonium Nitrate and Nitromethane, was spotted by the Missouri Highway Patrol and deputies from the McDonald County Sheriff's Department. The vehicle was traveling south on I-49. After repeated attempts to stop the vehicle were ignored by the driver, tire spikes were deployed near Jane, Missouri. When the vehicle became disabled, the driver detonated the explosives within the vehicle. The resulting explosion destroyed the vehicle and killed the driver.

"At that same time Arkansas Highway Police were in a high speed chase on a section of I-49 in Crawford Country, Arkansas. They were in pursuit of a northbound van of similar description. When the van was half way through the Bobby Hopper Tunnel, it detonated."

Seltzer paused and took a sip from a bottle of water on the podium. The pause started an avalanche of questions being shouted by the journalists. Seltzer raised his hands, palms out, to quiet the crowd. After the shouting subsided, he began again.

"As has been reported by the Arkansas Highway Department, sections of the tunnel have collapsed. It is unknown at this time if any civilian vehicles were present when the tunnels structural integrity was compromised. It is known that one Highway Police vehicle was in the tunnel. The total number of casualties is currently unknown, but we can assume the officer in the patrol car and the driver of the van are deceased. Rescue operations are underway for any possible survivors. However, it may be days before construction crews can clear the tunnel.

"Finally, at seven thirty-one, a white van was spotted by FBI agents approaching the campus of the University of Arkansas and Bud Walton Arena. The vehicle was traveling at a high rate of speed when it diverted from Razorback Road and drove toward the west entrance of the building. One of our agents fired his service weapon at the van as it approached his position. The van detonated prior to reaching the building. Several civilians were injured in the blast, but no fatalities, except the driver of the van.

"I will now take your questions."

Chaos ensued, but Seltzer remained calm and searched

for several journalists he had met with earlier so he could provide properly prepared answers. He spotted a female reporter from CNN and pointed at her.

"Director Seltzer," said Angela Newton, "what is the condition of the agent who stopped the van?"

"FBI Special Agent Sean Kruger is in critical condition in the intensive care unit in the hospital behind me."

Newton followed up with another question. "What would have happened if the van had detonated inside Bud Walton Arena?"

Seltzer blinked several times. "As all of you are aware, the Walmart Annual Shareholders meeting had just started when the incident occurred. At that time there were over fifteen thousand individuals in the building. Since then, structural engineers have been consulting with FBI investigators. It is their opinion that if the van had managed to drive into the building before detonating, the estimated casualties count would have been higher than we experienced during the 9/11 attack."

This statement caused even more shouting. Seltzer pointed at another familiar journalist.

"Director Seltzer," said Chris Jansing of NBC News, "can you tell us who uncovered this plot?"

"I can't get into specifics at this time, but it was a combination of numerous local law enforcement agencies and the FBI."

Another question was shouted, "Did this plot have anything to do with the recent attempt on Congressman Roy Griffin's life?"

Seltzer shook his head. "We are investigating, but right now, we don't think it does."

He felt bad about lying in front of the camera, put too

little was known at this point. He pointed to another reporter.

"What about the explosion in Kansas City, is that incident related?"

"Once again, we are investigating. As soon as we have completed our investigation, we will let all of you know."

A question was shouted by an unseen reporter, "Has any group declared responsibility for these attacks?"

Seltzer took a deep breath and paused briefly. "Not at this time."

The news conference continued for several more minutes with the same questions asked in different ways. Seltzer finally said, "Thank you," before he turned and walked back toward the hospital's entrance.

HIS EYES OPENED BRIEFLY, everything unfocused. The shape above him morphed into a woman looking down at him. She was dressed in a floral print pullover shirt with blue pants. He guessed she was in her mid-50s, with short grayish brown hair, a round face with rimless glasses and a friendly smile. "Welcome back, Agent Kruger."

His throat was extremely dry, and his lips felt like they would crack if moved. But he managed to say in a raspy voice, barely above a whisper, "How long?"

Her smile never wavered, "You've been with us for twenty-four hours."

He nodded ever so slightly and closed his eyes again.

The next time he opened his eyes, no one stood above him, but he felt pressure on his left hand. He looked over and saw Stephanie sitting in a chair next to him holding his hand. He croaked, "Hi."

She looked up from the book she was reading and smiled. She immediately stood, leaned over and kissed his forehead. "Hi, back."

"How long have I been here?"

"Three days; it's Monday."

He nodded, "Got any water?"

She nodded and held a cup with a lid and straw to his lips. He sipped cautiously. The water seemed to clear his head a bit. He stopped sipping and lay his head back on the pillow.

"Sean, how are you feeling?"

"Like shit. What happened?"

"You don't know?"

"I remember getting to Bud Walton Arena and talking to Tom Stark. Not much after that."

She explained what she knew and finally said, "You saved thousands of lives, Sean. I'm proud of you."

He smiled slightly, closed his eyes and drifted back into unconsciousness.

"THE NEWS MEDIA WANTS AN INTERVIEW."

Kruger shook his head. He was sitting up in bed, the IV still attached, but his focus was sharper and he wasn't drifting in and out of consciousness. Stephanie was sitting in the chair next to the bed. Her arms folded across her chest, her eyebrows pinched together as she glared at Seltzer.

Kruger said, "No, Alan, you know I don't do interviews, particularly from a hospital bed."

"Paul thinks it would be good for the bureau's image."

"Then let Paul do the interviews. I'm not."

Seltzer smiled, "You're back to being your old self. Good."

Stephanie stood and walked around the bed. Leaning close to Alan's face for emphasis, she said, "Back off, Alan. Sean almost died."

Kruger chuckled. "Someone told me I was clinically dead when I arrived."

Stephanie shot him a look of disfavor. "It's not funny. I could have lost you." A tear appeared in her eye. "I almost did."

"Sorry." Kruger turned his attention to Seltzer. "Have they identified the man driving the van?"

Shaking his head, Seltzer walked to the hospital room door and closed it. He came back to Kruger's bedside.

"No. There wasn't much left," he said. "They found several body parts and are using the DNA for a possible match. No one really expects it will be successful. We did get a break, however. An individual, who claims he was supposed to drive the van, turned himself in. He's being interviewed at the Tulsa field office. His information is consistent with what we know about the other two vans. We have those two drivers' names. All three men were from the mosque in San Francisco."

"Have they found the Imam?"

"No, probably won't either. Charlie called and said our friend in Springfield found a TSA surveillance shot of the Imam going through security in Oakland. We're trying to track his destination."

"He's gone, Alan."

"We know that. We want to know where."

Kruger nodded and reached for Stephanie's hand. She gently placed her hand on it, and they both stared at Seltzer.

Seltzer shuffled his feet and looked around the room. "Well, I guess I'd better get back to Washington. I've done all the damage I can do here." He shook Kruger's free hand and nodded at Stephanie.

As he opened the door, he turned. "Paul said the President sends his best wishes and is deeply grateful for your service. He'll be in contact when you feel better."

"He doesn't need to do that, Alan, I was doing my job."

"He knows that, but..." Seltzer smiled and walked out of the room.

Kruger looked at Stephanie. "I think I screwed up in reverse."

"What do you mean?"

"By stopping the last van, I've put us in the public eye. It will go viral. We're going to be bombarded with lawyers and promotional types who want to represent us. You wait and see, it'll get stupid."

"Oh, Sean, it might be fun."

He shook his head rapidly. "No, it will not be fun. As I told Alan, I was doing my job. A job I'm no longer willing to do."

She was quiet, her gaze remaining on him. After several moments, a smile slowly came to her lips.

Chapter Forty-Eight

KANSAS CITY, MO

Two Months Later

THE CONDO'S DOORBELL RANG. Kruger was sitting on the sofa reading and Stephanie was at the kitchen table working on adoption papers. She looked at Kruger with a puzzled expression, he shrugged, and got up to answer the door.

After looking through the security peep hole, he sighed and opened the door.

"Hello, Alan."

Alan Seltzer offered his hand and said, "How are you feeling, Sean?"

Kruger gave his old friend's hand a short two-pump shake and released it quickly. "Fine, Alan. Do you want to come in?"

Seltzer stood in the hallway hesitantly, then nodded and stepped past Kruger.

Stephanie frowned as she saw her husband's old boss

walk through the front door. She said, "He's retired Alan. What do you want?"

"Let's say I want to talk to an old friend who made a bad decision about his career."

Kruger shook his head slowly. "Can I get you anything, Alan? Coffee, iced tea, a beer?"

Seltzer shook his head. "No, thank you, I'm fine. I can't stay long. I'm interviewing a few local agents for the SAC position. I have a dinner meeting with one in an hour over in Overland Park. I'll need to leave shortly. But the director wanted me to stop by and tell you he was disappointed in your decision. He also wanted me to ask you to reconsider."

Kruger gave Seltzer a grim smile. "No, Alan, I'm retired."

Seltzer shook his head. "Not technically. The director put you on medical leave. He hasn't actually turned in your retirement papers."

Kruger stared at Seltzer, but was silent.

Stephanie stood and walked over to her husband. Her face flushed and she crossed her arms over her chest. "What are you talking about, Alan? He turned those papers in a month ago."

"I know, but the director wanted him classified on medical leave until he recovered from the incident in Fayetteville."

Chuckling, Kruger shook his head. "Is that what they're calling it? The incident in Fayetteville?"

Seltzer nodded and smiled slightly. "Yes, we're still getting requests from reporters wanting access to all of the files. So far, nothing has leaked."

"Why does the agency insist on hiding the facts the shootings in Washington, the KC bombing, the attempted assassination of Congressman Griffin and Fayetteville, are all related?"

"One of the President's advisors told him it made all of us look incompetent."

Kruger rolled his eyes toward the ceiling. "The only one looking incompetent is the person making the suggestion."

"I have a tendency to agree, but there is another more serious underlying reason."

"What?"

"There is a growing concern within the Bureau that these types of internal attacks are going to get worse and more common."

"I'm not following you."

"As we dig deeper into the background of the man who planned this whole episode, we're finding evidence this may just be the tip of the iceberg. After the financial meltdown in 2008, many of the safety nets for people living in poverty were taken away. There is a whole generation of young men and women who are growing up struggling to survive. Plus, television shows them what they don't have. They'll be reaching their late teens here in a few years."

"They're angry, aren't they?"

"That's how Aazim Abbas recruited."

"Was that his name?"

Nodding, Seltzer walked over to the sliding glass door that looked out over The Plaza and put his hands behind his back. He gazed out over the lights with his back to Kruger and Stephanie. He took a deep breath and slowly let it out. "Yes. He was a policeman in Bagdad at one time. We helped train him. We taught him how to detect terrorist and uncover conspiracies. We aren't sure of how Abbas recruited Ortega. We can't find any evidence they worked together or even met while Ortega was in Bagdad. But we're still looking."

Seltzer turned and looked at Kruger. "Ironic isn't it. We actually trained the guy on how to be a terrorist. He used our own tactics against us."

Kruger did not respond.

"My whole point is this: Ortega, Billy Reid and Cooper all returned to the states from overseas and couldn't find good paying jobs. Their training made them practically unemployable. Reid was a marksman, but he was also scarred from an IED attack. He was supposed to get plastic surgery to reduce his scarring, but his case fell through the cracks at the Veteran's Hospital, so he gave up.

"Cooper was an expert in explosives. Not a lot of work for someone like that, except maybe in construction. Unfortunately for him, there wasn't a lot of building going on in rural Alabama. Ortega was just mad at the world. We're still digging into his past."

Stephanie spoke up after being silent for a while, she said, "Alan, surely Ortega saw through this Abbas person's motives?"

"We don't think so. At least not at first." Seltzer turned to look at her. "According to Billy Reid, Ortega was avenging fallen comrades by killing the men who supplied shoddy equipment to the military. Reid knew it was a scam; all he cared about was the money."

Kruger frowned. "Why was Congressman Griffin targeted?"

"According to Billy, Ortega thought Griffin was responsible for accepting the lowest bid for military equipment."

"That's nuts. He was a freshman congressman."

"Once again, the power of persuasion by Abbas. He

knew Ortega's hot button. It didn't have to be true; it just had to make sense to Ortega for him to act."

Kruger hesitated for a moment and rubbed his forehead. "What was the real reason Griffin was targeted?"

"We don't know for sure, but we believe it was because he was a fervent supporter of Israel. His district around San Francisco is predominantly Jewish."

"That actually makes sense. What about the other three victims?"

Alan smiled grimly. "Every single one of them was rich, Jewish and gave heavily to Israel support groups."

Kruger nodded, but remained quiet.

"Do you remember how the owner of the warehouse in Tulsa claimed to receive a call?"

"Yeah."

"Examination of Ortega's cell phone reveals he was the one who called the owner."

"How did he know who it was?"

"We asked the same question. There is a security camera recording of him in the Tulsa County Assessor's office. Apparently he got the information there."

"Why would he do something like that?

Seltzer shrugged. "We don't know, but the call was made a few hours before he was shot."

"Second thoughts, perhaps."

"Yeah, probably." He paused for a few moments. "We got lucky at the Bobby Hopper Tunnel. Only seven fatalities. Two of which were the terrorist and the police officer in the patrol car right behind him."

"Five civilians and a police officer dead does not sound lucky."

"Normally, at that time of day, there's a lot of commuter traffic going into Fayetteville. Due to the high speed pursuit, the only other traffic in the tunnel was going south."

"Still…"

Seltzer just nodded. After a brief uncomfortable lag in the conversation, Seltzer walked toward the front door. "What should I tell the director?"

"Turn my paperwork in. I'm done."

"What are you going to do?"

Kruger shrugged.

"Okay, I'll tell him." He offered his hand, which Kruger shook. "Good luck Sean, we… I'll miss you. The Bureau won't be the same."

Seltzer opened the door, looked at his old friend briefly, then walked out. Kruger closed the door and leaned his back against it. "Am I doing the right thing, Stephanie?"

She walked up to him and placed her arms around his waist, but remained quiet.

Chapter Forty-Nine

KANSAS CITY, MO

Two Days Later

KRUGER WAS JUST FINISHING his morning run when his cell phone rang. He looked at the caller ID and frowned. He hesitated briefly before accepting the call, but finally pressed the answer icon.

"Kruger."

"Agent Kruger, this is Bill Monroe. I'm a Secret Service agent with the President's advance team."

"Good morning, Agent Monroe, what can I do for you?"

"The President will be in Kansas City tomorrow to address the American Bankers Association meeting at Bartle Hall. He would like to have dinner with you and your wife tomorrow evening. Will you be available?"

The only response Kruger could give was silence.

"Are you there, Agent Kruger?"

Finding his voice, Kruger replied. "He realizes I'm retired from the FBI, doesn't he?"

"I'm not at liberty to discuss his reasons. I'm merely coordinating your availability with his schedule. Will you be available to have dinner with the president?"

"Of course, when and where?"

––––––

"THANK you for joining me tonight, Sean. I'm honored to meet you, Mrs. Kruger."

Stephanie blushed and said, "Please call me Stephanie, Mr. President."

"Very well, please have a seat. I wanted to have a private conversation with both of you, that's why we're dining in my suite."

The room was the Presidential Suite at the Raphael Hotel on Ward Parkway, barely a ten-minute walk from their condos. There was a table with seating for four waiting for them as they entered the dining area. Pleasantries were exchanged as a steward poured wine. When he finished and stepped out of the room, the President said, "I was informed last week that, despite Director Stumpf's delay tactics, you have chosen to retire. Is this correct, Sean?"

Kruger nodded.

The President took a sip of wine. "I'm sorry to hear that. It's disappointing, but understandable."

Kruger remained silent.

"I don't believe I had the opportunity to personally thank you for preventing this country from experiencing another 9/11. Thank you."

"I didn't do it alone, sir. I had an outstanding team. They deserve the credit."

"I appreciate your attitude, Sean. Trust me, we need

more individuals like you in public service. Too many want the credit without doing anything to deserve it."

Kruger stared at his wine glass. Stephanie looked at him with apprehension.

"May I be frank with you, Sean?"

"Of course, sir."

"You are too young to be retiring. Particularly at this time. Since the incident in Fayetteville, we've uncovered a serious threat to our country. The short-sightedness of our congressional leaders after the Great Recession has created an environment of discontent in our inner cities. Plus the scrutiny of the news media over the past few years on isolated incidents of law enforcement excesses has also contributed to this discontent."

"I was told about this several days ago."

The President smiled. "Good, then I won't bore you with details. We have a mutual friend, the individual who recruited you for the FBI who—"

Kruger frowned. "You know Joseph?"

"Yes, very well."

"I knew he had connections, but I had no idea he knew you."

Chuckling, the President nodded. "Yes, we go back a long way. I assume you know what he does for me?"

"No, not really. He's always kept that part of himself a closed book. At least to me."

"And to everyone else, from what I understand. He's very trustworthy."

Kruger nodded, "That he is. What does all this have to do with me?"

"A valid question." The President paused and smiled slightly. "I want you to re-evaluate your decision to retire."

"With all due respect, sir, no. I've made a commitment to Stephanie and I will not break it."

"I respect that decision. But I'm not asking you to return to the FBI. There are other, let's say, opportunities, I would like for you to consider."

"What do you mean, other opportunities?"

"The reason I wanted both of you here is because it would require a move. You would be on the staff of a large university in a city in the center of the country. The position has already been approved by the president of the university and the head of the Psychology Department. They are completely on-board with the idea. You would have a flexible teaching schedule with plenty of graduate students to fill in for you. And you would report to me and only me."

Kruger tilted his head to the side. "I'm not sure I understand."

"Let me explain."

After the President completed his proposal, Kruger looked at Stephanie. She smiled, nodded and reached for his hand. Kruger returned his attention to the President and said, "I think we would like to pursue this further."

The President smiled.

Epilogue

Two Months Later

RETIRED SPECIAL FORCES MAJOR BENEDICT "SANDY" Knoll sat at a small table outside a busy bistro at the intersection of Boulevard Saint-Germain and Boulevard Saint-Michel. He sipped his espresso and watched an apartment building three blocks away. It was approaching noon, and traffic at the intersection was heavy.

At exactly 11:45 a.m., a man exited the apartment building wearing a white dishdasha and white taqiyah. Casually keeping an eye on the figure, Knoll heard two squelches from his ear bud as the white-clad cleric started walking toward the intersection. It was the signal from a watcher outside the apartment building confirming the man was their target. Raising his coffee cup to his lips, he spoke into a microphone attached to the cuff of his sleeve. "Package is on time. Confirmed as the correct item."

His words traveled to a nearby van which amplified the

signal and beamed it toward a satellite in synchronous orbit high above Paris. The satellite relayed the signal to another one high over Washington, D.C., all in a fraction of the time it took to speak the words.

In a room deep under the White House, four men sat in front of a flat-screen TV watching a detailed satellite image of the intersection in Paris. Twin small speakers broadcast Knoll's words. Joseph looked at the President of the United States and said, "What do you want to do, sir?"

The President was quiet. He glanced at FBI Director Paul Stumpf and CIA Director Admiral Jeffery Reardon, and both men nodded slightly. Returning his attention to the scene on the TV, the President said, "Proceed."

Joseph looked at his watch. It was 5:50 a.m. Eastern time. He leaned over and spoke into a small microphone.

"Green light."

Sandy Knoll heard the reply in his earbud and sat the coffee cup down. He placed a five euro note under the cup and waited. When the white-clad cleric passed by the bistro, Knoll casually stood and followed him.

The man under surveillance was Saleel Ghani, a militant Islamic cleric, whose last place of residence was San Francisco, California. He was also the Imam who had recruited three men to help Aazim Abbas attack Bud Walton Arena over four months ago. His arrival in Paris had gone unnoticed by the French General Directorate for Internal Security until he started inflaming French Muslims about pursuing jihad. Now on a watch list, his name had been passed on to the CIA and MI6.

The President said, "How did you find him, Joseph?"

"The third driver, a 19-year-old from San Francisco named Abdul Bahri, gave us his name. The DGSI notified us of Ghani's presence in Paris. Apparently, Bahri was not enthusiastic about volunteering for the mission. He told a team of FBI interrogators how Ghani shamed him into volunteering. Then when this young man expressed doubts about blowing himself up for the cause, Ghani threatened his family. When we learned where Ghani was, I sent Major Knoll and three members of this team to watch him."

The President remained quiet, his concentration completely on the TV monitor.

"They know where he's going," Joseph continued. "The Imam is a creature of habit. He's walking to mid-day prayers at his mosque. He does it every day at exactly 11:45 a.m."

Knoll kept his distance behind the Imam until he saw what he was waiting for. He quickened his pace and closed the gap until he was directly behind Ghani. A large delivery truck was speeding down Boulevard Saint-Germain toward the cleric. Ghani, as was his habit, walked close to the street to avoid being touched by infidels on the sidewalk. As the truck grew closer, Knoll stepped up behind the Imam and discreetly placed his hand on the man's back. With a puzzled look on his face, the Imam began to turn just as Knoll shoved him into the path of the large truck.

Joseph and the three other men in the room watched as the truck slammed into the stumbling Imam. The body was pushed ahead of the truck and crushed before the driver could apply the brakes.

They watched as Knoll continued walking away from the accident.

The President closed his eyes and said, "How many more were involved?"

Joseph did not smile as he spoke, "He is the only one we

are positive about. I'm sure there are more. But the trail is cold right now."

Standing, the President nodded.

"Find them, Joseph. Find them and make them go away."

Get a FREE prequel novella from J.C. Fields

vinci-books.com/ghost-in-the-mirror

Some shots echo forever.

Twenty years after executing a Desert Storm mission that continues to haunt him, former Marine sniper Michael Wolfe has retreated into the shadows.

But when FBI Special Agent Sean Kruger investigates a series of expert assassinations targeting military officers, Wolfe's name keeps surfacing.

vinci-books.com/seankruger3

A vanished plane. A brutal murder. A killer from the past returns.

When retired FBI profiler Sean Kruger is drawn back into the hunt for Randolph Bishop, the killer who escaped him years ago, the stakes turn personal. As his family becomes a target, Kruger faces a chilling battle of wits in *The Impostor's Trail*.

Turn the page for a free preview...

The Imposter's Trail: Chapter One

Paul Bishop parked the rented Kia Rio next to the lake and stared across the water in the pale early light of dawn following another sleepless night. Geese swooped in, flared their wings, and one by one, gracefully settled on the calm water. On any other day, he would have marveled at the beauty of the sight.

He once again opened the white envelope addressed to his brother, unfolded his hand-written one page note, and read it for the twentieth time. A tear slid down his cheek as he folded the letter and returned it to the envelope. This time he sealed the envelope, then placed it on the passenger seat next to the Taurus Millennium G2 9mm and stared at the gun. Returning his gaze to the eastern sky, he watched as the sun peeked above the horizon.

Looking back at the pistol, Paul picked it up, placed the barrel under his chin, and without hesitation, pulled the trigger.

The sound echoed off the hills surrounding the lake, startling several flocks of geese and ducks. Eventually, the clamor of their honking and quacking subsided and once again, the tranquility of early morning returned to the lake.

———

FBI Agent Sean Kruger stood in the middle of Paul Bishop's sparsely furnished living room. It was a small house located in the town of Wildwood, MO west of St. Louis. The house contained two bedrooms, a kitchen, laundry room, and one bathroom. Today the entire place was a beehive of activity, with members of an FBI forensics team and local detectives combing every room for clues about the owner. Referring to a small notebook, Kruger said, "Teri, can I ask you a question?"

Teri Monroe, lead technician for the FBI team, walked over. "Sure, what's up, Sean?"

"We've worked more than a few cases together over the years, haven't we?"

"More years than I care to think about." She smiled.

"Do you notice anything unusual about this place?"

She looked around and shook her head. "Nope. Looks like a man's house to me."

She looked back at Kruger. "Why?"

"It's unnaturally neat."

"We've seen it before." She shrugged. "The guy was a compulsive cleaner. Everything has its place, and every-thing's in its place."

Kruger shook his head. "The guy lived here twenty years. I don't see any pictures of family, friends, or pets. There's nothing personal in this house, absolutely nothing."

Monroe looked around the room and frowned. "Now that you mention it..."

Kruger checked his notes and continued, looking back at Monroe.

"There's nothing in this house identifying who the envelope is for. Just the name Randy. No last name. Who's Randy?"

He frowned and paced the small room. "Did Paul Bishop strip this place clean before he took his life, or did this Randy person do it?"

He stopped moving and focused on Monroe. "I need answers, Teri."

"Shit." Monroe shook her head. "Okay, everyone gather in the living room. We have a problem."

Of the four technicians gathering evidence, three were women from the St. Louis FBI office, and the fourth was a young skinny man who arrived at the scene with Monroe. Monroe waited until everyone was in the living room. "Agent Kruger just made an observation, and I tend to agree with him. Before we arrived, someone may have been in this house and taken evidence. We need to step up our game and determine if anything is missing. You know the drill. Let's get to it."

They all nodded and returned to their tasks.

"Charlie, would you stay here for a second?" Monroe pointed at the tall skinny kid. "Agent Kruger, this is Charlie Craft. He's young and inexperienced, but someday will make an excellent forensic technician for the FBI."

Kruger smiled and shook the young man's hand. "Nice to meet you, Charlie."

The young man stared at Kruger while he shook his hand. "Uh… Oh my… I mean… Uh, nice to meet you, Mr. Kruger."

"The name is Sean." Kruger chuckled. "My dad was Mr. Kruger."

Monroe grinned, "Mr. Kruger, please show Charlie how you would look at a crime scene." She winked at Kruger and walked away.

"Charlie," Kruger looked around the room, "what do we know about the man who owned this house?"

"He committed suicide and left a note confessing to the four killings known as the Quarry Murders. That was your case, wasn't it?"

Kruger nodded. "The reason we're here. What else, Charlie?"

Charlie shook his head. "That's all I've been told."

"Exactly. We know very little about this man, except he owned this house free and clear. No mortgage. We know his name: Paul Bishop. We know he had one credit card with a zero balance. We know he had a cell phone because of a bill found in his mailbox. We also know he owned a computer because the house has a Wi-Fi router. But we haven't found a cell phone or a computer, have we?"

Kruger remained silent as Charlie looked around the room. "Maybe he hid them off-site, or possibly they were stolen."

Kruger nodded. "I prefer to think the former."

"Why?"

"Good question. I'll answer it in a minute. One other fact we know about our Mr. Bishop: he has a clean background. Never been arrested, not even a traffic ticket, nothing. He didn't exist in the criminal system until they found his body with the note. It's rare. Most people get a speeding ticket at some point in their lives, but he didn't."

Charlie's eyes didn't waver as he watched Kruger.

"So here we are in his home of twenty years. It should reveal something about Mr. Bishop, wouldn't you agree, Charlie?"

Charlie nodded.

"So why is this house not telling us anything about Mr. Paul Bishop?"

Charlie shook his head. "I don't know?"

Kruger smiled.

"I think our Mr. Bishop has a secret. A secret someone doesn't want us to know."

While the forensics team systematically searched Paul Bishop's house, local detective Barry Winslow tapped Kruger on the shoulder. "Sean, we found someone at home who says she knows Bishop. I think you need to talk to her."

Kruger nodded and followed the detective out of the house. It was a picturesque neighborhood: a shady canopy of mature trees drooped over the street, with sidewalks on both sides of the road, nicely manicured lawns, and well-kept older homes. They turned to the south and walked diagonally across the street toward a house obscured by shrubs, flowers, and hanging baskets on the front porch. Alfonzo Cordero, another local detective, opened the door and introduced Kruger to the elderly owner.

"Mrs. Sellers, this is FBI Agent Sean Kruger. Agent, this is Norma Sellers."

Kruger smiled and offered his identification, which the petite woman examined with care. Though slightly stooped over, she stood barely as tall as Kruger's chest. He smiled. She probably didn't weigh as much as the German shepherd his parents used to own. Her silver hair was nicely done, and she wore a patterned dress accented with an open solid blue sweater. She handed his ID back. "I've never met anyone from the FBI."

"It just means I travel more than these detectives." Kruger smiled. "I'm basically here to assist them."

She returned the smile. "Can I offer you coffee, Mr. FBI Agent?"

"No thank you, ma'am."

"I offered these gentlemen coffee, but they turned it down too. You know, you remind me of my late husband. He was tall and slender just like you and a runner. Do you run, Mr. FBI Agent? Sorry, I've forgotten you name."

"It's Sean, ma'am. Yes, I run. What can you tell me about your neighbor, Paul Bishop?"

"Nice man. Friendly and always waved, a rarity in this neighborhood. After my husband passed, Paul always shoveled my driveway and sidewalk when it snowed. Never asked. He just did it. Wouldn't take a penny for his labors. He'd tell me he was already shoveling and got carried away. Then he'd laugh and continue shoveling."

Kruger nodded. "Do you know if he had any family?"

She frowned. "There was a woman living there when my husband and I moved into the neighborhood, but she disappeared several years later."

"Did he ever mention someone named Randy to you?"

She shook her head "Not that I recall."

Kruger nodded and smiled. "Okay. What can you tell me about the woman?"

She was silent, tapping her right index finger on her lips.

"When we moved into the neighborhood, oh, I guess it was nineteen years ago, we would see her on rare occasions. She wasn't very friendly—kind of snooty, actually. She never waved or spoke. One day she disappeared, and we never saw her again. I thought it odd and was going to ask Paul about her. But my husband told me to mind my own business."

"Do you know if they were married?"

"Oh yes. Paul introduced her as his wife when we first met them."

Kruger looked up at the two detectives. Winslow nodded and left the house. Kruger returned his attention to Norma Sellers. "Did you ever see him with another woman?"

She shook her head. "No. Can't say I did. Bob, that's my late husband, always said he thought Paul was queer. You know, uh, didn't like women."

Kruger nodded. Cordero jotted something down in a small notebook, and Kruger asked, "Did he ever mention a brother or sister?"

"No. Now that you mention it, he never talked about himself. He would ask about our health and was concerned when Bob got the cancer." She paused. "I will never forget, he stayed at our house during the funeral—kept the burglars away, you know. They wait for people to die and then steal from them during the funeral."

"I've heard that." Kruger paused for just a few seconds. "What else can you tell me about Paul Bishop?"

After a long silence, she shook her head. "Don't you believe a word they're saying about him. He was a gentleman, respectful and considerate. Not many men left like that anymore."

Kruger talked to Norma Sellers for another twenty minutes but failed to learn anything else of importance. He thanked her and left the house with Cordero. Once they were off the front porch, Kruger said, "Let's see if Winslow's found anything about the mysterious Mrs. Bishop."

They found Winslow sitting in the passenger seat of a dark green unmarked Chevy Impala police car. The door was open, and Winslow was hunched over, holding his cell phone to his ear with his shoulder as he rapidly made notes on a yellow five-by-eight notepad. When they approached, he held one finger up. Finally, he spoke into the phone, "No, that's what I needed. Thanks, Sharon. I owe you."

He smiled as he looked up at Kruger and Cordero. "We didn't think to look at divorce records. Bishop wasn't married here. They were married out of state. The divorce papers were filed here."

Kruger titled his head slightly. "And?"

"Timeline doesn't jive with the story Miss Sellers told."

"How so?" Cordero asked.

"She indicated the woman disappeared a few years after they moved in. The divorce wasn't finalized until six years ago. That's a ten or more year gap."

"Maybe she was confused," said Cordero. "Got her times wrong."

Kruger shook his head. "No. Her husband died six years ago. She mentioned a long period without Bishop being seen with a woman. Her husband thought Bishop was gay."

Cordero nodded. "Yeah," he paused. "There is that."

"What was her name?" Kruger asked.

Referring to his notes, Winslow flipped back a few pages. "Court papers state her name was Brenda Parker Bishop. Petition states reason for divorce was abandonment. It was filed by Paul Bishop, and her maiden name of Parker was restored. He got the house, and she got cash."

Kruger frowned. "I don't suppose there is any mention of her current address."

Winslow shook his head.

"I didn't think there would be. Dammit. How many Brenda Parkers can there be? Six or seven million?" Kruger slapped the roof of the police car.

All three men were quiet. Kruger rubbed the back of his neck. "Where were they married? Does the petition say anything about that?"

Winslow referred to his notes and nodded. "Illinois."

"She might have gone back to Illinois. Or, she could still be here in St. Louis. I'll have one of the techs start searching for her there. Why don't you two see if you can locate her here?"

Cordero nodded and headed toward the driver's side.

Just before they drove off, Kruger bent down to look into the car. "Have we been able to determine where this guy worked?"

Winslow shook his head. "Not yet. None of the neighbors at home knew him. Apparently he kept to himself. He'd wave, but they never spoke to him. The neighbors on both sides of the house aren't home from work yet. Maybe we'll get lucky with them."

Kruger nodded and looked back at the house. Yellow crime-scene tape was stretched around the yard. A white forensic van was parked in the driveway, along with several black-and-white police cars. The crowd on both sides of the house was growing. Curious onlookers were scattered in various yards on both sides of the street.

Cordero leaned over from the driver seat and remarked, "How many of your neighbors do you two know?"

Winslow looked over at him. "Not many."

Kruger smiled slightly. "I know one."

Grab your copy…
vinci-books.com/seankruger3

About the Author

J.C. Fields is a lifelong resident of Missouri. He has a degree in Psychology and extensive experience with computers.

His first short story was written while still in high school, and he continued writing throughout his university days. Writing took a back seat during the family-raising years. But in 2006, he opened his laptop and started putting words on paper again.

Research for the Sean Kruger novels started while traveling extensively throughout the United States. He also has weapons training in both short and long guns.

Currently, he resides in Southwest Missouri with his wife and their rescue cat, Asia.

Acknowledgments

This novel, like my first, would not have been possible without the assistance and efforts of others. While the writing itself is a solitary endeavor, getting the words right takes a team.

First, I want to thank the members of my critique group: Ike, Wayne, Bonnie, John D., Judy, and our newest member, Kwen. Your brutally honest comments and suggestions continue to both challenge and enhance my journey as a writer.

To my editor, Emily Truscott, thank you for your work in making this book a better reading experience.

Thanks are also sent to Norma Eaton for her tireless work in making sure my tendency to get comma happy is curtailed. You once again fine-tuned the manuscript before sending it to the publisher.

To Sharon Kizziah-Holmes of Paperback-Press, your continued enthusiasm and support are appreciated more than you can imagine.

Finally, and above all else, I give thanks each day for my wife, Connie. She continues to endure my early mornings, late nights, and weekend excursions into my office as I work on my manuscripts. She is truly my best friend and a wonderful partner in life.

www.ingramcontent.com/pod-product-compliance
Lightning Source LLC
Chambersburg PA
CBHW011742010726
47498CB00012B/2904